Joanna Johnson lives in a pretty Wiltshire village, with her husband and as many books as she can sneak into the house. Being part of the Historical Romance family is a dream come true. She has always loved writing, starting at five years old with a series about a cat, imaginatively named 'Cat', and keeps a notebook in every handbag—just in case. In her spare time she likes finding new places to have a cream tea, stroking scruffy dogs and trying to remember where she left her glasses.

The Marriage Rescue

is Joanna Johnson's gripping debut for

Mills & Boon Historical Romance!

Discover more at millsandboon.co.uk.

THE MARRIAGE RESCUE

Joanna Johnson

MILLS & BOON

First Published in Great Britain 2019
by Mills & Boon, an imprint of HarperCollins*Publishers*
1 London Bridge Street, London, SE1 9GF

© 2019 Joanna Johnson

ISBN: 978-0-263-26908-6

MIX
Paper from
responsible sources
FSC® C007454

This book is produced from independently certified FSC™ paper
to ensure responsible forest management.
For more information visit www.harpercollins.co.uk/green.

Printed and bound in Spain
by CPI, Barcelona

Chapter One

Selina Agres was going to die, and it was all her own fault. Hadn't she been warned, time and time again, to stay as far away as possible from those upper-class English animals?

Grandmother Zillah's words echoed in her ears as she rode for her life, her horse Djali's hooves pounding over waterlogged ground and leaving deep tracks in their fleeing wake.

Stupid girl.

It wasn't as though she hadn't seen the proof of their wickedness for herself, either.

The last clear memory she had of her mother was the way her eyes had changed at the moment of her death. Many of the other details she could recall were blurred: snatches of lullabies sung on summer nights, when the rhythmic swaying of their creaking caravan had rocked young Selina to sleep; the barest suggestion of a comforting floral scent she could never quite pin down.

But the memory of those eyes—so bright and sharp in life, missing nothing, holding a world of wisdom and humour—had clouded to a flat black, staring unseeing at the little girl who had gazed back, who had wondered where the light had gone from Mama's face...

She bent lower over the horse's neck, urging him onwards ever faster. A swift glance behind showed her pursuers losing ground, hindered by their own far clumsier mounts. Selina grasped at a tentative new hope: stubborn and scarred he might be, but nobody was as fast as her Djali over level terrain. He had been her mother's horse before she'd passed, then barely more than a colt, and Selina blessed Mama in that moment for training the bad-tempered creature so well. Perhaps they might survive this after all.

The wind tore at her clothes, an autumn squall that threatened the rapid approach of winter tugging her riot of midnight curls free from their ribbon and tossing the heavy tresses into her face. She flung them aside with desperate haste, her other hand tightening its death grip on the horse's reins.

She couldn't stop now. Just one more fence to jump and then it was all downhill to a thick copse of trees, if her memories of this wretched place were correct, and there she might just be able to hide—if she could only put enough distance between herself and those behind her... Twelve years had passed since she had last set foot on this land, and all she could do was pray her scattered recollections were right.

'Come on, Djali!' Her voice was loud, battling against the roar of the wind, belying the way her heart railed against her ribs like a trapped animal.

The horse plunged onwards, his breath coming short and fast in a pattern that matched Selina's own.

She hadn't even *wanted* to get so close. But what else could she have done? Left the poor girl alone in the forest? Perhaps she should have; look at where taking pity on a landowner's child had got her.

Seeing a Roma woman carrying a sobbing English child through the woods—Squire Ambrose Fulbrooke's own daughter, no less—of *course* his men had jumped to the wrong conclusion. The idea that the little girl had escaped her governess and got herself lost would never have occurred to them, whereas everybody had heard how the Roma were a community of thieves and vagrants. Of course she was stealing the child; what other explanation could there be?

Selina knew from bitter experience the prejudices that existed against her people. Shunned and almost feared, the Roma were well used to living on the fringes, making do in whatever ways they could. But they were strong, and that characteristic spirit was more than evident in Selina.

Almost from her first steps she had worked hard: foraging food for the pot, fetching water, helping Papa break in horses to sell. Her hands had grown calloused and her skin tanned, and with each passing year she had become more and more like the kind, capable mother ripped so cruelly from her.

Even Papa had commented on the resemblance once, years ago, on a camp a hundred miles from this damned estate, as he'd watched her lunge a new pony. The animal had been skittish and afraid, but with gentleness and determination Selina had brought him on well, and her father had nodded at her as he'd sat on the back porch of their wagon, pipe in hand.

'What do you think, Lina? Will you make a mount of him yet?'

'I believe so, Papa.' Selina had smiled across at him and wiped the sweat from her brow with the back of a hand. 'He's clever, and a good worker.'

'I think you might be right. You've a good eye for horses. You get that from me.'

He'd pulled on his pipe for a moment and Selina had seen the smile fade from his weathered face.

'Everything else comes from your mother. You're looking more and more like her every day.'

'Thank you, Papa.'

Selina's voice had been quiet and she'd turned back to the pony, wishing with all her heart she hadn't noticed her strong, tall Papa quickly pat a tear from his face with his old red neckerchief. The picture had stayed with her ever since, and never failed to bring a lump to her throat.

The fence was looming fast—a straggling construction that leaned back drunkenly at an angle that would make it difficult to jump. Selina cursed beneath her breath and chanced another raking glare backwards. They were still coming, three of them now. Two were dressed in the usual muddy colours of gamekeepers, riding out in front of a third too distant to see in any real detail. She thought she made out a flash of blue, stark against the muted grey of the sullen autumn sky. When had *he* joined the chase?

But it didn't matter how many there were. She would escape them all or die trying.

'Get up, Djali—good boy!' Clicking her teeth in command, Selina touched the horse with her heels. He was galloping flat out, lips pulled back from ivory teeth and mane flying, ready to take the jump.

She felt the rush of air as they left the ground.

It hit her squarely in the face—a stinging slap that brought tears to her eyes—but they were sailing over the lolling fence and nobody would catch them now.

And then they went down.

Djali struck the fence with a back hoof and veered to one side, stumbling to right himself. Selina pitched forward, tumbling from the saddle in a tangle of crimson skirts and bright woollen shawls.

She lay gasping, winded and dazed. She'd fallen from horses before, many times, but never from one so tall as Djali—one of the reasons he had been officially given over to her ownership on her eighteenth birthday, aside from sentiment, had been his surefootedness. After the fate that had befallen her mother, Papa hadn't wanted to take any chances with his only child.

What a cruel irony if I were to die here, too.

The thought crossed Selina's racing mind before she could stop it. A fresh bolt of terror tore through her heaving chest and her head swam as she struggled to regain her breath.

We never should have come back here, even if that murdering devil Charles Fulbrooke is on the other side of the ocean.

Her pursuers had seen her fall. She could hear them now, the unmistakable beat of hooves growing closer as she lay prone on the sodden ground, one arm flung out and the other twisted beneath her.

She pushed herself up, wincing as she felt a dart of pain crackle through the wrist that had borne her weight. *Where's Djali?* A wild scan of the grass showed him standing a short distance away, ears back as he eyed the approaching horses.

There was no time to reach him, Selina calculated. By the time she managed to get back into the saddle her hunters would be upon her and she would have nowhere else to turn. There was only one option open to her and she seized the lifeline with both hands.

Selina ran.

The copse lay mere feet away from her now; if she could reach the safety of the trees she would be able to climb high enough to conceal herself among the orange canopy of leaves that swayed in the chill wind. Djali would be fine, she knew. The obstinate creature was well capable of defending himself and would likely trot back to the campsite if she didn't reappear to guide him home herself.

Grandmother Zillah would be beside herself with worry when the horse came back without his rider, but there was nothing Selina could do about that now as she reached the first line of trees and plunged headlong through the rusty carpet of fallen leaves.

'After her!'

'Don't let her get away!'

Selina heard the rough shouts at her back and fought onwards, crashing through the undergrowth. Sharp boughs whipped at her face, drawing blood, but she kept running, searching for a tree whose lower branches would allow her enough purchase to haul herself up.

There! As if by divine providence a huge oak reared up in front of her, its gnarled roots thrust out and wide boughs sweeping down to hold out their arms to her. It was the work of moments to heave herself up, and she lunged upwards, ignoring the scream of her jarred wrist, moving through the leaves just as her pursuers lurched into view, now on foot, with faces flushed red with exertion.

'Which way did she go?'

'I didn't see!'

'You mean you *lost* her?'

Selina peered down through the branches at the two gamekeepers standing just metres from her hiding place. Secreted among the boughs, her crimson skirt blending with the autumnal colours of the leaves, she felt her palms prickle with sweat. If they looked up...

Why hadn't she just pointed the child in the

right direction and then left? She hated the land-owners for their wealthy arrogance, their hypoc-risy, for the way they treated her people and, of course, for their part in Mama's death. It hardly mattered that the Squire himself—owner of this vast estate and the imposing Blackwell Hall that sat within it—had not been directly responsible for the fate of Diamanda Agres; the upper classes were all cut from the same cloth.

For all Selina knew, Squire Ambrose had aided his brother Charles's flight to the Conti-nent after the events of twelve years before that had scarred her young life so violently, allowing him to neatly avoid any unsavoury accusations. If only Selina had treated the girl with the dis-dain she deserved, coming from such a family, and hadn't tried to return her to the great Hall, less than a mile away…

Damn. Selina sighed to herself. *You always were too soft.*

The sight of the little thing in her muddy gown, clutching a tow-headed doll, had moved Selina in a way she couldn't explain. Perhaps having lost her own mother at just eight years old had made her more sympathetic. The child had sobbed as she'd called for her mama, and Selina had had only a moment of hesitation be-fore bundling the mite up in her own shawl and making for Djali.

It wasn't the child's fault she'd been born to such a man, she'd reasoned. Not that the girl's father could do much harm now, Selina had thought grimly as she settled into the saddle. Squire Ambrose Fulbrooke had been six feet under for the best part of a month—a deadly combination of port and rich food had caused his heart to give out in the middle of a poker game, if the rumours that had reached the Romani were to be believed.

Apparently his son was in line to inherit, but no sign of the man had yet been seen, and in the absence of a master the Romani had judged it safe enough to make camp temporarily on Fulbrooke land—a judgement that, given her current situation, Selina now regretted with every fibre of her being.

The third man was approaching, kicking his way through the fallen leaves. One of the gamekeepers groaned, just loudly enough for Selina to hear. 'I knew he'd follow us. I said so, didn't I? And now he's going to see we let her get away…'

'Harris! Milton! What happened?'

Selina curled her lip instinctively at the sound of the man's voice. Cut-glass vowels and the confidence of a man born into luxury. He was one of *them*—she was sure of it.

A peep down through the branches confirmed her suspicions: the tall man standing with his back to her was the epitome of a well-bred English gentleman, dressed in a well-cut blue coat with breeches tucked into immaculate leather riding boots and with hair of a distinctive dark burnished gold. She frowned as a flicker of something stirred in the back of her mind, like a gentle breeze through long grass. That unique hair colour, so different from the Roma darkness...had she seen it somewhere before?

'Well? Don't keep me in suspense!' The voice was deep and edged with humour. 'I see my sister being carted off in the direction of the house by your wife, Milton, and then you two on horseback in hot pursuit of somebody—I ask again: What happened?'

'Well, sir,' began one of the gamekeepers, sounding nervous, 'we were just doing our rounds when we saw Miss Ophelia being carried off by a gypsy woman—sobbing her heart out, wasn't she, Harris?'

'Fit to burst, sir,' continued the other. 'So we snatched her back. The girl tried to tell us she came upon Miss Ophelia wandering all on her own, but of course we knew that wasn't true. Trying to steal her, she was.'

'So you gave chase, did you? Two of you against one woman and she still gave you the slip?'

The other men shuffled slightly. 'You know

what they're like, sir, those gypsies. Eels they are. Too tricky by half.'

'Yes. I can see how she would be difficult quarry.'

Although Selina couldn't see his face, she was sure the man was smiling. 'Never mind. All's well that ends well—my sister is back safely with her governess.'

'Thank you, sir. But you know...' The other man's voice lowered menacingly; the hairs on the back of Selina's neck stirred in response. 'If we ever come across her again, or find where those gypsies' grubby little nest is, well...'

'We wouldn't hesitate to teach them a lesson, sir. Be happy to do it.'

'Yes, Milton. I think I quite catch your drift.' The educated voice was cool—bordering on cold. 'Let's hope for everybody's sake that the woman in question is far away by now.'

'Yes, sir.'

'I think we should all be on our way. Bid you good day, gents.'

'Good day, sir.'

The men moved off. Selina listened to them go: footsteps on damp earth, then the telltale jingle of their horses' tack as they rode away, growing fainter and fainter until only the swaying creak of the forest remained.

She exhaled, long and loud. She was safe.

She'd ventured into the lion's den and escaped by the skin of her teeth.

'You can come down now, miss. It's quite safe.'

Selina froze. *There was still someone down there!*

Her heart checked for the briefest of painful moments before slamming back into a pounding rhythm so hard she was sure the man standing below her must be able to hear it.

She drew herself sharply against the oak's knotted trunk, pressing herself closely to the bark. A quick look down through the leaves allowed her nothing more than a view of the back of the uncannily familiar fair-haired head, its owner resolutely positioned at the base of her tree.

'I know you're up there. Don't be afraid. I won't harm you.'

Selina swallowed—a quick convulsion of her dry throat. *Celebrating too soon.* She was trapped. There was only one way down and he was guarding it; there was no way she could pass without being seen.

'Please, miss. You have nothing to fear from me.'

Selina's pulse was racing as she registered his words. What kind of simpleton did he think she was? Surely that was exactly the sort of claim he *would* make.

'Nothing to fear? You just hunted me for three miles like an animal—please excuse me if I don't hop down at the click of your fingers.'

There was a huff of laughter from below. 'I understand why it may have appeared that way. I'd be more than happy to explain if you would just come down.'

'I think not.'

Peering down through the leaves once more, Selina trained her eyes on her captor's blond curls. He hadn't moved so much as an inch, blast him. She herself was beginning to feel the sharp texture of the bark digging into her skin, forcing her to shift her position, and she could have cursed aloud when the movement sent a rotten branch crashing down through the canopy.

Hearing the sudden noise, the man whipped his head round, searching for the direction of the sound, and as his profile turned Selina saw the face of her tormentor clearly for the first time.

It was as though she had been winded all over again.

She *knew* him. Not by name—it hadn't seemed the right time for formal introductions many years ago, when Selina had come across a strange boy in these very woods and held a pad of moss against his cheek to stem the flow of blood that had seeped between his fingers.

How old had he been then? Perhaps twelve to Selina's eight? He had been the first gentry boy she'd ever seen up close, and the rare combination of his hazel eyes and golden hair, so foreign to Selina's childish mind, had burned itself into her memory. There could be no mistaking the fact that this man was the same person, and Selina felt a thrill of some unknown feeling tingle down the length of her spine as she watched him searching upwards, confusion rushing in to replace where moments previously she had felt only fear.

He's handsome. The thought came out of nowhere, taking her by surprise, and she shook her head slightly as if to clear it. *Don't be absurd*, she admonished herself fiercely, although nothing could stop the slow creep of colour she knew was stealing over her cheeks as she took in his defined jaw, in turn well matched by a straight nose and a mouth just teetering on the brink of a smile, and she felt another dart of the same unexplained feeling lance through her.

It was uncomfortably, unacceptably similar to the admiration she had felt once or twice before when confronted with an attractive man. On those occasions, however, she hadn't felt her heart rate pick up speed, and neither had she felt such a disturbingly instinctive appreciation for the fine colour of his eyes. How this gentleman managed to affect her in such a powerfully unexpected way she had no clue, but she knew she didn't like it.

He was hunting through the branches in earnest now, and Selina forced herself closer against the tree's rough trunk. She screwed her eyes closed, trying to bully her brain into ordering her whirling thoughts while her pulse skipped ever faster.

Who is he? Why is he here?

It was exactly her luck to have such an unlikely encounter, she acknowledged helplessly, even as the strange feeling crackled beneath her skin and she felt the urge to look down pull at her once again. *He* wouldn't remember *her*, that was for certain. She had been a skinny, dirt-streaked child, and he...

He now bore a scar, exactly where she had staunched the bleeding gash on his cheek—a pale crescent that somehow only served to enhance the otherwise unblemished perfection of his features...features that looked as though they had been designed to be traced by female fingertips.

Selina's own face felt uncomfortably warm as she sat motionless, horrified by the spontaneous reaction of her body. Each nerve tingled with the desire to take another peep at the man below, to make doubly sure her disbelieving eyes had been correct and he truly was the same person she had encountered all those years before—as well as to take another glimpse of the face that made her heart beat a frenzied tattoo against her ribs.

If it was him, could there be a slim chance her predicament might not be as dire as she had feared?

As a boy he had accepted her help and seemed grateful for it, she was forced to recall. There had been no sign of any upper-class prejudice then, only two children, both too young to fully grasp the social gulf that would divide them so completely as adults. Perhaps he might be as gracious now he was fully grown, and allow her to leave without too much trouble?

It was the most Selina could hope for, and she clung to that hope as she prayed for his disconcerting effect on her to wane.

Edward Fulbrooke frowned lightly as he craned his neck upwards. Where exactly *was* she? He'd known she was there the whole time. Poor Harris and Milton…it was the most obvious hiding place imaginable.

He'd arrived on the scene just after the two gamekeepers had thundered off, his own horse blowing powerfully from their afternoon ride. Milton's wife, Ada, had been attempting to drag a wailing Ophelia towards the Hall, and Edward had dismounted swiftly to aid her.

'Oh, Mr Fulbrooke. I'm that glad you're here!' Ada's voice had been barely audible above Ophelia's sobs, and Edward scooped the child up immediately in one strong arm.

'Ophie. That's enough. What's the matter?'

The little girl quieted at once, though her eyes—the same hazel as Edward's own—had glittered with unshed tears. 'Ned, the lady was only trying to help, and now they're going to *hurt* her!'

Ophelia had told him the full story. She'd been 'exploring' again, having escaped from the watchful gaze of her governess, and had walked so far she'd been unable to find her way back home. She had been about to give up all hope of ever seeing her mama again when a lady had appeared through the trees, dressed in strange clothes and singing a song Ophelia hadn't understood.

When she had seen the child she'd stopped and looked almost frightened, but after Ophelia burst into tears and explained that she was lost and alone the lady had wrapped her up snug in a shawl and taken her towards a waiting horse— a huge grey stallion, with great scars marring his flanks—and said she would take Ophelia safely home.

'But then Harris and Milton came, and they were so *angry*. Harris pulled me away and Milton tried to take hold of the lady. But she ran—and nobody would *listen* to me!'

Edward had set Ophelia back on her feet and leapt back into the saddle without a word. He hadn't doubted for a moment that the child was telling the truth; there wasn't a moment to lose.

He peered upwards yet again. Was that a scrap of fabric? It was hard to tell against the leafy backdrop.

'What is it that concerns you? Are you afraid I'll come chasing after you again?'

There was only silence from above, and Edward forced back a grin.

The pert creature. Sitting pretty as a picture up her tree, deciding whether the Squire's own son is worth coming down for.

The smile faded and a small crease formed between his eyebrows. The *late* Squire's son, now. He was still getting used to that, having returned from London only two days prior to find the Hall quieter than he had ever known it before.

'I can't deny I have some slight misgivings.'

The smoky voice was edged with an undercurrent of something Edward could not identify, and his frown deepened.

'Well, what if I gave you my word as a gentleman that I won't? Would you allow me the honour of an introduction then?'

Another silence stretched out, this time less amusing, and Edward raised an eyebrow. This was getting a little out of hand. He was well within his rights to *order* her down, trespassing as she was on his own land—or what *would* be his land once he took formal possession of his inheritance.

'Miss, I would have you know my word is my law. I would think myself beyond contempt if, once given, I were to break it.'

There was a moment's quiet. Then, 'I suppose there's no chance you'd leave and let me go about my business without an audience?'

'None whatsoever, I'm afraid.'

'Not very *gentlemanly* of you.'

'Alas, I remain unmoved.'

There was another pause. Edward was certain he could hear the grinding of teeth and allowed himself a small smile at her reluctance. She really was an unusual woman.

The branches above his head swayed suddenly, and then with a shower of falling leaves the woman dropped to the ground in front of him.

Edward felt his eyes widen in surprise. She was younger than he had expected: her tawny face, flecked with mud and with a long scratch across one cheek, belonged to a woman no older than twenty. Perhaps it had been the modest clothing that had confused him—she was certainly dressed like no fashionable young lady *he* had ever met. Her bright skirt was paired with a loose-fitting blouse, half hidden beneath a number of colourful tasselled shawls, and raven hair hung in thick waves about her shoulders.

Her effect on him was both immediate and startling. A distant part of his mind knew it was rude to stare, but for some reason he didn't seem able to tear his gaze away as he took in the vibrancy of the scarlet wool against the deep black of her curls, the delicacy of the bone structure beneath the dirt on her face and even the oddly intriguing lack of a wedding ring on the hand that clutched her shawls to her chest.

There was something about her that seemed to call to him, to make him want to drink her in, and he felt a sharp pang of surprise at the very thought. There she stood, a complete stranger and an intruder on his land. He ought to be unmoved by their chance encounter and yet there *he* stood, a full-grown man, apparently struck dumb by the power of a lovely countenance. For lovely it most certainly was.

Where had he ever seen its equal?

It was the strangest sensation—almost as though he had surrendered control of his senses for the briefest of moments before coming back down to earth with a bump. So she was handsome—what was that to him? He was only human, and now his rational mind must take charge again. Her beauty counted for nothing— just the same as any other woman's. He would not be making that mistake again.

She stood watching him with eyes as mistrustful as a feral cat's. There was a feline grace to her posture, too, in the way she held herself, ready to run at the slightest provocation, and it highlighted the contrast between her lithe elegance and his broad stature. Although he easily topped her by a good head and a half, the tense wariness of her frame radiated an untouchability that would have stopped most men in their tracks.

Thrusting his moment of madness firmly to the back of his mind, Edward offered a short bow. 'Thank you for indulging me.'

The woman inclined her head slightly but said nothing.

This might be a little more difficult than I thought, Edward mused. He wanted to thank her for trying to help Ophelia, but apparently conversing with her was destined to be like drawing blood from a stone.

She couldn't know who he was, he was sure. If she did she would be far more interested in conversation. The young women of his acquaintance always seemed to open up at the first hint of his name and prospects.

Not that it was necessarily a good thing. Edward had lost count of the number of ladies who had breezed up to him at balls and revels, affecting shyness, confiding that they had a dance reserved for him in the event that he might be 'inclined to take a turn'. Bitter experience had taught him not to be tempted.

'My name is Edward Fulbrooke,' Edward continued. 'I'm the son of the late Squire of Blackwell Hall, and this is my family estate.' He watched as something sparked in the woman's eyes—something akin to fear. 'Might I have the pleasure of knowing your name?'

He saw her throat move as she swallowed, his gaze drawn there by some impulse he couldn't control. The look in her eyes had been fleeting, but there had definitely been a reaction. *Was it something I said?* Far from impressing her, the revelation of his name had seemed to unnerve her even more. Why *was* that?

'Selina. Selina Agres.'

'Delighted to make your acquaintance, Miss Agres.'

The woman nodded again. An odd expression flickered across her face, mingling with the ever-present wariness; it was half watchful, half curious. She seemed on the brink of saying something before evidently thinking better of it, instead folding her full lips into a tight line.

'I'm afraid I might have frightened you earlier.' Edward spoke quietly, his voice uncharacteristically gentle; the last thing he wanted was for her to bolt before he'd had a chance to explain. That was the least he could do, given the circumstances. 'Please allow me to apologise for the misunderstanding.'

'Misunderstanding?' Selina's eyebrows almost disappeared into her hair. 'You and your men wanted nothing more than to hunt me down like a fox running from hounds!'

Edward frowned. 'That's not quite right. Ophelia told me what happened, and what your motives were. I went after Harris and Milton to—' He broke off. *To stop them from lynching you*, he concluded internally. Not a fit topic of conversation for a lady, traditional or not. 'They're very fond of her, and I was uneasy that in their concern for her safety they might get carried away. It was my intention to defend you, if necessary.'

Edward watched a spark of surprise kindle in Selina's eyes and felt another jolt of that unwelcome electricity as he saw how it enhanced their beguiling darkness. Their rich ebony was a colour rarely seen, and so entirely different from the china-blue set he had once thought the finest in the county.

Even if Harris and Milton hadn't told him Edward would have known at once that she was Romani. The realisation was oddly pleasing. Surely her presence indicated an encampment nearby? A fact that flew directly in the face of his late father's orders?

Passing groups of Roma had been a familiar sight to him on this land years ago, and Edward was momentarily lost in fond memories of brightly painted caravans pulled by gleaming horses, and the dark-haired boys his own age who had invited him, a shy, affection-starved child, to join their games. Although each group had rarely stayed for very long before moving on, Edward could still recall the brief happiness he had felt at their acceptance of him, all of them too young to have yet developed the prejudices of their parents.

His own father had disapproved enormously when Edward had told him of his newfound friends—but then, as usual, Ambrose's attention had been caught by something far more interesting than his lonely young son, and it had been an older Roma boy who had taught Edward to fish, and how to play cards, and any number of other things his father should have taken the time to share with his child so desperate for some tenderness.

A vivid pang of nostalgia hit him like a sudden blow as he remembered the friend he had made the last year the Roma had crossed Fulbrooke land—a little girl, younger than himself, who had cared for him after his fight with the neighbouring family's two sons. Edward felt a dull ache spread through his chest as he recalled how the pain of his cheek had been nothing compared to the crushing realisation that the other boys had been right: his mother was *not* going to return, and perhaps the unkind things they had said about her were more accurate than he'd wanted to accept.

Still, he'd given as good as he'd got. One cut cheek had been a fair price to pay for doling out a black eye and a broken tooth, and Edward almost smiled at the memory of his young nurse. She'd shown him more kindness in their short encounter than he had experienced in months, and again shown him the warmth of the Romani, almost unheard of among the upper classes.

There had been some unpleasantness soon after that incident, he recalled—some trouble with Uncle Charles and a Roma woman—and his father's reluctant permission for the travellers to cross his land had been swiftly revoked. If they had returned it meant Ambrose's grip on the estate was loosening, and Edward could truly step into his place.

He realised he was staring again. Selina returned his gaze uncertainly, a trace of a blush crossing her cheeks under his scrutiny, and Edward looked away swiftly, cursing his apparent lack of self-control.

'My sister has a bad habit of escaping. If you hadn't found her who knows what would have happened?'

Ophelia was the precocious daughter of Maria, the Squire's second, much younger wife. Little Ophelia had breathed new life into the ancient house and, at just seven years old to Edward's twenty-four, she held the key to her half-brother's heart in one tiny hand. She'd been quick enough to take advantage of her mother's absence from the Hall, visiting friends in Edinburgh, and go tramping about the estate on one of her 'expeditions'.

'It was never my intention to frighten you. Please forgive me if that was the case and accept my heartfelt thanks for your service to my sister.'

Selina shrugged—a fleeting movement of one slight shoulder. 'It was what anybody would have done under the circumstances.'

Edward nodded as though she had said something more gracious. She really did have the most disarming manner, he thought. Not at all polished, or even very polite, but there was honesty in her words, a lack of affectation that was oddly refreshing.

He shouldn't admire it; indeed, his interest in her was unnerving. *Get a hold of yourself, man*, he chastised himself uncomfortably. *You're not some green lad, swooning over a milkmaid.*

'Well. Thank you all the same.' After a moment's pause Edward delved into his waistcoat pocket, wrestling with something contained within.

Selina flinched backwards at the movement, glancing this way and that; she seemed on the point of darting away through the trees—

'No! Wait.' Edward held up both hands. Bunched in his right was a snowy handkerchief, which he held out to Selina as gingerly as he might on approaching a wild bird.

'You have some mud on your face, and a scratch—it's been bleeding.' He smiled wryly, one hand moving to the moon-shaped scar below his right eye. 'I know from experience that it's best to treat such a wound as soon as possible.'

Selina stiffened, and Edward saw another complex look dart across her countenance before she regained her composure.

'Oh. Thank you.'

She tentatively took the handkerchief from Edward's outstretched hand, her eyes never leaving his face. He watched as she dabbed at her cheek and cleared the dirt from her skin.

She may well be the most beautiful woman I've ever seen.

For all the scratches that marred her face, she was strikingly lovely in a way totally apart from the celebrated society belles of his circle. The notion was unsettling: hadn't he long thought himself immune to the charms of women? The fact that in that moment, with the trees whispering around him and leaves strewn at his feet, he found himself as vulnerable as any other man was alarming in the extreme.

He would disregard it. She confused him, straying dangerously close to stirring something deep within him that he wanted left undisturbed, and *that* he couldn't allow.

When she tried to return the handkerchief, he backed away with a shake of his head. 'You keep it. Call it a memento.'

'I'm not sure how much of today I'm like to want to remember.'

Edward bowed. 'I understand. Whatever else you might feel, I hope you won't forget that you have a friend in me. If I'm ever able to repay your kindness I shall endeavour to do so. I pay my debts.'

Selina's answering smile was strange and still mistrustful, as though she knew a secret she didn't intend to share. She was moving away from him, backing out of his reach in the direction of the place where Edward had seen her horse waiting for her. He watched her go, wishing the graceful movement of her stride wasn't so damnably intriguing.

'If that's the case, you owe me twice over.'

'Twice?'

She was almost out of sight. Edward frowned as she turned away from him, confusion clouding into his mind. *Twice? How was that?*

'Once for today. Once for before.'

She threw the words over her shoulder and with a whisk of her crimson skirt disappeared between the trees.

Chapter Two

Selina gazed up at the ceiling of the darkened caravan, arching in a perfect curve above her head. Orange embers glowed in the grate of the compact stove set against one wall, dimly illuminating the gilt-painted woodwork of the shelves and bunks to gleam like real gold. A sliver of moonlight fell from one not quite shuttered window, slicing down to leave a pale splash on the polished floor.

Like all Roma women, Selina kept her *vardo* spotlessly clean, and even Papa, when he came to call for a cup of tea, knew to wipe his boots before he was allowed to cross the threshold.

A sideways glance across the narrow cabin showed her grandmother was asleep, the mound of colourful crochet blankets she slept under rising and falling with each breath. In the eerie stillness of the night even that small movement was a comfort.

Selina sighed. *It's no use.*

Sleep evaded her, just as it had on the previous three nights. Each time she closed her eyes pictures rose up to chase each other through her mind: Edward as a young lad, on the day she had first encountered him all those years ago, attempting to smile through gritted teeth as she cleaned his wounded face, and then his adult counterpart, the blond curls just as vivid but his shoulders so impressively broad beneath his fine coat that Selina felt her heart beat a little faster at the memory.

Would that distinctive hair have been soft beneath her fingertips, she wondered, if she'd leaned down from her tree to touch?

The very notion made her breath hitch in her throat before she slammed the brakes on that train of thought, horrified by its wayward direction.

You can stop that this moment, Selina. What's the matter with you?

At least the mystery of who he was and why she had encountered him there had been solved. *Edward Fulbrooke. Ambrose's son and Charles' nephew.* Perhaps she should have suspected, she mused as the image of his face drifted unstoppably across her mind's eye once again, wearing the same dazzling smile he had flashed her mere days previously. But Edward's father and uncle shared the same chestnut hair and ruddy complexion, quite unlike his cool fairness. There was no physical resemblance. And as for character...

Certainly as a boy he had been agreeable, she recalled as she lay in the darkness. He'd looked surprised to see her there in the woods, hunting for wild mushrooms, and she herself had felt nothing but sympathy for him at the state of his bloodied cheek. In those days she'd had no real reason to fear the gentry; Mama had still been alive, and in her childish innocence it had felt the most natural thing in the world to go to him, to help tend to his wound and to feel a slow creep of pleasure at having made a new friend who delighted her with his strange old-fashioned manners.

But then they had killed Mama. The Roma had left the Fulbrooke estate, never intending to return—and Selina's hatred of the gentry had been burned into her heart like a brand.

It was just as well he didn't remember me. He might have wanted to talk, otherwise, and that would never have done.

Selina shifted beneath her bedclothes, attempting to make her body more comfortable than her mind. The fact Edward had been just as courteous as a grown man as he had been as a lad was as surprising as her apparently instinctive attraction to him—and almost as confusing. The upper classes were renowned among her people for their contempt of the Romani, fostering the animosity that raged on both sides.

Had her care of Edward as a child opened his mind to the possibility the Roma were more civilised than he would otherwise have believed? she wondered. Or perhaps she was giving herself too much credit, Selina thought wryly. Certainly she was giving *him* too much space in her head.

The fact that she had slipped Edward's handkerchief beneath her pillow meant nothing. There just wasn't anywhere else to keep it. Zillah, with her hawk-like eyes, would spy it at once if she left it on her shelf, and carrying it upon her person seemed unduly intimate. Perhaps she should just get rid of it, wad it into the stove, but the thought made her uncomfortable in a way she couldn't quite identify.

Beneath her pillow it would have to stay, incriminating embroidered initials and all, and Selina could only pray nobody would find it.

'You're still awake, child.'

Selina jumped, and sat up so quickly she almost hit her head on the low shelf above her bunk. 'I thought you were sleeping, Grandmother.'

'So I was—until you decided the early hours would be a good time to begin talking to yourself. A sign of madness, as well you know.'

'Sorry. I didn't realise I'd spoken aloud.'

'You didn't.' Zillah rose up in her bunk, arthritic bones creaking. 'You've been tossing and turning all night; any fool could tell you have something on your mind. I'd wager it's the reason why you rode back into camp three days ago as if the devil himself was after you.'

'It's nothing, Grandmother. Go back to sleep.'

'I will not. Make a cup of tea, girl, and tell me what ails you.'

Selina groaned inwardly. There really was no stopping Zillah once she got the bit between her teeth. A lifetime on the road—a hard path for any woman—had instilled in her an almost legendary resolve. There was no room for weakness in a *vardo*. At past eighty years old, with silver hair and a face lined with the countless creases of age, Zillah had a mind that was still sharp as a knife, and she was revered among the Roma for her experience and wisdom.

Of course she'd noticed Selina's absence from camp, and how distracted she had been for the past few days—how could Selina have expected anything less?

She swung her legs down from her bunk and shuffled, still cocooned in blankets, the few steps towards the stove. She could have made a fire in her sleep by now, she was sure, and it wasn't long before their copper kettle was whistling shrilly.

Two doses of strong, sweet tea were poured into china cups, and she conveyed them back to where her grandmother sat, swathed in a thick woollen shawl and regarding her expectantly.

'Well?'

'Well, what, Grandmother?' Selina hopped up into her bunk, cup clutched to her chest.

'I would like to know what it is that bothers you. Start from the beginning, and don't leave anything out.'

'I don't know what you want me to say.' Selina glanced at Zillah from beneath her lashes. Even in the darkness she could see her grandmother's eyes were fixed on her, gleaming bright as a pair of new pins. 'There isn't anything I can think of.'

Edward's face rose up before her mind's eye before she could stop it, his hazel gaze locked onto hers, and she frowned down into her teacup. How was it that the only man ever to make her blush was a gentleman, and a Fulbrooke at that? She had every reason to loathe his family, and yet the pull of Edward's powerful appeal was impossible for her to ignore.

No Roma man had ever tempted her so much, that was for sure. Although plenty had vied for the hand of Tomas Agres's pretty daughter, Selina had never felt more than a passing flicker of interest in any of them beyond a stolen kiss or two.

The only one who had ever made her think twice was a handsome youth named Sampson, and even his charms had quickly vanished when she'd overheard him boast of his confidence in winning her without even needing to try. Since her swift and loud rejection of him nobody else had dared approach her, for which Selina felt nothing but relief.

The only man whose good opinion she needed to consider was Papa, and that had suited her just fine—until Edward Fulbrooke had come striding back into her life, his handsome face making her question every rational thought she'd ever had.

'Are you absolutely sure?'

'Yes.'

'You lie,' stated the old woman flatly. 'Do you think I'm blind? That I've finally lost my aged mind after all these years?'

'Of course not!'

'Then don't play games with me, girl. I can read you like a book.'

Selina sighed, shoulders slumping in resignation. *Perhaps it wouldn't be such a terrible idea to talk things over,* she mused. There had never been any secrets between the two of them; living in such close quarters didn't really leave much room for intrigue. Besides, she had too much respect for Zillah to continue with such an unconvincing lie.

Edward's image surfaced once again, all disarming smile and broad shoulders, and she forced it back roughly. It was definitely because she was overtired. She wouldn't waste a single, solitary second thinking about him *or* the musculature hidden beneath his coat under usual circumstances. The distress of that day must have disturbed her more than she'd realised, and now her mind was playing tricks on her. Perhaps the benefit of her grandmother's wisdom would help her regain her mental equilibrium. She just wouldn't tell her every detail.

'Very well.' Selina took a sip of tea and braced herself for the inevitable. She had no doubt it would not be pleasant. 'There was an incident while I was scouting for food.'

'What kind of incident, child?'

'I was set upon by two men. They chased me for a few miles, then I managed to climb a tree and hide until they left.'

'Did they hurt you?' Zillah's voice was soft in the darkness—ominously so.

'No. No doubt they would have done, had they caught me, but another man came and threw them off the scent. I suppose it's to him I owe my escape.' She hadn't thought of it that way before, she had to confess, and, looking at events in such a light, didn't it make her earlier behaviour towards Edward seem a little ungrateful?

Not to mention rude, she chided herself. *You didn't do much to show him Roma aren't really insolent and ill-mannered.*

But, no. One good act could never hope to negate generations of malice. Even if Edward *had* surprised her that day, there was nothing to say he wouldn't revert to his class type on any other. Besides, she thought grimly, if he'd known where they were camping would he have acted entirely less chivalrously?

'I see. And this heroic figure of a man—what of him?'

'What do you mean?'

'I mean what of him, Lina? Why did he intervene? What manner of person was he? Roma?'

'No, Grandmother.' Selina's mouth twitched at the thought as a sudden recollection of Edward's refined features flitted through her mind, his lips curved yet again into a distressingly attractive smile. 'Most definitely not Roma.'

Zillah's eyes narrowed. 'Come along, Selina. At my age I don't have time for guessing games. What is it you think you cannot tell me?'

Selina took a deep breath.

'He was gentry.'

There was silence.

'Grandmother…?'

'Speak on, girl.'

The mound of crochet blankets shifted as Zillah turned to face her directly with a close scrutiny Selina could have done without.

'What strange circumstances led such a high and mighty gentleman to concern himself with the likes of you?'

'I found his sister lost in the woods. I was trying to return her to where she came from and I was seen. The men who saw me assumed I was trying to steal her—and they weren't pleased.' Selina shivered suddenly and drew her blankets round her more tightly. What exactly would they have done if they'd caught her? The endless possibilities made her feel sick. 'The gentleman saw where I was hiding but sent the men away before they realised. He said his sister had told him what happened, and if I ever needed help I was to call on him.'

Zillah gave a short caw of laughter. 'Call on him? What does he think we would ever need *him* for?'

She clucked to herself for a few moments, evidently tickled. Selina tried to smile, but found her face was cold.

'And did he have a name, your new friend?'

'He—yes. Grandmother, he was the late Squire's own son.'

Every trace of mirth died from the old woman's face. 'Selina! Say you didn't tell him we were camped on his land?' Her voice was earnest, and her eyes fixed on Selina's own. 'I had not thought he would come so soon. If he learns we're here we'll have to move. With winter coming, and the babies so ill, we can't—'

'I would never endanger our people,' Selina breathed. 'I gave no clue where I had come from. He has no reason to suspect we're on his land.'

Zillah gazed at her a moment longer, before exhaling slowly. 'Good.'

It would be disastrous to move the camp now, and both women knew it. Winter was approaching fast—the hardest time of year for those living on the road, whose lives were a trial at the best of times.

All their menfolk, with the exception of just two elderly grandfathers, were away working on the Oxford Canal, undertaking the backbreaking labour of widening it. Even their adolescent boys had gone, taking up shovels and picks and toiling alongside the grown men. The work was hard, and the hours long, but they were able to make a few coppers to take back to the waiting women on their short visits home that would allow them to buy provisions for the entire winter—including costly coal to feed the stoves that kept their caravans warm.

Such opportunities didn't arise every day, and Selina's father had jumped at the chance. Even the prospect of returning to the Blackwell estate, with all its nightmarish memories, would be worthwhile if it meant securing the survival of the camp. If the Roma moved on now the men would have to give up this precious source of reliable income.

It isn't just the men's jobs at stake, though, is it?

Selina bit her lip as she thought of the women who'd had the misfortune to bear autumn babies: three of them, all born within a few days of each other, struggling to breathe in the raw mornings and coughing their hearts out at the first suggestion of a frost. They would never survive the jolting journey along pitted roads if the camp had to move. The chill would get into their tiny lungs and one of the women would be sewing a miniature shroud before they knew what had happened.

No. There was no way they could leave now.

'I mean it, Grandmother.'

With a supreme effort Selina once again attempted to banish Edward from her mind. He had no place in her world; their chance encounter could so easily have ended in disaster.

'You know nothing in this world is more important to me than the safety of our people.'

Zillah seemed about to reply when the silent night was shattered by a terrible scream.

* * *

Edward couldn't sleep.

That damned letter from Father certainly hadn't helped, he reflected drily. How unfortunate that even now the Squire's missives brought so little happiness to their recipients.

Edward's mouth set in a grim line as he recalled the weight that had settled in his stomach when he'd heard the news of his father's passing. Their relationship had been strained in life. Each had been as stubborn as the other, and Ambrose's unsuccessful attempts to control his son had damaged their already shaky bond.

Edward remembered the many times his father had pushed him to the limits of his patience with his demands. His move to London, ostensibly to take care of their business in the capital, had allowed Edward to put a distance between them, and that was the only reason their relationship had managed to survive at all. They had disagreed on so many things, and their heated arguments had been the cause of more than one servant running for cover.

But Ambrose was the only father Edward would ever have, and in his own way he had begun to mourn the man who had caused him so much frustration; or at least he had, until anger had seeped in to mingle with his complicated grief.

He threw back the red coverlet and left his bed. The cold night air raised goosebumps on his skin and he shrugged his way into his best brocade dressing gown. The fire in the grate had burned down to ash, and he toyed momentarily with the idea of calling for a maid to bring it back to life before dismissing the thought in irritation. When had he become the kind of man to consider dragging a girl from her warm bed in the middle of the freezing night solely to pander to his own needs?

He'd been in London too long; it was as well he'd returned to Warwickshire when he had. The capital, with all its diversions and frivolous pursuits, had threatened to turn him into a 'perfect' gentleman—selfish, hedonistic and mainly decorative. Now he was back where he belonged he could feel the countryside and its ways seeping back into his bones, gently erasing the hardness city living had threatened to instil in him.

Edward struck a match and lit the candle standing on his desk. The light illuminated the Squire's final letter, lying on the green leather top, and Edward picked it up. He'd read it a dozen times already, and it did not improve with further scrutiny.

His father's solicitor had seemed almost apologetic when he'd handed it over, having taken it from his ancient safe at the reading of Ambrose's will. It was written in a bold and flowing hand, and Edward ran his eye over the last communication he would ever receive from the man to whom he had been so deeply vexing.

As my only son and heir, you have repeatedly disappointed me in your duty to continue the line of our great and noble family. Nothing in your life could be more important, and your persistent failure to marry has provoked me to act.

I have instructed Mr Lucas to amend the terms of my will and add a condition on your inheritance. If you have not taken a wife within two months of my death the entirety of your inheritance will revert to my brother, your Uncle Charles, in his position as next in line.

He dropped the letter back onto the desk and extinguished the candle. He'd half expected it. His reluctance to marry had been like a red rag to a bull for Ambrose, for whom the continuation of the family name had been almost an obsession. Pretty heiress after pretty heiress had been paraded under Edward's nose, but of course the damage had been done long before then.

His mother had been the first to crush his faith in gentry women, but the Right Honourable Letitia James had driven the lesson home with brutal clarity. With her blonde ringlets and china-blue eyes Letitia had the face of an angel but not the morals to match, and her thoughtless betrayal of Edward with a richer suitor had opened the wounds he had hoped she would help him to heal. She was the only woman he had ever entertained marrying, and her actions had only proved to Edward his reticence had been justified.

Edward felt a hot pulse of anger course through him as he wrenched his mind away from past pains and recalled the full contents of the letter. Unable to dictate terms while alive, Ambrose had in death finally managed to find a way to bend Edward to his will, and recognition of the fact that he had no choice but to obey caused Edward's hands to curl into fists. He wasn't a simpleton; he knew he would have to wed eventually. It was the notion of being ordered, instructed like a child, that turned Edward's blood to fire.

In fairness, I suppose my bride might not be entirely like Mother or Letitia, he mused grimly as he dropped into his favourite armchair by the cold hearth. *You never know. Her pretty ringlets might be dark instead of blonde, for instance.*

The thought of dark hair stirred something in the back of his mind.

The girl from the woods. Selina. Now, that's

the sort of woman a man might be persuaded
to marry, were such a feat ever to be managed.

What had she meant, he owed her twice? The
words had puzzled him ever since their chance
meeting. Surely they had never met before. Edward knew he would never have forgotten one
such as her. It must have been simple mischief
on her part, doubtless for her own amusement,
and he had resolved to put her from his mind.

Unfortunately the Romani girl had persisted
in working her way into his thoughts with vexing regularity since their encounter three days
before. The memory had troubled him to begin
with—what was he doing, allowing a woman so
much space in his mind?—until he had reassured
himself that it meant nothing.

It was simple human nature to admire a pretty
face, and that was surely all his idle thoughts
amounted to. Couldn't a man enjoy the mental
picture of a handsome woman without it meaning anything more? He was in little danger of
ever seeing her again—and besides, his disin-
clination for spending too long in the company
of young ladies ran deep.

Thoughts as to her suitability as a wife were
as laughable as they were entirely hypothetical.
Still… She wouldn't be self-centred and idle like
the women of his class, he was sure of it. She
certainly wouldn't spend too much money on

dresses and amusements—in a stark contrast to the wasteful extravagance of the gentry. Of course it helped that she was beautiful, but a beautiful wife was often more trouble than she was worth—and besides, it wasn't as though he had any intention of *loving* a woman. He doubted he was even capable anymore, his heart having twice been battered by thoughtless rejection.

The only female with any sort of claim to his affections was little Ophelia, and he resolved there and then never to allow her to be moulded into an upper-class Miss. If she were to be subjected to endless lessons in etiquette and how to be a true lady he feared his sister would one day become conditioned to be more concerned with herself than other people. Just like his mother.

Edward grimaced. *Now you're getting maudlin,* he chided himself. Ophelia was nothing like the first mistress of Blackwell Hall and thank goodness for it. His sister would never be so cruel as to abandon her own child and run away with another man, leaving without so much as a goodbye for the boy she'd left behind, who had spent months waiting in vain for her return and defending her reputation with his fists.

At least she'd done him one favour—even if accidentally. From her harsh teaching he had learned a valuable lesson: he knew never to fall in love with a woman lest she leave and shatter his heart all over again. That was his mother's legacy.

Letitia had been the only one to break through, and Edward had dared to believe she might be a better woman than the one who had given him life. But instead she had proved herself almost a copy of his mother, and after her duplicity he had rebuilt his defences with even higher walls.

Edward drummed his fingers on the arm of his chair as thoughts of Letitia flitted through his mind. The notion that he had once thought she could be his bride seemed so ridiculous now he might almost have seen the humour in it if she hadn't ripped open the emotional scars he'd borne since childhood.

She knew how Mother's leaving had affected me, and yet she betrayed me in exactly the same way Mother betrayed Father.

If what he'd felt for Letitia had been love he could do without it. For when the loved one left—as apparently was inevitable—the pain was almost too much to bear.

The gilt clock on the mantelpiece struck two, but Edward was only half listening to the feeble chimes. The idea of another fashionable young lady parading around his countryside sanctuary appalled him. This was where he came to escape the cloying falseness of high society—the notion of inviting it into this last outpost of peace was unthinkable.

He sighed and rubbed his aching forehead with one hand. 'Think, Ned,' he said aloud. 'Put that Cambridge education to use for once in your life.'

Inspiration wouldn't come.

Edward got to his feet and paced the floor, boards creaking as he moved. 'Think! This is your future. Do you really want to be bound to such a creature for the rest of your life?'

Anger at his father's last actions churned within him once again, and he felt his chest tighten with the now familiar mixture of grief and rage. The Squire had been dead almost one month already; only a few weeks remained for Edward to find a suitable match or risk forfeiting his inheritance forever.

He could barely even remember Uncle Charles, the man to whom all his future could be lost. The only communication they had shared in the twelve years since Charles had left for the Continent was the occasional letter, never concerning anything warmer than news of business affairs. The injustice of his situation made Edward curse out loud.

He crossed to the window and drew aside one heavy curtain. There was no sign of dawn. Darkness would cover the estate for hours yet—until the sun sulked into view and its pale autumn rays signalled the start of a new day.

His rooms were at the front of the Hall, positioned to make the most of the natural light, and from the window Edward could just make out the line of manicured trees that stood to attention on either side of the long drive leading up to the Hall's imposing front door. He gazed out at the night, watching the trees stir gently in the moonlight.

A movement further down the drive caught his eye. He frowned. Even from a distance he could tell that whatever was out there was approaching the house at some speed, and getting ever closer. Edward squinted, straining his eyes against the gloom. Was it an animal of some kind?

Yes, he could just see it now: a great horse, bleached bone-white by the moon, galloping towards the Hall as though fleeing the fires of hell. Its rider was swathed in a cloak, with only her hair uncovered, flying out behind her like streamers in a storm—

'Selina?'

A thrill of something unknown flared in Edward's chest. It was definitely her—the closer she drew, the more Edward's certainty grew that the figure flying towards him was the girl from the woods. Now she was in range he could even recognise her horse: a huge grey beast, flecked with scars and knotted with hard muscle, speeding down the gravelled drive with a gracefulness that belied its size.

Momentarily frozen in surprise, all Edward could do was watch her approach, his confusion growing with every moment. He hadn't expected to see her again, and yet here she was. A less sensible man might have called it fate, and the unwanted suggestion was enough to galvanise him into action.

His heart pounded in his ears as he wrenched on his breeches, a rapid succession of thoughts chasing each other through his mind. Why was she here? At this hour? And why had she approached so swiftly? Something must be gravely wrong. She had given the impression that she distrusted his offer of friendship. What events could the intervening few days have wrought to bring about such a change?

A disloyal corner of his consciousness registered the thought that he was, despite his rational mind, *pleased* she had sought him out. Whatever it was she wanted, it was to him that she was turning. He dismissed the thought as soon as it arose—*ridiculous notion!*—but the echo of it stubbornly remained.

A thunderous sound at the front door drove him onwards in even greater haste. *She'll break it in two if she's not careful*, he thought in wry amusement as he thrust his feet into long leather boots.

The creak of an inner door being hurriedly flung open signalled the emergence of Blackwell's aged butler, Evans, and Edward couldn't restrain a grin at the prospect of the faithful retainer confronted with Selina.

Poor Evans. He smiled. *He won't know what's hit him.*

She was trying to pull away from the butler's firm grip when Edward reached the top of the grand sweeping staircase that led down into the entrance hall, all the while waving something in Evans's heated face—something white. Or at least it might have been white originally, but now it was streaked with mud and perhaps... dried blood?

'Mr Fulbrooke!' Selina spotted him and her attempts at escape doubled. Her hair was windswept and tangled from riding and her eyes were wild. 'Mr Fulbrooke! Please, sir, I must speak with you—let me *go*!'

Evans was trying manfully to restrain her, but the woman appeared to be as strong as an ox. The older man's face was puce with effort, and one of his slippers had come clean off in the fracas.

'You can't just push in here, waking the whole house—'

Selina paid him about as much attention as Edward would have paid a gnat. 'I brought this with me. We met in the woods—do you remember? You gave me this—this handkerchief!'

'Of course, Miss Agres.' Edward reached the bottom step and gently laid a hand on the butler's heaving shoulder. 'Thank you, Evans, you've done very well, but Miss Agres is a friend of mine. Please let go of her.'

The other man's face was a picture of surprise, and he opened his mouth as if to argue. Edward watched as the butler took a good look at Selina, taking in her disordered hair and unusual dress, but years of unfailing service prevailed and he hesitated for only a moment before sweeping into a low bow and stepping away.

'Please forgive me, miss. I should never have laid hands on you had I realised you were known to the master.'

Edward turned back to her, a smile forming on his lips. But it flickered and died when he saw the expression on her face, and he registered for the first time how her entire body trembled as though she suffered from an ague. Her slim form, so perturbingly attractive to him upon his first sight of her, now seemed to radiate a vulnerability unlike the defiance of their previous meeting. Was it for that reason he felt a glimmer of protective concern?

'Miss Agres? What's the matter?' She was

very pale, he saw with alarm—could she be ill? The pallor served to highlight the rich darkness of her eyes, a fact that did not escape him. 'You seem unwell. Won't you please sit down and I—?'

'There's no time!' Selina burst out.

She was wringing her hands, and Edward had to fight the unwelcome urge to take them in his own and hold them still.

'Please, Mr Fulbrooke, come with me at once! You said you'd be a friend to me, and that your word was your law—I need you to prove it!'

Edward gazed down at her. He had been right; something truly terrible had occurred. There could be no other explanation for her coming to him, and in such a state of obvious distress.

'You must try to calm yourself.' He spoke with such firmness that Selina's agitation seemed to check a little. 'I will, of course, do anything within my power to help you, but first you must explain to me the particulars.'

Selina took a deep breath and clenched her hands into fists. Behind her, Edward caught sight of the below-stairs maids peeping from the servants' corridor, their eyes wide with curiosity.

'Evans. Would you please ensure the maids return to their beds and tell Greene to saddle my horse immediately? I have a feeling I'll be going out, and I'm not sure when I shall return.'

Chapter Three

Selina glanced across at Edward, riding next to her on his sleek thoroughbred mare. Even in the silvery moonlight she could see his sharp jaw was tightly clenched as he bent low over his horse's neck, urging her on at full speed. She swallowed. Even at this pace they might still be too late.

At that first cry Selina had vaulted from her bunk and thrown on her clothes. Something within her had known what was happening even before the woman had stumbled up the steps of her caravan and hammered on the door, shouting out what she had seen and moaning in fear.

'They're coming! They're coming for us! What will we do? How can we defend ourselves?'

'We can't.' Zillah had stumped the short length of the cabin, unbolted the split door of the *vardo* and taken the wailing woman outside firmly by the shoulders. 'The only hope we have of surviving this is to lock ourselves in and pray for a miracle.'

'Is that *all*?' The woman had stared at Zillah, and Selina had seen the horror in her eyes. 'Is that all we can do?'

'Yes. With the men away we have no protectors. We don't even have any tools with which to arm ourselves—curse our foolishness! We should have planned for this.'

In the dim light Zillah had looked haggard with fear, and for the first time in her life Selina realised her grandmother was afraid. The knowledge had shaken her to the core. If weathered, unflappable Zillah was frightened, their situation must be every bit as bad as Selina feared.

'We bolt our doors and we pray.'

'And if they break down our doors? What then?'

Zillah closed her eyes. 'Then we try to save the children. Whatever the cost.'

That was when they'd heard it: men's voices, perhaps ten in all, punctuated by the excited baying of a pack of hounds. The woman had paled and fled back to her caravan, to drive home the heavy bolt across her door and gather her children round her, as though there was something she could do to keep them safe.

'So this is where you're hiding, is it?'

'Did you think we wouldn't find you, child-stealer?'

Selina's blood had run cold. She had known those voices—Harris and Milton, Edward Fulbrooke had called them. She'd remembered their threats, and her stomach had begun to knot in animalistic terror.

'We've brought some friends with us. Why don't you come out and meet them? Such a shame you ran from us before—if you hadn't we wouldn't have needed to come and find you...'

Selina's heart slammed into her ribs now, as she and Edward rode onwards. They were so close. Was there a chance they would get there in time? She imagined the children, cowering behind their shaking mothers as the sound of the men's mocking laughter echoed around the camp and heavy clubs began to whistle towards shuttered windows—

She gasped for air. *No.* She couldn't allow herself to think like that. If she went to pieces how would Edward find the camp? She had to stay strong and do whatever it took to protect her people. She had already taken the biggest risk, in the name of salvation.

Zillah had stared at her, eyes wide with horror. 'What? What did you say?'

'You said yourself—we need a miracle!'

'That would be no miracle, girl, only mad-

ness!' Zillah had backed away from her. 'You
would go to *them* for help? Our enemies?'

'What choice do we have?' Selina cried. 'He
gave me his word; I mean to test it!'

'But, Lina—'

'This is all my doing. I'm the only one with
even the smallest hope of getting us out of this
unscathed.' Selina had grasped both of Zillah's
hands in her own and felt them tremble. 'Do you
think I would go if there was any other way? You
know I would not. You know I don't make this
decision lightly.'

From outside the caravan both women had
heard a fresh scream, followed by a bray of boor-
ish laughter.

'Grandmother, please. I have to try.'

Zillah had peered up at her, an unreadable
expression in her ebony eyes, and given a shud-
dering sigh. 'Your mother wouldn't want this,
Selina.'

'Perhaps. But I know she wouldn't want anyone getting hurt if I had a chance to protect
them.'

She'd slipped from the caravan and out into the
meadow. Keeping to the shadows, she'd called
softly to Djali and been up onto his back and
gone from the camp before anybody could stop
her.

She felt Edward's eyes upon her, although she

didn't dare turn her head to look. She'd been grateful when he'd saddled up and followed her—more grateful than he would ever know— and amazed, too. She hadn't *really* expected him to keep his word, but to try had been her only option. What had been the real chances that an upper-class gentleman would honour his promise to a Roma?

She had obviously underestimated him in that moment, but that didn't mean she trusted him. The canker of suspicion ran too deep, and even now Selina had the unpleasant feeling of having jumped from the frying pan into the fire.

Even the horror of her current circumstances hadn't managed to completely obliterate her disloyal senses, however. A furtive glance towards him was like a swift punch in the guts. Once again she was assailed by the handsomeness of his face and the powerfully masculine frame of his body, and she felt her throat contract as she caught a glimpse of a tantalising expanse of toned chest: Edward's shirt had apparently been thrown on in great haste, with a few buttons left unfastened. There was a smattering of hair there, far darker than the gold on his head—*fascinatingly* so, in fact...

Selina wrenched her eyes away before he could turn and catch her looking. Even more mortifying than she ever would have believed was the realisation that she was *enjoying* the sight of him improperly dressed. It caused her great agitation, and her cheeks were flushed with both shame and guilt as she rode next to him in pained silence. Shame for appreciating such a trivial thing at such a time, and guilt at being appreciative of such a man at *any* time whatsoever.

Her instinctive attraction to Edward seemed to be tightening its grip on her, not loosening as she had hoped, and her grip on Djali's reins tightened likewise at the thought.

'Are we getting close?'

Selina swallowed hard, trying to force her voice into some semblance of normality. 'Yes. The camp is just beyond the line of trees up ahead.'

Edward nodded and spurred his horse onwards. Refusing to be outpaced, Djali surged forward too, and the horses flew neck and neck across the final stretch.

As they approached the screen of branches Edward began to slow. 'Miss Agres. Stop.' He pulled his mare up short.

Frowning, Selina did the same, and watched as Edward dismounted and hooked his reins over a branch. 'I want you to wait here.'

'What? No!' She slipped down from Djali's back and moved to stand at his head. 'Mr Fulbrooke, there's no way I'll be leaving my people to face this alone!'

'Be sensible.' Edward's voice was steady. 'If what you have told me is true, these men were drawn here by your presence. What effect do you think it will have if you suddenly appear in front of them?'

Selina opened her mouth, but her reply was quickly cut off by Edward's outstretched hand. He stood so close he could have touched her if he'd chosen to. His proximity made Selina's heart skip an unwilling beat and she quickly took a step backwards.

'The last thing either of us wants is to make things worse. I would consider it a personal favour if you would stay here until I come to find you.' He looked away. 'I would also like to know that you're safe.'

Selina blinked at him. He actually sounded concerned for her welfare. In all probability it was an affectation, born out of some misguided upper-class notion of honour, although she might have been fooled, had she been the foolish type, into believing he was genuine. And yet—to her shame—the notion that he might harbour some kind of regard for her wasn't unpleasant. Certainly some small part of her—a disloyal part, she thought crossly—hoped, against her better judgement, that he might be sincere.

Why, Lina? Because he's handsome? Selina scoffed at herself, irritated by her own brief weakness. *You should know better than that. Why should he feel any kind of concern for you? And why should you want it?*

'I'll stay here,' she said reluctantly. 'But only because I know you speak the truth. I can well imagine what would happen if those men laid eyes on me again.'

Edward nodded. 'I'm glad. Now I'll go and see what can be done to help your people.'

Selina stared at the ground. Edward's boots really were the best she had ever seen, and it was much easier to look at them than into the eyes of their owner. 'Thank you.'

'Don't thank me yet.'

There was an edge of grim humour to Edward's voice, and Selina chanced a glance up at his face. His firm jaw was fixed, and even in the pale light of the moon she could see the set of his expression. He looked determined, yet calm, and the combination only served to emphasise the handsome lines of his features. Selina twisted her fingers together beneath the cover of her cloak.

'We need to make sure I'm successful first. I intend to seek out every man who thinks he has the right to do this, and show him the error of his ways. Now, please, hide yourself. I hope to be back soon.'

Selina watched as he moved cautiously through the trees and vanished from her sight. *Well, I did what I could.* It was all up to Edward now, she supposed as she settled herself against the thick trunk of a spreading oak.

And what of Mama? Zillah's earlier rebuke echoed through Selina's mind. Would she really be so appalled? Or would she understand that family came first and must be protected even if at great personal cost?

Edward had taken her by surprise so far, she could not deny it. His conduct towards her had been far better than she would have expected from a gentleman—and a Fulbrooke, come to that. His face was undeniably pleasing, though his fair looks were in stark contrast to the dark Roma handsomeness, strange but not unappealing in their novelty.

Not that you should care for such pretty manners, or notice the colour of his eyes, she reminded herself sternly. It took more than such trivial things to impress her. It was just an observation, and one she would continue to strive to banish from her mind.

She shivered. A glance down at her hands showed that they still shook—with cold or fear? she wondered. She strained her ears, both hoping and dreading to catch a whisper of a clue as to what was happening beyond the trees, but there was nothing save the quiet breathing of the horses and the sigh of leaves stirring in the night air.

Selina squeezed her eyes shut. *Oh, Mama. What would you have done?*

Edward felt the brutal atmosphere change to one of shamefaced fear almost as soon as he stepped from the camp's shadows into the light of Harris's torch and swept it from his hand with rough force. One glance at Edward's flame-lit face—rigid with cold fury—was enough to make the group of men, frozen in the act of battering the spoked wheels of a caravan, decide that perhaps the Roma had learned their lesson, and Edward might almost have laughed at the instantaneous change of their voices from jeering to pleading.

'We were just trying to protect Miss Ophelia, sir,' Milton ventured meekly, attempting to hide a club behind his back as his friends shuffled from foot to foot, their eyes sliding past Edward to fix on the ground.

'Do you think me a simpleton, man?'

Edward turned to him, feeling the rage that bubbled within him course hotly through his veins. The Roma women inside their caravans must have been beside themselves, he thought disgustedly. What kind of man could take pleasure in such a thing?

'We both know this has nothing to do with my sister and everything to do with your need to bully those you feel beneath you. Am I wrong? Do you disagree? Answer me!'

The gamekeeper stared down at his boots, the ashen shade of his face visible even in the moonlight. 'I... I'm not...'

'Not a bully? Of course you are. You all are. What other possible explanation could there be for *ten men* to go to the effort of seeking out and then attacking a camp full of women and children?'

Edward glared down at the man from his great height. The image of Selina's terrified expression and shaking body flashed before him and he felt his fury surge upwards. Even if the Romani woman hadn't been such an undeniable beauty— which, he had to admit to himself, was part of the reason he had extended the hand of friendship in the first place—he still would have interceded on her behalf. How dared these men take it upon themselves to behave so appallingly on *his* estate? And, to add insult to injury, to pretend they did so out of loyalty to his sister?

'You didn't do this for Ophelia.'

He gestured across the camp, catching glimpses of the damage as he turned. Cooking pots and blankets lay strewn across the ground, evidently kicked about by heavy boots, and more than one lantern had been hurled down to burst into shards of glass. The caravans had fared better than he had feared, at least. The half-hour it had taken for Selina to return with him hadn't left the men enough time to destroy any of them, although several now bore the marks of savage blows to their wooden walls.

'Not for her. You did it because *you* wanted to.'

It was an ugly truth, Edward knew, but a truth nonetheless. He'd heard tales of abuse before, from the Roma boys he had played with as a child, when their easy laughter and unselfconscious warmth had seemed poles apart from the stiff propriety of playmates in his own class and their welcome of him had left a permanent impression of their decency.

There was no basis for this mistreatment— no justification at all. But folk inherited their intolerances from their fathers, as had their fathers before them, and prejudice was passed down through generations to rest in the hearts of men such as Harris and Milton—men with little power of their own, whose low social standing fanned the flames of their desire to find someone, *anyone*, they perceived to be worth less than themselves to bear the brunt of their frustrations.

He surveyed the men surrounding him, taking

in their various attempts at contrite expressions, and felt his rage renew its vigour. He could dismiss them—throw them off his land just as they had wanted to drive off the Romani—but they had wives who had committed no crime other than making a dubious choice of husband, and children, too, reliant on their fathers' employment for survival. To remove the men from his service would be to punish their families, some of whom had served the Blackwell estate for generations, and he felt a twinge of conscience at the thought of that.

Damn it all. These animals should count their blessings.

He looked down at them, his face set in an expression of grim dislike. 'I have decided on this occasion to let you off with a warning. Make no mistake, however,' Edward went on. 'I will not tolerate this kind of behaviour on my property. If I hear anything of this nature has happened again, next time I will not be so lenient.'

The light of their torches illuminated the men's faces, each sagging with relief.

Only Milton looked mutinous, and Edward raised a challenging eyebrow. 'Something troubles you?'

'No, sir.' Milton shook his head quickly, although resentment gleamed dully in his sunken eyes. 'Thank you for your kindness, sir.'

'Very well.' Edward nodded his head in the vague direction of where the estate workers' cottages lay. 'You may all return home now, to reflect upon what I have said.'

The men slunk off, dogs creeping at their heels. No doubt to tell their wives of Squire Fulbrooke's unfair and malicious treatment of his well-intentioned, faithful servants, Edward imagined. He snorted as he watched them go, slouching away between the trees. It was almost an anti-climax, how easily he had been able to intervene. They were cowards indeed.

Long grass knotted about his boots as he fought his way back up the bank and through the line of trees to where Selina waited, a silent shape at the base of an ancient tree.

'Mr Fulbrooke!' She leapt to her feet when she saw him coming, one hand at her throat and the other on the tree's trunk to steady herself. 'What happened? Is the camp—?'

'Do not fear.'

Edward could hardly keep himself from reaching out to touch her shaking hand. She looked as though she might faint, he noted in alarm. Not that he would blame her if she did. She'd had the most terrible experience, and if anything he was rather impressed by how well she'd handled it.

The notion almost made him frown. 'The men have gone and your camp is safe.'

'Gone? Safe?'

Edward looked at Selina a little more closely. Pale and beautiful in the soft light of the moon, she appeared to be swaying now. 'You look a little faint. Here, take my arm. We can walk together.'

'No.' Selina shook her head wildly. 'I'll ride—it'll be quicker. I have to get back *now.*'

'You're in no fit state to ride anywhere. Let me help you. You're no use to anybody unconscious.'

'But Djali—'

'Will follow us, I'm sure. Now, come. Take my arm.'

She hesitated, suspicion sparking in her eyes once more. Edward sighed, supressing a flicker of irritation. *Mistrustful as a feral cat.*

'Miss Agres. I have risen in the middle of the night, ridden for miles and dispersed a mob—all in the name of your safety. Do you really think it likely that I undertook all that only to lunge at you on the pretence of offering my arm?'

Selina's eyes flashed, and she opened her mouth to reply before evidently thinking better of it. She took a shaky step forward and, with the air of one with a gun to her head, slipped her hand beneath his arm and gripped tightly.

It was a warm little hand, Edward noted with a jolt of surprise. The night was chill, but the patch of forearm covered by her palm suddenly didn't seem cold at all. It was an unexpectedly pleasant sensation. Usually having a woman on his arm felt intrusive, but Selina's touch, although firm, was not invasive.

He wondered for a moment at how it was that her grasp was so much more bearable than anybody else's had ever been. If he were to be honest with himself, it was more than merely bearable… At the first touch of her fingers he'd felt a sharp pulse of something unexpected shoot through him—a bewilderingly quick nameless rush that had caused him to frown in surprise. He glanced down at Selina, searching her face for any indication that she had felt a similar sensation, but she studiously avoided his gaze, the faintest suggestion of a blush colouring her cheeks.

'Can we go now, please, Mr Fulbrooke?'

Edward smothered a smile at the careful politeness of her tone. 'Of course. Watch your step.'

The slight pressure of her hand on his arm was the only way Edward knew she walked beside him. Her steps were almost silent, graceful as any wild animal.

It was only a short distance to walk: down a small slope, through a band of trees and then out into the secluded meadow that Selina's Roma community had thought so safe.

Edward surveyed the scene in front of him. Fires had been lit in his absence, their orange tongues dancing in the night air, and a group of women stood to one side, conversing in low voices that flared with both sorrow and relief. Among them a young girl was singing softly in a tongue Edward didn't recognise, gently rocking a baby on her hip. An old man, bent almost double with age, seemed to be tending to an injured horse, while a small boy carefully swept up a heap of spilled oats from an upended sack. Another cluster of women were gathered around one of the caravans, its painted sides still gleaming cherry-red in the firelight but heavily dented by brute force.

He approached cautiously. Despite Selina's presence at his side he could almost feel the cold stares of the women upon him, their fear and uncertainty palpable.

'Grandmother!'

Selina slipped away from him and the place where her hand had rested on his arm felt suddenly cold. She had held it there for mere minutes, and yet he felt a curious sense of loss at the withdrawal of her touch. Edward pulled his coat closer about himself, shrugging off the uncanny sensation. He must be getting tired… His mind was beginning to play tricks on him.

Selina was in the arms of an old woman, being folded into a fierce embrace. The woman was small and frail-looking, but with a similarity around the cheekbones that suggested a family connection. The embrace ended and the two began to talk. He heard the rise and fall of their voices, soft at first, but swelling to such a pitch that the neighbouring Roma glanced across in concern.

He thought he saw the glint of tears on Selina's face, shining like rubies in the light of the fire, and turned away. *You shouldn't be here,* he warned himself. *You've played your part.* Selina and her grandmother evidently had much to discuss, and none of it his business. He should enquire as to whether he could be of any further assistance and then leave these people in peace.

'Mr Fulbrooke?' Selina stood close to him, her fingers working in apprehension. The fire lit up one side of her face, making flames dance in one jet iris while throwing the other into shadow. 'My grandmother told me what happened, and what you did to help us. We are so grateful.'

Edward smiled. 'It was a pleasure.' The tears had gone, he saw: she'd rubbed them away with the back of her hand when she'd seen him looking. There was softness under her tough facade, he was sure. Why was she so determined that he not see it?

'We are forever in your debt.'

'There is no debt, Miss Agres.' He shook his head. 'You were kind to my sister when she was in need and I've just shown the same kindness to you and yours.'

Selina nodded, although Edward saw unhappiness in the lovely oval of her face. The sight niggled at him, creating an uncomfortable feeling of concern that took him by surprise. 'Has something else occurred?' he asked.

'Something else?'

'You were so relieved before we arrived in camp. Now you've spoken with your grandmother and you seem distressed again. What has she said to you?'

'It's nothing that need trouble you.' Selina's voice was quiet and she looked away from him across the camp.

Edward followed her gaze to where a little girl was attempting to coax her trembling dog out from beneath a caravan, the wheels of which were scarred by the blade of an axe.

'It's only—they said they'd be back.'

'What?'

Selina turned to him, her eyes huge with worry. 'As they were leaving Grandmother heard them. They said it was only on your land that you would feel obliged to protect us, and that as soon as we moved they would come to find me.'

Edward felt his pulse quicken. Those two-faced, disobedient rogues. How *dared* they make new threats? How dared they try to get around his express word? And yet…

There isn't much I can do to prevent it, he thought darkly. Edward couldn't control what they did outside his estate, and short of catching them in the act he would have no concrete proof of their involvement in any future incidents.

Selina's voice was hoarse. 'It's all my fault.'

'It is not.'

'Oh, but it is.'

She smiled then, a tight stretch of her lips filled with such sadness and fear that Edward felt another sharp stab of that *something* lance through his chest, only to flicker and fade the next moment.

'Why do you say that?'

'Because it's me they want. And they'll continue to hound us, over and over, until they find me.'

He gazed down at her. Out of the corner of his eye he could see the group of women watching him, Selina's grandmother among them. Nobody seemed willing to come nearer, and the contrast between their wary distance and the way women of his own class clustered around him at any given opportunity was so absurd a part of him wanted to laugh.

The sight of Selina's rigid face stopped him. 'What is your plan?' he asked.

She sighed—a long drawn-out shudder of breath that seemed to come all the way up from her toes. 'I'll have to give myself up to them. There is no other way.'

'You cannot possibly!' Edward stared at her, hardly able to express his disbelief. 'You cannot mean that!'

'What choice do I have?' Selina stepped away from him, her face shuttered and blank. 'Apparently I've made fools of them—and they won't stop until they've proved they're the victors and I've lost.' She shook her head slowly. 'They'll continue to terrorise us when we leave here, and with the health of the babies and our menfolk's jobs we can't get far enough away to escape them. This is the only way.'

Edward passed a hand through the tousled thatch of his hair. Selina had given him a brief outline of the Roma's current situation as they had ridden out from Blackwell. To move the community now would indeed spell disaster.

'So, you see, it's what I must do. Grandmother forbids it, of course.' There was a ghost of that terrible smile again. 'But I won't allow a repeat of what happened tonight.'

It was unthinkable. Edward paced a few steps away from her, noting with perverse amusement the way the group of women standing nearby flinched backwards. She couldn't. The very idea that Selina would consider sacrificing herself for the good of her community was madness.

A commendable sentiment, Edward thought, *but utter madness.*

The fact that he couldn't see how to prevent it from happening pained him more than he cared to admit. He had no choice other than to acknowledge that she was a remarkable woman, quite unlike any he'd met before, and the notion of her in such danger was abhorrent to him. Of course she would face that danger bravely—there was that damned flicker of admiration again—but still...

If only there was a way he could reliably intervene...a set of circumstances that meant Harris and Milton could never touch her and she would be permanently out of their reach...

They would continue to hunt Selina, of that he was certain. Their lust for vengeance for her perceived victory and the pull of that generations-strong prejudice was too powerful. Neither common decency nor the pleas of their wives would prevent them from attempting to punish Selina and the other Roma. She had escaped them not once, but twice, and now their resolve would be firm.

No doubt it was the rumours of his family's mistreatment of the Roma that had made the men feel safe in persecuting them, Edward mused darkly. Charles had done something terrible, and Ambrose had all but chased the travellers off his land. Their prejudices had been clear to all—perhaps people suspected that Edward shared their sentiments.

The idea that he might so easily have followed their unthinking bigotry was uncomfortable. *Thank goodness I was taught better than that,* he thought, his eyes on Selina's silent face.

His childhood Romani friends had done him that favour, by including him in their play and allowing him to be himself in a way frowned upon at his austere home.

And that little Roma girl who showed me such rare kindness will never know the difference she particularly helped to make.

Her tender care of him was something he hadn't experienced at Blackwell Hall; his mother had been only occasionally attentive, in a detached sort of way, and Ambrose had never so much as lain an affectionate hand on his shoulder.

The thought of his father caused a pain in his chest Edward could have done without, and resentment swelled within him once again as the contents of that enraging final letter ran through his head.

Having been temporarily replaced by the severity of Selina's situation, his own troubles now returned to the forefront of his mind with a vengeance, and Edward felt his insides twist with renewed anger at the late Squire's meddling. Time was running out for him to claim his inheritance—a needless pressure born out of one man's obsession with control.

But Edward was his own master and always had been—that was what his father had hated so much. To *make* Edward obey him in death in a way he hadn't managed in life would have been Ambrose's final victory.

An idea exploded into Edward's consciousness with such vigour he could have sworn he heard it. *Of course.* It was so simple—and wouldn't it neatly solve Selina's problem at the same time as his own?

He would obey his father's will to the letter—right down to the final dot of the final 'i'. He would marry as instructed—but not to the kind of woman Ambrose would have so ardently desired, nor one in any way reminiscent of the lady who had taken his heart only to grind it into dust.

It was risky. People wouldn't like it. Certainly his father would have been beside himself with rage. But the opinion of society had never mattered much to Edward and, given the desperate circumstances of both parties involved, it now mattered even less. There was even some satisfaction to be taken in knowing he was, as always, acting according to his own wishes—dictated to by nobody but himself.

'Miss Agres?'

Selina had turned away from him. Standing before the fire, only her silhouette was visible to Edward's gaze, outlined in sparks and tongues of curling flame. He could see the tension in her back and knew it was only by sheer willpower that she was maintaining her composure.

'Yes.'

'I think I may have a solution to your current dilemma—depending on your answers to two questions.'

'Have you?' Her tone was flat and devoid of curiosity. 'And what would those questions be?'

Edward ignored how dull she sounded, feeling his hopes beginning to build. 'The first is: What is your age?'

She didn't turn to look at him, her eyes still fixed on the flames before her. 'How is that of any relevance?'

'Please. Humour me.'

She sighed, as though it was an effort to find the words to reply. 'Very well. I am recently turned twenty.' The fire crackled, sending sparks swirling into the night sky. 'Your second question?'

Edward reached for her. At the first touch of his hand on her shoulder Selina jumped and swung round to face him, a frown of distrust clouding her features. Edward smiled as the expression in her dark eyes, at first wary and fearful, turned to frozen astonishment as she watched him drop to one knee and take her small hand in his own.

'Selina Agres. Will you marry me?'

Chapter Four

'I— *What?* What did you say?'

Selina gaped at him, feeling her mouth drop open in shock. Had she misheard? Surely he could *never* have said what she thought he'd—

'I said, will you marry me?'

She stared downwards, first at Edward's intent face and then at their hands, joined together in a clasp uncomfortably like that of a pair of lovers. His hand was so much larger and yet it held hers so gently—*almost tenderly*, a disloyal voice in the back of her mind murmured.

To her horror, a sensation not unlike the warmth of a fledgling fire kindled beneath Edward's firm fingers, flickering against her skin and stealing upwards towards her arm. The feeling crept higher, warming her against her will, until it reached her chest and settled there, burning inside her with an inexplicable heat that sent her heart fluttering.

On the very edge of her field of vision she could just make out Zillah, watching them in uncharacteristically mute shock, for all the world as though she couldn't believe what she was seeing. Selina wasn't sure she believed it either. He couldn't be serious—of course he couldn't. Whatever had possessed him to make such a cruel joke at such a moment?

'Have you run *mad*?' The flickering embers of sensation sparked further, beginning to smoulder, and Selina snatched her hand from Edward's grasp, cradling it against her body with the other as though he had truly burnt her with his touch. 'Or do you think to mock me?'

'Neither, I hope.' Edward rose lightly to his feet again, and Selina took a step backwards, out of his long reach. He didn't attempt to come closer, but instead regarded her calmly as she glared at him. 'I asked in earnest.'

'No! Of *course* my answer is no—how could you have expected otherwise?'

'Because I think it would be helpful to both of us if you were to accept my offer.'

She stared at him, taking in the sincerity of his expression, and some private part of her regretted that such a face should be wasted on a madman. How on earth could he imagine his question to be *helpful*? Surely a proposal of marriage was the absolute opposite of a helpful suggestion? And yet there Edward stood, apparently entirely sober and set on his ridiculous request.

Selina's heart thrummed in her ears as she stood, silent, hearing the hostile muttering of the watching Romani women as they hovered a short distance away. Edward must have been able to hear them too, but he gave no sign as he waited for her reply, arms folded across his invitingly broad chest.

'How could that possibly be helpful?'

Edward glanced towards the nearby cluster of Roma and dropped his voice to a low murmur. 'It would solve problems for both of us.' He nodded engagingly, the light of the fire on his hair making it shine like burnished gold. 'I think we could both benefit if we were to come to an understanding.'

Selina narrowed her eyes, taking in the calm patience of his face. What problems could a pampered gentleman have that would reduce him to pinning his hopes on a Roma girl, of all people?

When she didn't reply he continued. 'I am in need of a wife in order to meet the terms of my father's will and retain my inheritance.'

Edward spoke lightly, but something in the set of his jaw increased Selina's suspicions.

'I thought if you were to help me navigate the issue I could do something for you in return.'

Navigate the issue? Selina opened her mouth

to speak, but found she had no words. He must be a madman indeed; what other explanation could there be?

Her voice, when she finally trusted herself to speak, was strained. 'I see. Or rather, I don't see—not at all. Why me? What do you think you could do in return that would ever persuade me to accept you?'

His answer was not one she had anticipated.

'I am willing to extend an invitation for your people to stay on my land, under my protection, so your camp will not have to move during the winter months.'

Edward spoke quietly but with a conviction that made Selina pause.

'You, in turn, would be safe with me at Blackwell Hall until the spring, when we might annul our marriage, and then you would be free to leave with the rest of the Roma. By that time your menfolk will have completed their assignments, and your people will be able to travel far enough away to avoid any further trouble.'

Selina felt all the breath leave her body as she froze, pinned to the spot by his words. *No.* He couldn't offer her that. How could he?

'You jest. You can't promise me—'

'I can, and I do.'

Edward's face was grave, and Selina felt her

heart check as his solemnity only served to en-hance her appreciation of his sharp features.

'Without your help I will have to forfeit this entire estate. I ask for you to become my wife in name only, and not forever. My father's will specifies that I must marry, but it gives no in-dication of how long I must retain a wife after the fact.' A glint of something like wry humour passed over his face. 'Please believe I have ex-plored every loophole in the legalities. An an-nulment can follow in the spring, so long as we admit you were under the age of twenty-one and did not have your father's permission to marry.'

Selina swallowed. He had played his cards well—he must have known that this was the one thing he could offer her that she would be tempted to accept. A whole winter without the worry of being moved on? The men would be able to keep their jobs, and the sick Roma babies would be safe—even the threat of the gamekeep-ers' mob would vanish. The only thing standing in the way was herself.

If she were to accept Edward's offer she would be ensuring the immediate future of the entire camp. Wouldn't that be worth the sacrifice? All their lives in exchange for living a lie for a few months?

But what would those few months cost her? To live with Edward, to *marry* him, would be to go against everything she had felt about the gentry ever since that fateful day twelve years before.

She could see, if all pretence to the contrary was abandoned, why a woman might be tempted by his offer, and even *she* might have considered it had he belonged to any other class. His physicality was compelling, and there was something in his look that seemed to call to her.

Even as he stood before her, awaiting her reply with quiet dignity, Selina felt drawn to him in a way that she couldn't explain. Never before had a man managed to affect her so powerfully, pulling her in even as she tried to dismiss him. It was beyond confusing, and a temptation like none she had ever known before.

But to marry him would be to forget almost an entire lifetime of suspicion and resentment and willingly enter into the lions' den of her worst enemy. And what of Mama? Selina's heart ached at that question.

Edward's a Fulbrooke, and it was a Fulbrooke who killed Mama—or as good as killed her.

That his face made her want to stare shouldn't matter one bit, and the fact that the urge to reach out and touch the scar that gleamed on his cheek still called to her wasn't something she should even consider.

'Selina—Miss Agres. It comes down to this: *you* don't want your people to come to any harm and *I* don't appreciate being forced to marry according to somebody else's wishes. If you accept my proposal both of us will be delivered from situations not of our choosing.'

'But why ask *me*?' Selina burst out, uncertainty and frustration boiling over into vexation. His effect on her was unnerving, and his request even more so: it just didn't make *sense*. 'There must be hundreds of women of your acquaintance. Why do you think *I'm* your best option?'

'Because you are. I have no desire to be bound to a wife. You don't *want* to be married to me. You place upon me no expectations and you will ask nothing of me other than that I honour our bargain. In turn, I will ask nothing of you other than that you marry me. You will have your own private bedchamber and I will not attempt to impose on you as a husband might expect to do. All I require is your help to allow me to keep my inheritance away from my uncle.'

If her fall from Djali had been painful, the mention of Charles Fulbrooke was like a drop from ten times the height. Selina felt her face freeze into a tight mask of horror and all words were stolen from her dry mouth as she stared up into Edward's face. An iron fist seemed to be squeezing her chest, and it felt like a lifetime before she was able to draw enough breath to answer him.

'Your uncle? Your *uncle* will inherit if you fail to marry?'

'That is correct.' Edward's speech was clipped, as though he was holding himself under control. 'He has been abroad these past twelve years, but I don't doubt he would be delighted to return here to take my place as Squire.'

Return here? Selina's blood was like ice and it froze her to every last bone. *The man responsible for Mama's death to return to a handsome inheritance? To a position of power?*

Surely it couldn't be allowed. Surely such good fortune could never come to such a monster as he?

And yet of course it could. Selina knew little of upper-class affairs, but even she couldn't fail to grasp the importance placed on the continuation of family names. They weren't so different from the Roma in that regard, in truth. The Agres family was ancient and respected, and Selina knew her mother had been proud to marry into it. Whatever past crimes Charles might be suspected of, the Fulbrooke inheritance would pass to him with ease should Edward somehow fall short of his father's expectations.

But I could prevent it.

The thought stole through Selina's mind like a cold wind, chilling her as she turned it over inside her head.

I could stop that man from returning here and from claiming the Fulbrooke fortune. Wouldn't that be the most perfect revenge? His inheritance blocked by the daughter of the woman his prejudice helped to kill?

The temptation glowed within Selina like a burning flame, chasing from her the chill of moments before. Perhaps some of its light showed on her face, for Edward peered down at her with something like confusion and she felt another powerful wave of that mysterious *something* engulf her from head to toe.

It would mean marrying a gentleman—a member of the same class she had been taught to fear for so long—but Edward had yet to show any sign of the cruel streak she had expected, and his physical effect on her was something she could not ignore. They had been almost friends once…could some shadow of the gentle lad he had once been still remain?

'What do you think, Miss Agres? Can you see—?'

A flurry of movement at her side caught Selina's attention a split-second before she felt the grip of a bony hand clench around her bicep.

'That's quite enough of that.' Zillah's words were directed squarely at Edward, who looked down at her in surprise. The old woman glared at him as she jerked Selina by the arm. 'Come away now, Lina.'

'Grandmother—' Selina began to speak, but her words were abruptly silenced.

'No, girl. We're grateful for his help, but that doesn't mean he can take liberties.' Zillah thrust her chin towards Edward. 'You *know* what he is.'

'What I *am*?' Edward's brow creased in visible confusion, although his tone was courteous as ever. 'Perhaps you could explain what it is about me that troubles you, ma'am?'

Firelight glinted off Selina's dark hair as she tossed it back from her face, her cheeks slightly flushed. 'You're gentry, Mr Fulbrooke.' She spoke slowly, deliberately, as though explaining something to a child. One of her hands was attempting to prise the fingers from her arm, but the old woman held fast. 'Roma do not mix with gentry—for good reason. You must know this.'

'Exactly so,' Zillah rejoined firmly. 'I don't know what your designs on my granddaughter are, but I can tell you now they won't be successful.'

For a moment both generations of Roma women fixed Edward with black eyes: one pair filled with challenge, the other with uncertainty. It was the gaze of the latter that he returned.

Edward inclined his head politely. He would

have to tread carefully, he thought, if he was to have a hope of achieving his aim. 'I understand your reluctance to engage with me, ma'am, under the circumstances. But I would very much appreciate it if you were to allow me to continue my address to Miss Agres.'

Zillah snorted. 'Continue your *address*? If there's something you wish to discuss with Selina, you can do it in my hearing. You may have done us a good turn tonight, and for that you have my thanks, but that doesn't give you leave to fill the girl's head with nonsense.'

Edward bit his tongue. *Remember your manners.* If he were to stand any chance of securing Selina's agreement to his plan he would need to find a way round her grandmother. She could hold the key to his inheriting. A wife was all the will required, and in Selina there was a chance for him to marry without the risk of forming any dangerous attachments that might end in disaster. He could see how she chafed under the grip of the old woman's hand, and how her brow was furrowed in thought. If he could just navigate her captor, all might not be lost.

He bowed. 'You're quite right. I've been exceptionally rude. I should, of course, have consulted you before I made an offer to your granddaughter. Perhaps I could have a moment of your time now, to discuss terms?'

Edward could see where Selina had inherited her spark from—he had no doubt her grandmother would have liked to give him a swift kick in the shins if she'd thought she'd get away with it. He wondered if Selina felt the same sentiment, and steeled himself against the smile that tried to curve his lips upwards.

'Now isn't convenient. You can see we have much to do before morning comes, and I have important things I need to discuss with Selina myself.'

'Grandmother.'

Selina's voice was firm, quite as resolute as Zillah's, and Edward marvelled at the world of determination he heard beneath the surface of that one word.

'I haven't finished my conversation with Mr Fulbrooke.'

'I don't see that he can have anything else to say. Our troubles are no longer any of his concern.'

Edward seized his chance. 'I would like to *make* them my concern.' He stepped a little closer and saw how the old woman bridled but stubbornly stood her ground. 'I offer your granddaughter sanctuary, Mrs Agres, and a promise that by marrying me she will have the full protection of the Fulbrooke name, extending to everyone living in this camp.'

'We are more than capable of solving our own problems, Mr Fulbrooke.' Zillah drew herself up to her full height, still not reaching Edward's shoulder. 'We will find a way to deal with this ourselves.'

'Grandmother!' With a final sharp tug Selina broke free from the old woman's grasp and backed a few short paces away from her. 'You're not *listening*. Think what this could mean for you all.'

Edward saw how her chest rose and fell rapidly and heard the edge of desperation in her voice. He nodded at her, feeling a creeping glimmer of optimism. The fact that Selina hadn't dismissed his proposal out of hand was encouraging.

'I have no intention of trying to force Selina into doing anything she doesn't want to do. Her wellbeing is a large part of why I make this offer.'

The old woman looked from her granddaughter to Edward and back again, taking in the girl's agonised expression, and Edward saw her hesitation.

'I want to keep her safe. I will make sure she's treated with every respect during her time with me, should she choose to come.' He turned to Selina and saw a shadow of doubt flicker across her beautiful face. 'I know you don't care for me, or for anything I stand for, but believe me—that is an advantage for both of us.'

Selina shook her head impatiently. 'That is what I do not understand. Why not choose a woman you *want* to marry? Why not find one you think you could love? And who could love you in return?'

It was the worst possible thing she could have asked, and it hit him squarely in the target of his heart. It was a fair question, he allowed ruefully, and he understood why she'd asked it. Perhaps he might have said the same in her position. But he couldn't...*wouldn't* bring himself to answer her boldness with the truth: that he no longer knew what it was to love anybody but his poor half-orphaned sister, and that even if he *could* open his heart to another it was not worth risking the pain of another rejection.

The only person he would ever admit that to was himself, he thought bitterly as he watched Selina's face turn from agitated to bemused at his silence. How could he ever put into words the damage his mother's abandonment and Letitia's later betrayal had done to him? And even if he managed to find a way, who could be trusted enough with the knowledge that between them they had irrevocably shattered his trust in the women of his own class—and perhaps women entirely?

The memory of the sickening swoop of his insides when he had learnt of Letitia's duplicity raked through his mind—and how the pain had gradually been replaced by a numb despair that was scarcely more bearable. There was no chance he would ever make himself vulnerable in that way ever again.

He forced a smile, but he knew his eyes must be cold as he replied. 'As I said before, I don't wish to take a wife at all. If I must, I'd rather know the lady won't form an attachment to me that I can't return.'

'Well. You needn't fear for me there.'

Selina turned away from him, worrying at her lower lip with small white teeth. She seemed to be weighing his words. Edward waited with all the patience he could muster as she slowly paced back and forth, the firelight playing across her as she moved.

'If I were to take your offer—'

Zillah started, her face haggard with disbelief. 'You can't be thinking of *accepting* him, girl?'

Selina took the old woman by the arm, leading her the few paces towards what Edward assumed must be their caravan. She persuaded Zillah to sit on the wooden steps and squatted next to her on the ground, their heads close together in an age-old picture of intimacy.

Edward, taking a moment to pass a hand across his tired eyes, missed the fleeting glance Selina threw his way before she bent to whisper into her grandmother's ear. The old woman grew very still, listening intently. Edward could have sworn he caught the words 'inheritance' and 'uncle', and he saw Zillah flinch as though in pain. But in the next moment her face took on an expression of reluctant contemplation, and she clutched Selina's hand in her bony fingers.

'But what of you? What will become of you, Lina, up there in that big house?'

'I will manage.' Selina's face shone pale in the moonlight, her brow creased into a determined frown. 'My only other choice is to allow the mob to find me and to draw them away from the camp myself.'

'I won't allow it!'

'Then don't you see? Accepting Mr Fulbrooke is the lesser of two evils.'

Selina glanced at him entirely unapologetically and Edward attempted manfully to hide a small smile. Did she not know he was the most eligible bachelor in the county, or did she simply not care? *The latter, most likely*, he thought in wry amusement. *The lesser of two evils, indeed.* If it was a loveless marriage he desired—and desire it he did—Selina would certainly oblige him.

'So, do you have an answer for me, Miss Agres? Do we have a deal?'

Selina's eyes were huge in the firelight as she rose to her feet and came slowly towards him.

Gazing down into them, Edward saw a world of reflected flames, leaping and tumbling in the ebony depths of her pupils, and he wondered for the first time if his offer was the solution to their problems or the start of another, far bigger than any before.

He frowned as a sudden twist of unease settled in his stomach as he looked down at the captivating woman who stood before him, her slender form still radiating a wariness that stirred him in a way he couldn't quite explain.

'You guarantee the safety of this camp?'

'I do.'

'You give me your solemn word that I can leave as soon as spring comes and the weather allows us to move on?'

'I give you my word.'

Selina sighed slowly, deeply, as though it pained her to breathe. Zillah watched from her perch a few steps away, and it was to her Selina turned with a face full of tender anguish.

How must it feel to be loved like that? Edward wondered as the old woman slowly nodded her head just once, unsmiling as a judge.

The gesture seemed to mean something to Selina—or perhaps everything; for he saw her blink rapidly, as though her eyes were suddenly sore, and when she fixed them on him he saw grim determination in their depths.

Chapter Five

Edward raked his hand through his hair and yet again turned his eyes to the door of the empty chapel. He half expected her not to come—wouldn't that serve him right for bribing her into marriage in the first place? He slipped his best silver pocket watch from his waistcoat and peered down at the ivory face for the tenth time in the space of a few minutes.

Exactly eight o' clock. Time to be married.

He had obtained the marriage licence as quickly as humanly possible after Selina's reluctant acceptance of his suit two days previously; there had been no time to be wasted in waiting three weeks to have the banns read. The common licence had been costly, but Edward was willing to pay almost anything to ensure his plans went ahead.

'Begging your pardon, sir.' Evans stood at Edward's elbow, dressed in his Sunday best and looking as though all his Christmases had come at once.

Perhaps it was an odd decision to ask his butler to stand as witness, Edward mused vaguely, his attention on other things, but Evans had served the Fulbrooke family faithfully for almost forty years and he could think of nobody more reliable to perform the task. Besides, Evans would do what was required, no questions asked—which was more than Edward could say of any of his gentry friends, who might pry a little too deeply into his choice of bride.

'I believe I hear footsteps outside.'

The sound of feet on wet stone grew louder. Edward fixed his eyes on the cross mounted to the wall above the reverend's head and determined there and then that, no matter what, he would not turn around. He didn't dare risk it. What if Selina took one look at him and decided she couldn't go through with their arrangement? If he could just wait until she reached the altar their fates would be fixed.

The church door creaked as it swung inwards on aged hinges and Edward felt the hairs on the back of his neck prickle. *Here she comes. My wife-to-be.*

At his side, Evans moved to gaze up the aisle towards where Selina had paused, presumably to gather her courage before making her approach.

The wait seemed to go on for half a lifetime. Edward shifted his weight from foot to foot, affecting restless excitement, although his heart raced with apprehension and, aggravatingly, with the tamped-down desire to once again lay eyes on the woman who had so piqued his interest, despite his efforts to the contrary.

What was taking her so long? If she could only keep her nerve for a few more moments... Wouldn't it be worth it? Wouldn't this gamble pay off and make her people safe from harm for the entirety of a cruel winter? And he from the threat of losing his inheritance?

Finally, *finally*, he heard Selina begin the long walk down the length of the church and he exhaled involuntarily—he hadn't been aware he'd held his breath. He glanced sideways. Evans was staring in Selina's direction, his expression a mixture of curiosity and frank admiration. Edward shook his head to clear it. There was a buzzing in his ears, a whisper that tempted him to turn.

No. Look straight ahead. I mean it.

He turned around—and his breath seemed to catch in his throat.

Selina's face was ashen under a circlet of heather, her eyes ringed with shadows clearly the work of a broken night's sleep. She appeared to be gripping her grandmother's arm with the strength of a drowning man clutching a raft, and even from a distance Edward could see the rapid fluttering of her pulse beneath the thin skin of her throat.

But her steps were measured and steady, her hand perfectly still as she held her small posy against her chest, and her head was held up with a determination that was almost defiant. In the dim light of the votive-lit church the oval of her face was luminously pale, and her strained expression only served to highlight the fine lines of her jaw and cheekbones.

Edward swallowed. How could he have thought she wouldn't come? She was a warrior—she might be afraid, but she was damned if she would let him see it, and Edward felt a new respect for her flicker into being. His own nerves still thrummed within him, but Selina's resolve inspired a fresh sense of purpose that forced his lingering doubts into submission. If she could find the strength to honour their bargain there was no way he would fail her at the final hurdle.

What man wouldn't be proud to marry a woman such as that?

Even as he attempted to force his lips into some semblance of a smile the sudden shock of that thought reverberated through his mind. Of course he wasn't proud—that was entirely the wrong word, and he had been foolish to think it.

The strength of Selina's will was no more to be admired by him than any other facet of her personality and he would do well to remember it. The fleeting thought that she looked positively angelic in her bridal gown would be likewise dismissed as entirely irrelevant—and dangerous.

Take that as a warning, Edward cautioned himself, a frown pinching his fair brows together. *Don't allow that nonsense into your head again; you know better than to be fooled by a pretty face.*

If Selina was pleasing to his eye—as was undeniable, he admitted reluctantly—it was not something to be encouraged. Their marriage was to be nothing more than a convenient lifeline for both of them, and he had no intention of feeling anything more for the woman who now approached him as though marching to war. Feelings led to nothing but pain, and not even his body's perturbing reaction to this Roma woman would convince him otherwise.

Selina swallowed hard as she saw Edward turn to look at her, her heart leaping within her and her throat as dry as if she'd thirsted for a week. *Only a few minutes and he will be my husband.*

How many women would give anything to be in her situation? she wondered as she moved down the aisle towards him, trying to ignore the rush of blood in her ears that obliterated all other sound but her own heartbeat. Rich *and* handsome. Perhaps she too would have considered herself lucky had they not shaken on their bargain like two hagglers at a market.

The unfamiliar sensation of lace against her legs only served to add to the strangeness of the moment. The dress had been Zillah's, made decades before by her own two hands for her wedding to Selina's long-dead grandfather. The lace had yellowed slightly with age, and Selina knew the cut was no longer fashionable, but it tied her to her people and to the Roma way of life; it gave her courage and she needed all the courage she could get.

She felt her legs tremble as she neared the altar and redoubled her grip on Zillah's arm. The older woman's hand came up immediately to cover her own, and she held it tight with the birdlike claws of her fingers.

'Steady, girl,' she murmured, too low for any of the three watching men to hear. 'You hold on to me. I've got you.'

Selina nodded, intent on reaching her goal. *Just put one foot in front of the other. You're almost there.*

Her eyes felt gritty with tiredness, the night before having been spent curled up with Zillah in wordless comfort in her bunk. There hadn't been much to say—both women knew what had to happen, and that no amount of talking would change what lay ahead. She would be leaving everything and everyone she loved and putting her trust in a man she barely knew.

At least he didn't expect her to consummate the marriage, she thought as she closed in on the altar, with Edward looming ever larger at her right-hand side. He'd intimated as much, and she recalled how her cheeks had flared hotly with girlish embarrassment. No Roma man had ever dared venture into such a conversation with her before, and she would have boxed his ears if he had.

A small voice in the back of her mind whispered that Edward looked well in his wedding suit. The pale blue of his waistcoat was paired well with his fair hair, and cream breeches emphasised the lean shape of his legs—a detail Selina couldn't help but notice with reluctant admiration.

Part of her—a very secret, apparently feral part, over which she had terrifyingly little control—had been anticipating seeing him again. Edward's broad frame and clean-cut jaw had robbed her of sleep the night before almost as much as her apprehension, and now he was before her Selina could feel the same ready blush he always seemed able to provoke in her simmering below the surface of her pallid cheeks.

The small smiles he insisted on shooting her were kindly meant, she imagined, and his mute expression upon first seeing her had been undeniably flattering—enjoyable, even. Not that any of that mattered, she reminded herself sternly as her stomach fluttered disloyally. What use did she have for flattery or for a handsome face? They both knew why they were doing this—it was a business transaction and nothing more. She was no blushing bride tripping happily to the altar, even if he *did* cut a figure most women would look twice at and be glad to get to know better— as she herself might have been, in truth, had the circumstances been different.

'I wasn't sure you'd come.'

Edward's voice was quiet, almost a whisper in her ear that stirred the hairs at the nape of her neck. He was standing so close Selina could have reached out and touched him, and the entirely too-tempting urge to do so was one she fought with every fibre of her being.

'Truth be told, neither was I.'

She felt the air shift as Zillah moved a few paces away and then she turned to Edward, both of them tense and silent before the clergyman, who cleared his throat with a dry cough and began to speak.

'Dearly beloved...'

Selina saw the man's lips move as though she were in a dream. He seemed to go on talking for a long time, although she knew it could only have been a few minutes before she heard Edward's voice and watched with blind eyes as he reached for her hand.

She hesitated. *Last chance, Lina.*

She could still turn and run, and there would be nothing Edward could do about it. He couldn't force her to marry him—what if she chose not to? What then?

Papa would be spared the pain of learning of her marriage when he next returned to the camp. There had been no question of sending him a letter to tell him of her situation—neither he nor Selina could read or write, and she hadn't been able to bear the shame of dispatching one of the children with a message.

Edward's gaze was warm as he looked down at her, although she thought she could detect a thread of uncertainty in his expression. *I doubt this is easy for him, either,* she realised, with a feeling uncomfortably close to sympathy growing inside her.

How was it that he actively sought a wife who would never love him? She knew he wasn't ignorant of the knowledge that he was everything she loathed, living his life of genteel idleness, with servants to pander to his every whim and enough money to feed a Roma camp for a full lifetime, let alone one winter. Heaven knew, he could surely have his pick of women, with his good looks and even better prospects. There was no doubt about that.

Selina felt another pang of that instinctive attraction Edward seemed able to inspire in her without even needing to try. Despite his explanations, it didn't make sense.

But she wouldn't run. The bait on the hook was too precious. With just a few months of worry she would buy a safer future for her people, and for that she would have done almost anything.

She placed her hand in Edward's and almost gasped aloud at the jolt of electricity that thrilled through her at the contact. His palm was warm and she could feel the steady beat of his pulse in the thumb that brushed her knuckles, a gentle caress of reassurance that took her by surprise. Even as her lips moved in the vows that would save them, all she was truly conscious of was that small movement of his skin on hers, lighting up her every nerve and inviting her to enjoy the sensations of that tiny comforting gesture—and then a ring was slipped onto her numb finger and the deal was done.

* * *

The sound of a tray being placed down somewhere close to her head roused Selina from her sleep. Dimly, as though muffled by something soft, she heard the trickle of liquid being poured, punctuated by metal clinking gently against china.

Selina raised her head slightly from her cloudlike pillow and slowly cracked open one eyelid. Blinding sunlight poured through the windows of the unfamiliar room she was in, and she instinctively brought a hand up across her face to shield her eyes—her left hand, where a slim gold band winked cheerfully at her from the third finger.

Blackwell Hall—Edward.

She had spent the rest of the previous day packing her admittedly meagre possessions into a trunk supplied by Edward—her *husband*—and saying tearful farewells to her family and friends. He'd come to claim her as night had fallen, and they had ridden together in silence up the long drive to his great home, Djali bearing her steadily onwards to meet her fate.

She'd fully expected to lie awake all night, with the events of the day running ceaselessly through her mind. Instead, however, it appeared that distress had sapped her energy and she'd been asleep as soon as her head had hit the pillow.

A young woman hovered at her bedside, holding a teacup and saucer in her hands. At Selina's questioning glance she held out the cup to her uncertainly. Selina noticed her hand trembled slightly.

'Who—who are you?'

'Dinah, ma'am.' The girl bobbed a neat curtsey. 'I'm to be your maid.'

'My *what*?'

Selina's eyes were still bleary from sleep, and she rubbed at them with a clenched fist. Looking at the girl clearly for the first time, she took in her short stature and round, honest face, sprinkled with a constellation of freckles. They must be around the same age, and she found she liked her immediately—although the deference in her tone made Selina wince. She hadn't been *ma'am*-ed in her entire life, and she would have been quite content to keep it that way.

'Your maid, ma'am…if you please.' Dinah peered at her nervously, apparently anxious for her reply.

My maid? Truly?

She stared blankly at the girl. Was it some kind of joke? Surely Edward knew she could fend for herself, for goodness' sake. Why had he sent her this poor creature, who now looked every bit as uncomfortable as Selina felt?

'But I'm not in need of a *maid*.'

The very idea of it—a Roma with a servant?

It was almost an insult, and Selina bridled internally. Of course women born to upper-class life needed help: gentry ladies were more ornaments than functional beings. But surely Edward didn't dare lump her in with them?

'Oh, please, ma'am! Don't send me away!'

The girl seemed close to tears, and Selina regarded her with baffled horror.

'I'm a good worker, honest, and I've waited so long for a chance to wait on a real lady and not be in the kitchens anymore.' She whisked a handkerchief from the pocket of her drab dress and patted at her eyes.

Selina hesitated, unsure of what to do, then set her cup down on her bedside table with a sharp click of porcelain against varnished wood.

'Are you saying you *want* to be my—?' She couldn't finish that sentence; it was too ridiculous for words. Dinah nodded vigorously into the cloth folds that concealed her face, only increasing Selina's amazement. 'I see. Well…if it means that much to you… I would never want to—to—*deprive* you of—'

The girl whipped the hanky away and peered short-sightedly at her, her expression so absurdly hopeful that Selina had to fight the perverse desire to laugh.

If only the girls at home could see me now.

At Blackwell for less than twelve hours and

already somebody's superior. 'But I've never had a maid before, and I'm certainly no real lady. I think you might be disappointed.'

'Never, ma'am! If you'll have me, I promise you won't ever regret being my mistress.' Dinah picked up the cup again and placed it back into Selina's hand, her homely face creased in determination.

Selina smiled ruefully. 'I'd really rather be your friend than your mistress, Dinah. I have a feeling I'll need all the friends I can get.'

The girl didn't understand—she could tell by her face—and it probably wouldn't be a good idea to elaborate further, Selina supposed. Instead, she slowly sipped her tea as she allowed her gaze to wander around the bedchamber she had slept in. It had been night when she'd arrived, and it was only now, in the cold light of day, that she was able to see her surroundings clearly.

She could barely believe how huge the blue-papered room was. The contrast between the cabin of a *vardo* and this vast cavern of a bedchamber was immense; Selina wasn't sure she liked it. She felt too exposed. Where was the cosy snugness of a caravan? Certainly nowhere in *this* room, for all its fine furnishings.

Admittedly, the huge oak-framed bed she had slept in was the most comfortable she had ever experienced—and, she realised with a jolt of shock, the first proper one, with luxurious pillows and a richly embroidered powder-blue coverlet, but it wasn't a patch on the familiar nest of her own bunk.

She traced the design worked on the borders of her blankets with one finger as Dinah fussed busily in the background. *My own bunk.* How had Zillah slept last night without Selina lying there opposite? The two had shared a cabin ever since Diamanda had died, never missing a night in twelve years. Had she managed to snatch a few hours of rest after such an emotional day? Or had she lain there, staring up at the ceiling, wishing her granddaughter home, until the first light of a new day had crept beneath her shuttered windows?

Selina felt a lump rise in her throat and forced it back harshly. *No.* She had to be strong. It wasn't as though she would be away forever, and besides: it was because of Zillah she had to stay. Wasn't it for all the Roma? If she could just focus on the end goal, and keep her nerve despite the circumstances...

'Mr Edward has asked if you'd honour him with your company for breakfast, ma'am. I'm to do your hair and show you to the dining room.'

Dinah was waiting at a fine-looking dressing table—*her* dressing table, Selina realised with a start—in front of one floor-to-ceiling window, and the built-in looking glass reflected Selina's face back at her as she sat there in the great island of her bed.

'Has he?'

The maid was too busy rearranging a set of silver hairbrushes to notice Selina's frown. So it had begun already—Edward acting the husband, summoning her to him for…for what? *The pleasure of my company?* The notion made Selina's heart skip a little faster, before she dismissed it quickly. *Of course not. He's just being polite.*

A flicker of something suspiciously close to disappointment passed over her and she shook her head slightly against it. There was no reason to suppose Edward *wanted* to spend time with her, even if her own thoughts on the matter were confused at best.

The idea of seeing Edward filled her with an uncomfortable mixture of dread and, mortifyingly, an anticipation that only made her irritation at herself grow in strength. *You really must try harder to master this effect he has on you, Lina*, she chastised herself privately. It was already becoming an annoyance she could have done without, having to battle her rational mind against her apparent weakness for Edward's slow smile, or the way his hair curled delightfully at the base of his neck…

Oh, for heaven's sake, girl. She pinched the

back of one hand—hard enough to snap herself out from her reverie. *Enough!* Aside from during the wedding ceremony she had barely exchanged two words with her new husband—what would they possibly find to talk about for the duration of a whole meal?

She thought back to their silent ride up the drive to Blackwell Hall, and how her heart had thumped within her chest as the grand old building loomed closer and closer. Edward had treated her kindly then. Even she had been able to recognise that his actions had been sympathetic as he rode near her, making no attempt to force her to talk but instead allowing her to wrap herself in quiet as fear and worry had risen up to twist her lips into a silent grimace.

She'd cursed herself for her weakness when she'd realised he'd seen, but other than the look of concern that had crossed his face he'd given no sign that he had noticed her distress. She'd been grateful for that at least—but not for the simultaneous realisation that the expression had made Edward look even more handsome than ever, if such a thing were possible.

Now, as she sat swathed in blankets that cost more than her entire wardrobe put together, she recalled how he had handed her down from Djali's wide back with more gentleness than she would have thought his strong frame capable of.

The candlelight that had spilled from the windows had illuminated the striking lines of his face, and Selina had once again felt the curious sensation of flames licking at the base of her spine at the touch of his hand on her waist as he guided her, still in calm silence, upwards.

The memory was strong, and it made her shiver despite the fire that blazed merrily in her bedroom grate. How was she to manage a normal conversation with the man over breakfast? Selina wondered bleakly. Everything she had thought normal for twenty years had been taken from her overnight, and she could barely look at him without staring.

She took a deep breath and made to get up, approaching her dressing table cautiously, gingerly settling down on the seat like a wary cat. Her reflection in the looking glass gazed back at her sombrely, dark eyebrows drawn together above eyes clouded with doubt. What was she *doing*, allowing herself to be groomed like a doll? Pulling a comb through her thick curls and then binding them back from her face with a ribbon was as far as her hairdressing skills stretched. Occasionally she made a braid for special occasions, but most often her hair was left to its own devices, playing around her shoulders like a raven cloak.

Dinah brandished one of the silver-backed brushes. 'How does Mr Edward prefer it? You'll be wanting to look your best for your first full day as a married lady!'

Selina screwed up her nose. How was she to know Edward's thoughts? The idea of inspiring her new husband's admiration was a tempting one—would it *really* be so bad to want to make a good impression?—but reality flooded back to hit her.

She doubted he would notice if she were to come down to breakfast with no hair at all. Her presence in his house was a mere puzzle piece, part of a bigger picture and a necessary evil. He had made it clear he wouldn't have chosen her otherwise. What she looked like would matter less to Edward than a bonnet would to a horse, and she would be foolish to think otherwise, despite any confusing or borderline panic-inducing stirrings to the contrary.

She forced a smile at the waiting maid, aware of a curious sensation of something suspiciously close to disappointment circling inside her. 'I don't believe he minds one way or the other. You do as you see fit.'

Edward toyed with the silver salt shaker in front of him, wondering as he spun it exactly what feminine mysteries could possibly take so long as to delay breakfast by a full half-hour. Perhaps Selina hadn't slept well and was finding it difficult to rise from her bed in the great blue chamber he had picked out for her.

Arriving home in the darkness of the night with a mysterious new bride had caused a few whispers among the staff, as he had expected, but at least nobody had seemed surprised at Selina being given her own separate rooms. His father and Maria had never shared a marriage bed other than for the begetting of little Ophelia, and he supposed their chaste example had set the tone.

He was interested to see his new wife this morning—a little too interested, as he had silently chided his reflection as he'd stood before his glass an hour earlier, waiting for his valet to make the vital decision as to which waistcoat would be most suitable for the day ahead. Some slight apprehension was to be expected, he'd thought; which was just as well, as he had felt a strange flicker in his stomach at the thought of Selina seated opposite him at the dining table.

He'd frowned to himself as the garment was buttoned around him—the cream today, Wellburn had resolved. It was only because he was anxious to be an attentive host, he had told himself, and in no way was he eager to see Selina for her own sake *per se*. It was merely good manners that had demanded he rise at a proper hour and invite his wife to take breakfast with him on the morning of what he recognised must be a very difficult day for her.

Difficult for me, too, in truth. His first day as a married man was an interesting thought, and one that gave him pause. Should he pretend to be pleased to see her? Should he remain a little cool and aloof? The knot of tension in his stomach tightened a fraction more as his uneasiness grew.

Bored now, with both his irritating trepidation and his wait, and getting more so by the minute, he glanced around the room, debating whether it would be a terrible display of bad manners to skim through his morning correspondence as he waited. There was another letter from his father's solicitor, and Edward almost smiled as he began to mentally compose his reply, stating his acquisition of one legal wife.

But any thoughts of his triumph were driven from his mind by a jolt of *something* in his chest as the door to the dining room finally opened and Selina stepped over the threshold.

His first thought as he rose to greet her was how different she looked, with her hair bound up away from her face. This was swiftly followed by a painful twist of his insides as he saw how much the style suited her.

Parted sharply down the middle, with a thick nest of curls pinned up at her crown and a bunch of ringlets hanging at each ear, the distinction between the elegant style and the wild mass of waves Edward had previously associated with Selina was stark. As was the contrast between her hair and her clothes: the dress she wore had seen better days, and was still half covered by a number of woollen shawls each more colourful than the last.

Edward wondered if a more unusual—or beautiful—woman had ever graced the dining table. The thought was a dangerous one, and yet again, to his alarm, Edward felt the same dart of attraction that managed to disturb him more and more each time he set eyes on her. It was getting stronger, if anything, and Edward felt his apprehension increase.

He would have to master these twinges of weakness. Nothing good could come of them, and there was no way he was willing to allow them to develop into anything worse.

'Good morning. I hope you slept well?'

'Like the dead, Mr Fulbrooke, would you believe?'

Her colour was better today. The shadows beneath her eyes had faded slightly and the bloom of her cheeks had chased away the pallor of the previous day. She certainly looked more well-rested than he had expected, and he felt his spirits lift imperceptibly as he pulled a chair out for her near his own place at the long white-swathed table.

'Please. Won't you call me Edward? I would very much like you to feel as comfortable as possible during your time here.'

He really *did* want her to feel at ease, he realised with a start. Seeing her there, so out of place in his world, gave him a sudden pang of sympathy that surprised him. She was like an exotic bird of paradise in an aviary of dowdy sparrows, and it was an uncomfortable feeling to think he had somehow forced her into a cage.

He pushed the thought away briskly. *She chose to agree to this, don't forget. She didn't have to marry you.*

Part of him had wondered what state she would be in upon waking in such unfamiliar surroundings, but she looked calm enough, despite the air of wariness that seemed to accompany her whenever he was near, and he couldn't help but feel pleased when she dropped into the proffered chair with only the smallest of hesitations.

He took his own seat again and nodded at the servant who hovered in the doorway. The man withdrew immediately, his footsteps swift and quiet, and Edward was left alone in the novel company of his distracted new wife.

She was squinting down at the array of cutlery laid out in front of her in obvious bemusement, touching each piece in turn, and Edward noticed her lips move as she counted to herself in a soundless murmur.

He watched her for a moment in silent amusement.

'Is everything to your satisfaction?'

Her head jerked up at the sound of his voice, a crease appearing between her dark eyebrows as she appraised him. 'I've got too many spoons.'

It was almost an accusation. Edward hid his smile behind the fingers of one hand. 'Ah. No. Each spoon is for a different part of your breakfast.'

'Why? Why not just use the same throughout?'

'I—I don't really know.' It didn't make a lot of sense now he thought about it, and he had to cast about for an answer. 'That's just how it is.'

He opened his linen napkin and laid it across his lap, more for something to do with his hands than for any other reason. He felt a vague unease now she was before him, a slight awkwardness in his own skin such as he had last experienced as an adolescent. It reminded him uncomfortably of how he had used to feel at that age when confronted with a pretty girl: a little ungainly, and more than usually aware of his movements. He'd grown out of that, of course. So there was no real reason he could think of for Selina to affect him so—or not one he was willing to admit.

When he looked up from his lap he saw she'd picked up one of the confusing array of spoons and was turning it this way and that, moving her head to catch the upside-down image of herself caught in its silver curve. He suppressed a smile. The magic the maid had worked on Selina's hair had evidently made quite an impact on her.

'That hairstyle suits you.'

The words left his lips before he could stop them, earning him a startled look and a clink of metal against wood as Selina dropped the spoon abruptly. Edward frowned to himself. He'd had no intention of speaking aloud, and now he had unnerved her.

Control yourself, man. What ails you?

She spoke more to the tablecloth than to him, her dark brows drawn together. 'I've never worn it like this before. It feels a little strange.'

They lapsed into an awkward silence that lasted several moments. More for a way to break the tension than anything else, Edward cleared his throat. 'I've been meaning to ask you something.'

Selina looked up from her study of the table, one suspicious eyebrow cocked. 'Oh, yes?'

There was more than a touch of wariness in her tone, and Edward could have kicked himself for his mistake in allowing his inner thoughts to spill out of his mouth. Still, at least her silence allowed him the chance to ask a question that had been bothering him since they met.

'That first day, when you found Ophelia. You said that I owed you twice over—once for then, and once for before.' Edward leaned his chin on his hand, watching for her reaction. 'What did you mean?'

She held his gaze for a moment in a look so dark and penetrating that Edward felt the sensation she was attempting to read his mind. He couldn't quite tell whether or not he enjoyed being the object of her undivided attention. It felt a little like chess—both of them unsure as to the intentions of the other, each waiting to see what the other would do next.

He wondered idly if she knew how to play. If not, he felt sure he would enjoy trying to teach her. Her instinctive caution would make her a natural.

Selina's eyes were slightly narrowed when she finally answered. 'You truly don't recall me at all, do you?'

There was a ghost of amusement in the ebony darkness and Edward's heart rate picked up at the sight. Selina amused—that was certainly a new development, and one that served to soften the usual guardedness of her face. He couldn't deny it was a pleasant effect.

'I suppose I should be glad I look so different now. I'm less bruised and muddy than I was at eight, at least.'

It took a moment for Edward to understand Selina's answer, and when it hit him he could only stare, piecing together the fragments of memories only recently rediscovered.

'The little girl in the woods, all those years ago—that was you?' His hand flew to the scar on his cheek, a small raised island in the otherwise smooth skin of his face. 'You were the one who treated my wound? Who stopped the bleeding with moss?'

Selina nodded almost shyly. 'An old country trick. I learned it when I was very young.'

'I can't believe it.' Edward shook his head slowly, amazement plainly written across his handsome features. *That little wraith had been Selina?*

She was certainly more altered than he ever would have thought possible, with all traces of the tomboyish creature he remembered gone, to be replaced by distinctly feminine grace. It was uncanny.

'Why didn't you tell me before?'

She shrugged, her eyes slipping past his to fix

again on her gleaming silverware. 'I didn't think it was important.'

'Not important?' Edward sat back in his chair, disbelief still running through him. 'How could you think so?'

He felt the temptation to revisit that day pulling at him, the desire to talk over fond memories strong.

Surely she should know how much her care then meant to me? How much I appreciated what she did?

It had been such a difficult time for him, those few weeks after his mother's abandonment, and Edward was gripped with the sudden urge to tell Selina how much her kindness had soothed his troubled younger self—but then a renewed sense of caution crept over him and he closed his mouth with a snap.

A conversation like that would be too intimate, too friendly—it would invite Selina closer, and the odd sensations he felt whenever she was near warned him that they were quite close enough already. He couldn't take the risk, he thought as he glanced at her, taking in once again the gloss of her hair and the tawny perfection of her skin. To be polite was one thing, but to relive their shared past might foster a relationship that could all too easily stray into dangerous territory, and that he could *not* have.

The dining room door opened and a small procession of servants entered, each bearing a silver platter with the exception of one, who wielded a great teapot.

Under cover of the ensuing clattering and arranging, Edward lowered his voice and continued. 'Did you know me all along? When did you realise that I—that we—?'

'As soon as I saw you.'

Selina's voice was quiet too, and Edward could have sworn he caught a hint of colour flush across her cheeks.

'Your hair and eyes, both so light… I remembered you at once, and when I saw your scar I knew I hadn't been mistaken.'

Outwardly calm, Edward nodded. Inside, however, he felt a spark of satisfaction kindle. He dismissed it in alarm. That was exactly the kind of thing he should be trying to guard against—apparently with good reason. If he had made a lasting impression on Selina it was nothing to be proud of: no small number of upper-class women would have said the same thing, and the realisation was enough to pour cold water over any misplaced vanity.

The interest of women of his own class was something he never wanted to experience again, or to return. Selina should be no different.

It was an uncomfortable train of thought. Indeed, this entire meal was rapidly becoming even more uncomfortable than Edward had expected. With her new hairstyle and that gleam of humour, Selina was only growing more attractive by the moment, and Edward cast about for something, *anything*, to replace the disquieting direction of his thoughts.

Glancing at her as he poured out a cup of tea, Edward watched as Selina carefully buttered a freshly baked roll and spooned a little honey onto her plate. She was using entirely the wrong cutlery out of the range available to her, Edward noticed. If she was to successfully play the part of a squire's wife there was much for her to learn. He would definitely need to call in reinforcements—and he knew the perfect person to help him.

'I was hoping to reintroduce you to my sister today, if you've no objection.'

A large window directly behind Edward showcased the stunning grounds at the back of the Hall, and Selina toyed momentarily with the idea of leaping straight through it to escape into the green beyond.

Slightly dramatic, possibly? she debated as she crumbled the remnants of her bread roll into fragments, avoiding Edward's enquiring look. *But more appealing than the alternative?*

If only he'd stop staring at her with those

blasted attractive hazel eyes she'd be much more able to think up some excuse. She didn't want to see Ophelia. It wasn't that she blamed the child for her current situation…it was more that she would serve as a reminder of things Selina would prefer to forget—including how she had got herself into this mess in the first place.

The way the little girl had called for her mama that day in the woods had struck uncomfortably close to the bone, conjuring memories that Selina had kept hidden for so long, and she was in no rush to repeat the experience.

Edward was still watching her, arms folded across his expansive chest, apparently in no hurry for her answer. She saw her uncertainty must be showing on her face, for one of his eyebrows was raised in the barest suggestion of a challenge.

'I realise she's a terrifying prospect, but she'll be very excited to see you again. You made quite an impression the last time.'

'I can imagine.'

'An impression' was probably something of an understatement. If Ophelia was anything like the young girls back at the camp, she had probably talked of little else since their dramatic first meeting mere days previously.

Had it really been less than a week since actions had swung into motion that would change her life forever? Selina spun the ring that gleamed on her left hand, feeling the unfamiliar sensation of metal against skin.

Silhouetted against the window, Edward's sharp profile was more striking than ever, and Selina quickly turned her attention back to her breakfast plate. Lounging in his natural habitat, Edward was a picture of masculine confidence, his every movement exasperatingly eye-catching and his every glance a physical touch to Selina's skin.

She groaned inwardly. This was *not* the plan. How was she to maintain a dignified distance from her new husband when everything he did was so damnably fascinating? Even the way he managed to juggle the bizarre number of spoons was more impressive than she would like.

Selina felt herself glowering down at her lap as heat snaked up from her neck to cross her face with burning fingers. There was an imposing fireplace directly at her back, and Selina found herself fervently hoping Edward would blame the crackling flames for her rosy cheeks and not his apparently swoon-inducing presence.

'Perhaps I could call for her now and she could help me give you a tour of the house? When you've finished eating, of course.'

She eyed him as he moved to the fireplace and tugged at a bell-pull hanging to the side of it, crossing the room in a handful of easy, long-legged strides. He really was very tall, and when standing next to the stocky servant who answered the summons he looked taller still.

The other man soon withdrew, and Edward turned back to her so quickly Selina had to scramble to avert her eyes in time. It wouldn't do for him to think she was looking. The fact that she had been, and had been undeniably pleased by what she had seen, made her shift uncomfortably in her chair.

She hadn't been prepared for his earlier compliment, and his praise had caused the aggravating embers that seemed to flicker in her stomach whenever he was near to glow brighter, their heat warming her insides. She'd quickly sought to dampen them, determined that some throwaway comment would not succeed in affecting her so worryingly, but the ashes remained, and Selina felt a nagging sense of unease that it would be all too easy for Edward to stoke them up again.

The idea rankled even as some distant part of her wondered how far his kind words were the truth, and how far they had been motivated by simple good manners. Her discomfort intensified as she realised she hoped it was the former.

'She'll be down directly. I hope you're prepared for lots of questions? I'm told she's been asking her governess when she can see you approximately every ten minutes ever since she woke this morning.'

A reluctant smile threatened to unfurl on Selina's lips. Perhaps seeing the little girl again would be better than she expected. It certainly sounded as though she was already Selina's most fervent admirer, and it could only be a good thing to have such a powerful ally. Besides, with Ophelia in the room she wouldn't be Edward's sole focus, and that would definitely be an improvement on the current way his gaze seemed to fix on her with unnerving regularity, with correspondingly unnerving results.

Chapter Six

Gravel crunched under her feet as Selina hurried away from the Hall, casting about her as she dipped her head down and pulled her worn cloak closer about her body. It was a grey day, the air oppressively still, and clouds brooded ominously overhead, threatening rain. A robin called from a tree as she passed through the grounds, its red breast vivid against withered leaves, but she knew she had no time to stop and listen.

She rounded a manicured hedge and ploughed onward. Shooting a fleeting glance over her shoulder in the direction of the Hall, she saw nobody had followed her. Only the huge old house was watching her go, its gleaming windows glinting like eyes in the stone walls. She wondered for a moment which of the windows was hers, where she'd stood that morning and gazed out at the green beyond before slipping down the creaking stairs and out through the heavy oak garden door.

The grounds were stunning—even Selina, whose preference was for the untamed beauty of the countryside, could appreciate the artistry that had gone into the well-laid beds and meticulously landscaped lawns. Trees and shrubs of all descriptions stood about in perfectly placed groups, and Selina knew the sight of the grounds in summer, when all the flowers were in full bloom and emerald leaves stirred in warm breezes, would be breathtaking. Not that she would be there to see it.

A sweet little stone arbour stood beyond an avenue of fruit trees, with classical statuettes set into alcoves on each wall. It was at one of these statues that she glanced out of the corner of her eye as she approached, and slowed her stride to a quiet, careful step. As she drew closer the mound of striped material she'd spied from a distance grew more distinct, nestled behind a Greek goddess she couldn't have named even if she'd wanted to.

Placing each foot with pinpoint precision, Selina inched forward. Her breathing was too loud. She forced herself to slow the rapid beat of her heart, fluttering against her ribs as she closed the final distance.

She pounced. 'Got you!'

With a high-pitched shriek of glee Ophelia struggled in Selina's arms, trying in vain to escape her sister-in-law's tickling fingers. 'Stop! Stop! Stop it!'

'Stop what? This?' Selina redoubled her efforts and the little girl's laughter gurgled in her ears, her skinny legs flailing.

'Yes! Stop it!'

'Do you admit I'm the Queen of Hide and Seek?'

'Yes!'

Setting the child back on her feet, Selina paused to get her breath back. A stray curl had escaped during their game, marring the fresh masterpiece of hairstyling Dinah had created for her that morning, and she swept it back behind her ear.

Ophelia was clutching the side of the arbour, still breathless with laughter. She looked Selina up and down, frowning now, and her eyes grew round with innocent horror.

'You've torn your dress, Lina!'

'Have I?' Looking down at the cream muslin she wore beneath her old cloak, Selina saw the skirt was rent from hem to knee, displaying what she imagined would be considered a scandalous amount of bare leg among Edward's set.

'You'll have to change quickly, before anyone sees you!'

Just in time Selina managed to stop herself from reflexively rolling her eyes. During her first week at Blackwell Hall, Ophelia had taken it upon herself to begin educating her on exactly what it took to be a real upper-class lady. It didn't seem to matter how many times Selina tried to explain, as gently as possible, that she wouldn't be there for longer than a few months, and therefore didn't need such an in-depth knowledge of different types of spoons. It was a concept Ophelia seemed cheerfully determined to ignore.

Short of sitting down with the seven-year-old and outlining the terms of her marriage of convenience in brutal clarity, she couldn't think of a way to drive the point home without upsetting the little girl she had already begun to care for, despite her initial misgivings.

Perhaps it was because she reminded Selina of the Roma children she had left behind at the camp. All of her cousins had little ones, three of them girls, and she loved the way their hands would find their way into her own and the seriousness with which they confided in her their precious secrets.

Looking down at the girl in front of her, Selina felt a sudden pang of loss at the thought of those she'd left behind and forced a smile to unwilling lips. She should be grateful they'd been able to form such a bond. Ophelia's sunny company brightened days that otherwise she didn't know how she would have managed, as well as providing a welcome distraction from the incessant thoughts of another certain somebody Selina seemed unable to master.

'Don't worry. I can mend it when we return to the house.'

The little girl's face expressed exactly what she thought of *that* statement. 'Why don't you just ask Ned to buy you some new ones? He buys me dresses all the time!'

Selina shook her head, feeling, as always, the same jolt in her stomach at the mention of Edward's name.

Damn it, Lina. Get a hold of yourself.

'Because N— *Edward* is your brother. He's allowed to buy you pretty things.'

'But you're his wife. Isn't he allowed to buy you things, too? I'd wager he would if you asked him. I don't think there's a kinder brother in the whole world!'

Selina raised an eyebrow but held her tongue.

His money is the last thing I want. Of course he had offered to purchase some gowns for her—beautiful things befitting her new station—but she'd refused. Her shawls and modest dresses had always been good enough for her, and would continue to be so within the privacy of Blackwell and its grounds, where the only eyes on her were those of Edward and his sister.

Perhaps the servants might gossip at her plain attire, but people would always find something to talk about, whatever one did, and it hardly seemed worth the effort to avoid it. Besides, spending her husband's money was what a *real* wife did, and there could be no gain in muddying the waters.

The time they spent together was tolerable enough, after a fashion, although heaven knew how much she didn't *want* to notice the strong shape of his thighs in his riding breeches, or how the green of his coat highlighted the rich colour of his eyes. She found things much less vexing when Edward left the Hall on business of his own, as he had that morning, and she was excused from spending time with him that always seemed to result in blushing confusion.

'It's—it isn't quite the same, Ophie. I don't want him to do that for me.'

The clouds were drawing in overhead. Selina could smell rain in the air—a scent she loved more than almost any other—and with her eyes closed and her nose turned towards the sky she prayed fervently for the weight she had carried these past two weeks to fall from her shoulders.

To be out in the open, free from the atmosphere of the brooding house, should be like a soothing balm to her troubled spirit. But thoughts of Edward still niggled at her, despite the cool breeze in her hair, and she felt no more able to force them back as the temptation to appreciate Edward's clear profile and impressive height became almost too uncomfortable to bear.

'What are you thinking about, Selina?'

Ophelia's little voice piped up beside her and Selina jumped a touch more guiltily than she was comfortable with. 'Oh. I—'

A deep rumble of thunder echoed suddenly through the grounds, just as the first drop of rain landed squarely on the toe of Selina's boot. Ophelia's fearful gasp at the sound rescued Selina from having to speak further, for which she was truly thankful. She would hardly have been able to tell the truth—*I'm thinking about your brother, Ophie. Again. Indeed, I can't seem to put him out of my mind.*

Selina's lips twisted into a wry smile that might have been mistaken for a grimace. *No. That would never have done.*

Even as she took the little girl's hand in her own and led their charge back in the direction of the Hall, Selina's mind whirled with unstoppable pictures of Edward as he'd looked that first morning in the woods, with no light of recognition sparking in his eye but still as courteous as though she'd been born a lady. There could never have been any mistake on that score, but that hadn't seemed to matter to him.

Once again Selina wondered *why* he had chosen *her*—a woman he truly hoped would never love him and whom he would never love in return—to take as his bride. She knew she shouldn't be flattered—he had made it plain it was nothing more than a business arrangement— but she still wasn't sure she trusted his bland explanation. There must be more to Edward than met the eye...

Rain pattered down upon their heads as they skirted a rapidly growing puddle and fled up the gravel path. Another boom of thunder sounded in their ears and Selina's attention was momentarily distracted from the jumble of Edward-shaped thoughts as Ophelia squeaked again at the loud noise.

'Almost there, Ophie. Don't be afraid!'

The two of them surged forward, the little girl clinging tightly to Selina's hand as they rounded one hedge and then another, as quickly as their legs could carry them.

Selina collided with the broad male chest in front of her so hard she would have rebounded had its owner not reached out to catch her. She flung out a hand to steady herself, instinctively grabbing hold of the closest thing she could grasp—which unfortunately turned out to be

Edward's firm and unyielding bicep, barely disguised by the damp fabric of his riding coat.

All the blood in her body felt as though it had rushed to her face as she gaped up at him, momentarily mute with surprise. His hand cradled the small of her back, holding her upright, and her own hand lay across the powerful muscle of his arm, feeling the strength beneath her cold fingertips.

Looking into his face, Selina saw how the rain had darkened the gold of Edward's hair. A stray lock curled across his forehead, and she was gripped with the sudden urge to reach up to brush it away. Her heart rate, already raised from running, sped up another notch as a slow glimmer of warmth unfurled itself from where Edward's hand held her close to him—a terrifyingly delicious feeling that would have robbed her of speech had she not already been rendered silent by his unexpected touch.

She blinked rapidly, forcing her body to respond to her orders. She should move her hand and step away, and she should do it *now*.

'Ned! I thought you'd gone into Warwick today?'

For the second time that morning Ophelia's voice interrupted the tension of Selina's thoughts. The moment broke and Selina stepped away from

Edward smartly, shrugging out of his grasp with a low murmur of thanks.

'That was certainly my intention.'

Edward smiled down at his sister, although Selina was sure his lips looked a little fixed and she felt herself cringe. *Why did he have to see me being so clumsy?*

'Mr Lucas was called away on urgent business so I came back early. Miss Jenkins told me you ladies were out walking, so when the rain started I thought I'd better come to escort you back.'

He glanced across at Selina and she wondered with a jolt of dismay if he could somehow hear how rapidly her heart was beating in her chest. Her skin still tingled where Edward had touched her, and it was a monumental effort to pretend to be unfazed by the realisation that his arms had felt every bit as strong as they looked.

'We should hurry back—we'll catch our death, staying out in this weather.'

It was on the tip of Selina's tongue to reply that no Roma had ever died from a bit of rain, but at the last moment she thought better of it. She still wasn't sure she trusted herself to speak with any degree of normality, and her heart was still hammering with disloyal fury, so it was in silence that she joined the others in a dash back to the looming shadow of Blackwell Hall and in through the garden door.

* * *

Edward stood with his back to the roaring kitchen fire, all too aware of the slim figure of his wife crouching to one side of him, warming her hands by the hearth. He still hadn't got used to using that word—*wife*—despite Selina's now week-long residence at the Hall. Although she kept to only a few of the vast number of rooms the house boasted, and moved around them with a cat-like, almost silent step, the house felt more full, more lively, and it puzzled him how one extra person could make such a difference.

Her uncertainty at being caged within four walls was still plain to see, and he had noticed how much time she chose to spend out in the open air, going to visit her horse in the stable yard or walking in Blackwell's beautiful gardens. When he'd spied her from the window of the upstairs gallery that morning, however, something in her manner had piqued his interest.

At first the sight of Selina slipping down one of the paths away from the house had caused his brow to crease—what was she doing that made her movements so furtive? It was almost as though she didn't want to be seen... That alone had given him cause for concern. A quick glance up and down the long wood-panelled gallery had showed Edward he was on his own, apart from the painted portraits of his forebears that hung on every wall, and he had leaned closer to the lead-patterned window to get a better view of what Selina would do next.

She'd looked to be heading for the little stone arbour only just visible from the house. Edward had squinted slightly, following with his eyes as Selina slowed her pace to a stealthy creep, pausing for a moment before lunging downwards at something he hadn't quite been able to see. When she'd straightened up again everything had become clear—she held Ophelia in her arms, and even from a distance Edward had been able to make out his sister's familiar delight at being involved in a tickling contest.

He had drawn back from the window. A smile bloomed across his face, apparently without his permission, and he had carefully smoothed it away.

Selina's patience with the girl continued to impress him. Much as he loved his sister, he couldn't deny there were times when her mother Maria's influence was evident, and he feared she would eventually turn out to be a copy of her haughty mama. It was only little things—a forgotten thank-you to a servant here, a flash of temper at a trifle there—but Selina's firm but kind manner with the girl had already brought obvious improvements.

He found himself wondering again why Selina

was so determined to keep that softness hidden from him. Given her revelation that she had been his mystery nurse all those years ago, he knew her heart was kind, but evidently something still held her back from allowing her to be her true self with him now.

Raindrops sparkled against the darkness of her hair as Selina brushed the moisture from the hem of her cloak and handed it to a waiting maid, who smiled shyly at Selina's use of her first name. Edward's brows twitched together briefly—at Blackwell a week, and already on Christian name terms with the servants? Apparently she had set out to make a friend of everybody except himself.

The thought was uncomfortable in a way he couldn't quite grasp.

'What shall we do now? We can't play outside anymore today.'

Ophelia peeped up at him earnestly, her hands held towards the fire glowing in the kitchen grate. Her hair had started to steam a little, he saw with interest, and her face was ruddy from exertion.

A swift glance towards his wife showed the same high colour in her complexion, and one ringlet slipping down to curl in front of her ear. She seemed to be holding the skirt of her dress together with one hand. It looked as though it had torn, and Edward caught a glimpse of an impressive expanse of bare leg before—with more than a shadow of reluctance—averting his eyes.

'*You* need to go back to Miss Jenkins, Ophie.' Leaning down, he gently pinched his sister's baby-soft cheek. 'You need to get into some dry clothes, and then you have to do your lessons.'

'Lessons?' Selina was leaning against a hulking dresser now, arms folded across her narrow chest. Her eyes were bright with interest. 'What is she learning?'

Edward shrugged. 'Drawing. How to read music, singing, how to dance—lots of things.'

Selina seemed about to speak when Ophelia dashed forward and took hold of her hands, her face alight with excitement. 'I can *show* you! I've learned a new step this week—come and dance with me and help me practise! Miss Jenkins will be so pleased with me if I've got better!'

'Oh…' Selina shook her head. 'I'm sorry. I don't think I can help much—I don't know any of the dances you learn.'

'Really?' The little girl's face creased in disappointment. 'Can't you dance? At *all*?'

'I can. Just not like you.'

Edward could have sworn he saw a glimmer of amusement in her eyes. *Pert thing.* He knew perfectly well what *her* style of dancing involved, and its passionate nature couldn't be further from

the sedate steps beloved by the gentry. To watch
her dance would be a rare treat, he imagined.

A sudden picture of Selina twisting in wild
rhythm flitted through his mind, her hips swaying and her black hair falling about her like a
curtain as she moved. He blinked it away distractedly. That was *not* an image he should dwell
on—too enticing by half, and it strayed dangerously close to stirring thoughts within him that
he was still trying his hardest to repress.

Selina continued, thankfully oblivious to the
direction of his thoughts. 'Roma have a different way of going about dancing, and I don't think
your brother would like me to teach you *that*.'

'Oh…'

The little girl still held Selina's hands, although her shoulders had slumped despondently.
Edward was just about to console her when the
blonde head snapped up again and the beam re-
surfaced like the sun appearing from behind a
cloud.

'*Ned* could teach you!'

Selina started, the sudden movement causing
the dresser she was leaning against to creak ominously. 'Ah, no… I really don't think—'

'Come along, now, Ophie.' Edward cut into
Selina's stumbling excuse. He was only too
aware of how distasteful she'd find the idea of
dancing with him, and didn't feel it necessary,

or flattering, to dwell on it. 'Don't embarrass Selina. She will never be able to dance like we can, and that's that.'

Out of the corner of his eye, Edward saw Selina frown.

'Now, it really is time for you to go back to Miss Jenkins. I'll look in on you later today and you can show me your new step.'

Ophelia sighed the sigh of a most dejected soul, but nodded obediently and left the kitchen, pausing only to receive a piece of freshly baked gingerbread from the indulgently smiling cook.

Edward watched her go, following the progress of her slippered feet as they pattered up the kitchen steps and disappeared from sight. Turning back towards his wife, Edward was surprised to find her wearing an expression of frank irritation.

'Is there a problem?'

The downturn of her lips deepened. 'You know, if there's one thing we Roma pride ourselves on it's our skill at dancing. If I chose to learn I could perform just as well as you or any of your upper-class ladies.'

Edward shrugged. What did it matter? 'If you say so. I just know you would never make that choice.'

'And how do you *know* that? Perhaps I might want to try!'

Edward eyed her narrowly. One of Selina's hands had come up to rest on her hip and her face was set in the same expression of determined challenge she had worn as she'd walked down the aisle towards him on their wedding day. The reluctant admiration he had felt for her ever since rose up within him once again, renewed in strength and mingled with a sense of frustration.

Wasn't the whole reason he had chosen Selina as his wife *because* she was the very opposite of everything he had previously admired in a woman? The spectre of Letitia flitted through his mind before he could banish her laughing ghost. He had no intention of allowing such feelings to unman him ever again, and yet at every encounter with the new Mrs Fulbrooke she somehow managed to get under his skin, to provoke in him a reaction he felt an aggravating inability to control.

It was unacceptable, and it troubled him more than he cared to admit.

Taking in the firm set of her jaw, Edward felt the beginning of an idea dawn upon him. Perhaps he could be the one to unnerve this proud Roma for once, taking the upper hand she always seemed to have without even trying.

'Oh? Well, if that's the case I'll teach you myself. We'll begin at once, shall we?' Without pausing for an answer Edward made for the kitchen stairs and began to climb. 'I'll let you go to change your dress. Meet me in the Great Hall.'

He heard her sharp intake of breath at his back and couldn't restrain a quiet laugh. Two could play at her game. If she insisted on turning such an insignificant thing into an argument he would call her bluff. Perhaps it was time for Selina to learn that she wasn't the only one who could be pig-headed.

She was hesitating near the door when Edward entered the Great Hall, having changed her gown and exchanged her muddy shoes for clean ones. Selina's previously damp hair had almost completely dried, he saw as he stepped close to her, and he noted with fresh admiration and discomfort just how much the new style suited the sharp lines of her bone structure.

'Shall we begin?'

'Yes. Let's.'

The defiant glint had returned. Whatever panic she had felt in the kitchen at his abrupt statement had evidently been squashed.

Edward smiled inwardly at her attitude. *Let's see how brave you are when we're actually touching. If you don't combust with horror on the spot I'll consider it a miracle.*

'Very good. We'll start with a simple waltz. It's a new dance, brought over from Europe and considered in some circles particularly scandalous.' He sketched a short bow, almost but not quite missing the cynical flicker of one dark Romani eyebrow. 'Take my hand and then place the other hand on my shoulder.'

Reaching towards her, Edward was barely able to hide his smile at the fleeting look of mortification that flashed across her face. But then she grasped his hand, and suddenly it didn't feel amusing anymore.

With one palm in his, and the other lightly placed at his shoulder, the space between them was closed, and for the first time Edward was struck by the flawless fragility of her body. Supple and delicate, she felt light in his hold, but balanced with an underlying core of wiry strength that took him by surprise. It was a combination that momentarily robbed him of speech. Her waist was warm beneath his touch, and he was close enough to be able to count the dusting of freckles scattered across the bridge of her nose should he choose—an action he suddenly found quite unacceptably and quite unexpectedly impossibly tempting.

The immediacy of her effect on him was bewildering, as was the intensity of feeling that swept through his nerves, setting every sinew in Edward's entire body alight. He felt the way her body moved as she breathed, inhaling and exhaling in a steady rhythm his own wanted to copy, and he marvelled at how the curve of her waist fitted perfectly into his hand, as though they had been designed to meld together in seamless heat.

The urge to further explore the secret geography of her body came upon him in a rush of confusion and he forced it back, disturbed by the wayward direction of his disloyal thoughts.

'Like this?'

Edward felt the hair on the back of his neck prickle at the sensation of Selina's breath on his cheek. His own breath seemed to be coming more quickly than he could account for, and he had to swallow hard before answering. At such close range he could see each individual hair that shaped the lines of her brows, now pinched together slightly in concentration.

Why had his heart rate picked up to such a ridiculous degree, leaping within him like an animal in a trap? It wasn't as though it was the first time he had danced with a girl, and he had never experienced such a reaction before. Perhaps he had caught a chill during his cold morning ride across the fields—or perhaps it was something else entirely...something that he thought to guard so strongly against.

'Exactly like that. You're a natural.'

Looking down at her face, so close to his own, Edward saw Selina's uncertain expression. Her eyes had been averted while she considered the placement of her hands, but now she met his gaze full-on, with her head tilted back and lips slightly parted: lips, he realised at that moment, that were the prettiest he had ever seen.

Black eyes stared up into hazel, and for the longest moment of Edward's life neither of them moved. The silence was deafening, and the world seemed to halt on its axis as each of them drank in the sight of the other. But then Selina's long lashes came sweeping down, veiling her from his scrutiny, and Edward fixed his eyes on a spot on the opposite wall above Selina's head.

At a loss as to what to think, feel or do, he began to teach, all the while steeling himself against the whirl of new sensation that caused each nerve ending to stand to attention.

Selina moved, twirled and stepped as though in a dream, just as she was instructed—it was just as well she wasn't required to think independently, for her mind appeared to be playing tricks on her that she couldn't decipher. Her cheeks were suffused with inexplicable heat, and the place on her waist where Edward's hand lay felt as though it were smouldering under her gown.

It was entirely out of the question for her to peep up into her partner's face again. That one long look had shocked Selina to the core. She had been close enough to brush his face with her lips, and noticed for the first time how the deep hazel of his irises was flecked with tiny chips of gold. The intensity of his gaze had thrown her, and it had been all she could do to look away.

Now, as she turned gracefully in Edward's hold, following some dimly-heard instruction, she could scarcely breathe for inhaling the scent that seemed to emanate from him: a combination of soap, rain and spices from the kitchen that was horrifyingly, delightfully, extremely attractive.

Stop it.

Stop. It.

So what if his hand was large enough to almost span her entire waist? It meant nothing. The same went for the impressive musculature she could feel moving beneath the fabric at his shoulder. Nothing. It meant nothing. She would allow it no space in her mind. She would never allow herself to forget what he was—*who* he was: an unwilling husband, from a world so far removed from her own there could never be any real accord between them even if he had *wanted* a loving wife.

But the firm grip of his hand around hers sent a strange thrill down her spine, and her eyes *would* stray across the achingly impressive expanse of his chest, and there was precious little she could do to slow the hummingbird beat of her heart, pounding within her as the flames in her belly licked higher and higher and burned brighter with every step she took.

The whirl of confusion inside her mind held her attention for a moment too long and, distracted, Selina felt her breath catch as she missed a step, her foot coming down on the hem of her gown to make her stumble.

There was never any real danger of her falling, so quite why Edward seized her so firmly she couldn't say. But the next moment all such thoughts vanished as she found herself closer to him than ever before, and when she dared look up into his face it was all she could do to stay upright. His eyes found hers and she saw something flicker in them she had never seen before.

Edward's lips were gentle as they came down to slant across her own.

What? What's happening?

Selina's eyes flew wide in shock before drifting closed, as she was lost in a wave of sensation that threatened to overcome any rational thought she had ever had. His hands were warm as they held her close to the firm chest she had only allowed herself the briefest of moments to consider, so dangerously enticing had she found it, and Selina felt her own hands twitch with the desire to slide over Edward's coat, to delve inside and trace the hard planes of his body with wondering fingertips.

Her heart pounded in her ears as the flames inside her roared with approval, stoking themselves higher to burn her from within. She was sure she must have stopped breathing, and some tiny voice in the back of her mind screamed at her to pull away, but that suddenly seemed such a silly waste of time when she could be spending it exploring the fascinating terrain of Edward's lips. There was nothing she could do to stop herself from standing on her tiptoes and reaching for Edward as ardently as he reached for her.

Just when she was sure she would either pass out or crumple into a heap on the floor, Edward released Selina's mouth and drew backwards, his breath coming hard. He ran a hand through his hair and shook his head slightly, his eyes fixed on Selina's flushed and dazed-looking face.

Selina's vision was blurred, and she fought to pull herself together. She had never experienced anything like that before. Nobody had ever made her see stars and feel as though her legs might fold beneath her. They stared at each other, neither able to move or say a single word to break the aching tension between them.

The sound of the dinner bell ringing made them both jump.

Edward released Selina from his grasp and she immediately stumbled away from him, fanning herself with one hand. She barely knew where to look—certainly not directly at the man in front of her, who seemed as much at a loss for words as she was. Edward's face was flushed—and with more than the exertion of dancing, Selina thought, mortified.

He was the first to speak in the beat of silence that stretched between them—one Selina could no more have filled than she could have snatched back the last few minutes, never to be repeated.

'Well...' He cleared his throat distractedly. There was another painful pause. 'So—what do you think of "gentry dancing"?'

Was he truly going to act as though nothing untoward had just happened? she wondered in disbelief. As though both of them hadn't just lost control and made their situation even more awkward than ever before?

She stared at him as icy fingers of shame snaked down into her stomach. *That was a mistake. Enormous. Unforgivable.* But if Edward could pretend nothing was amiss then, heaven help her, so could she.

'I like it well enough, I suppose.' She almost choked on the words, her mouth dry. A few more curls had escaped Selina's hairstyle, and in a passable show of nonchalance she reached up to twist them back into place. 'Will you want me to return the favour and teach you a few Romani steps?'

'I'm not sure I could keep up.' Edward had managed to muster a small smile, but Selina caught the impression of something hiding beneath the surface. 'I should go and change. Thank you for a very…interesting morning.'

He bowed to her and moved away, long strides taking him quickly from the room.

He had never behaved in such a way before. Usually he would allow her to go ahead of him, his good manners evident in his every action. Now it seemed as though he couldn't get away fast enough; hardly surprising, given the circumstances.

Selina watched him go, waiting for her breath to return as a feeling she couldn't identify gnawed at her. It was a new sensation, vaguely uncomfortable, and it circled in the pit of her stomach like nothing she had ever experienced before. Whatever it was—and however stupid she had been to cause it—she wasn't sure that she disliked it…

Chapter Seven

Edward lowered the correspondence he had been reading to the dining table and tapped his teeth absently with the end of his letter-opener.

Word of his marriage was spreading fast. The letter in front of him was the third he had received containing congratulations and a barely disguised hunger for information about his mysterious new lady, and he had no doubt that there would be many more to follow.

A sideways glance through the expansive window overlooking the Hall's grounds showed Selina crouching near one of the raised beds, gently patting Edward's favourite old dog on his grizzled head. The sight made his lips begin to curve upwards—a movement he quickly halted in vexation. Ever since their alarming kiss a few days previously Edward had found himself uncomfortably affected by small things Selina said and did—a glimpse of her being affectionate to old Tips should not be so pleasing to him, he was sure.

At least the ice between them had thawed slightly as a result of their impromptu dance lesson. Selina had been less chilly in her manner with him, and he had even caught her watching him on a couple of occasions without looking as though she was plotting his doom. The strange sensations he had suffered while they danced had been unfortunate, but surely only the natural result of holding so closely a pretty—very pretty... more than pretty—girl. He would not be so foolish as to allow it to mean anything more.

He would not be so foolish as to repeat his most catastrophic lapse in judgement either.

Edward pinched the bridge of his nose as the image of Selina's face appeared before him, scarlet with shock, kiss-swollen lips parted breathlessly. Once again it sent a shard of discomfort into his gut. What had he been *thinking*, allowing himself to lose control so unforgivably? It could never happen again.

The sensation of Selina's lips beneath his own had been achingly sweet, dangerously exciting. The last woman he had kissed had been Letitia, of course, and Edward felt himself grimace as the memory of blonde ringlets and sky-blue eyes rose up, an unwelcome reminder of a past he had no desire to revisit. Letitia's kiss had been chaste, though, and oddly cold. Selina's had been a burst of fire, and Edward felt the embers of that disconcerting *something* spark within him at the thought.

He should never have kissed her—that much was true—but he couldn't deny how much he had enjoyed it, and how even now he knew it would be a struggle to curb the desire to surrender to his urges again.

He suppressed a small sound of irritation and sat back in his chair, pushing away the letter in front of him. *You need to be more careful.* His mistake might so easily have led to something worse. His attraction to Selina might not be under his control, but how he chose to react to it certainly was, and he had let himself stray perilously close to the pain of a rejection he never wanted to experience again just for the sake of a fleeting thrill. Aside from his own determination never again to be vulnerable to a woman's whims, Selina's Romani sensibilities would never entertain a gentry suitor—and he shouldn't forget that.

He heard footsteps on the boards outside the dining room and moments later Selina entered, enveloped in her customary shawls and with the elderly whippet trotting at her heels. She took her usual seat at the table and nodded across at Edward, who passed her what he now knew to be her favourite delicacy from the selection laid out for luncheon—a little sugared bun topped with caraway seeds. It was far too sweet for Edward's taste, but Selina could eat at least two at any given opportunity.

'Thank you.'

She laid the morsel neatly on her plate and hesitated for the barest of moments before picking up her knife and fork. Glancing at her out of the corner of his eye, Edward saw she had selected exactly the correct cutlery. Ophelia would be delighted that her seemingly relentless lessons had borne fruit.

Unaware of her audience, Selina took a fragment and dropped it into the waiting jaws of the dog lying at her feet. Edward raised an eyebrow. Apparently not *every* etiquette lesson had hit its mark.

'I received another letter in the afternoon post. About my very sudden, very private marriage.'

'Oh.'

'Oh, indeed.' Edward took another forkful from his own plate and scanned the page once again.

Apparently yet another acquaintance of his father had heard the news that young Master Fulbrooke had taken a wife—a wife nobody seemed to know much about. Was such talk true? There were rumours, he informed Edward darkly; hideous calumnies that the lady was not quite the *thing*.

Edward rolled his eyes. It was true that the only people officially informed of his marriage so far were his servants and, of course, his father's solicitor, for the purpose of the will. But it had been necessary to spread the news as soon as possible, to ensure Harris and Milton didn't get any ideas of new ways to attack the Roma camp and target Selina.

He could only imagine the looks on their faces when they had heard who the young Squire's new wife was. Edward would have paid a hundred guineas to have been there to witness it when they realised she was well and truly out of their reach.

He looked up. Selina had progressed to feeding Tips small morsels of bacon—rather brazenly, in Edward's opinion. The dog's skinny tail wagged and he peered up at the Roma girl with adoring eyes.

'I've been thinking. We're going to need to be seen together. People have started asking questions, and the only real way to answer them is to let people see you with their own eyes.'

Selina's hand stilled on its journey back to the meat platter. 'Seen together? Where?'

'Society venues, I'm afraid. I don't care for them any more than you do, I can assure you.'

'If you don't like them, must we go?'

'It would be a good idea. People are curious about you. I'd much rather we met them where we can leave if we like, rather than sit through hours of dull visits.' He raised an eyebrow at her rigid face. What could be her objection? 'Unless, of course, you'd prefer to receive endless streams of visitors here, with no chance of escape until they leave?'

The notion of a host of nosy society busybodies descending on his house made Edward want to curl his lip. Unless he debuted Selina in public, however, he couldn't think how such a thing was to be avoided. It was customary in his circles to welcome a new bride, and there was little point in trying to avoid it, however much he might want to.

Her silence was more unnerving than any words she might have spoken. Edward allowed the quiet to stretch for a few moments before leaning a little closer to her chair. It had been raining again, and he just caught the appealing scent of damp earth and cut grass that clung to her, enticing him to lean closer still.

He sat back again smartly. 'Come along, Selina. It isn't the end of the world. You never know—you might even enjoy yourself.'

'Might I?' Her voice was quiet, restrained. 'Do

you truly think I'm likely to find any enjoyment in meeting all your high-class acquaintances?'

Edward frowned. He understood her reluctance—given the choice he wouldn't venture out either—but certainly the prospect of a society outing wasn't *so* bad.

'Selina. This is part of our bargain. I have shielded you from your troublesome situation, and now you need to play the part of a squire's wife for me—only until you leave.'

'You don't know what you're asking.' A touch of something like a warning had crept into her tone, and the hands that lay on the table had balled into fists. 'Marrying you and taking your name is one thing. Your insisting on parading me about like one of your society ladies is quite another.' She lifted her chin and looked him directly in the eye. 'I don't want to go. I don't want to be around those people.'

Frustration broke over Edward like a wave, surprising him with its intensity. He'd allowed himself to believe they had managed to make some headway, to find at least some tiny shred of accord between them. Evidently he had been wrong, and he disliked the heavy feeling of disappointment that mixed with his annoyance.

'I'm afraid I must insist. We needn't stay very long, and you needn't enter into any deep conversations, but you must be seen with me as my wife until we have our annulment.'

He saw the anger that rose up in her face. It looked to Edward as though it was mingled with something else—something complex that was almost like anxiety. But what was there for her to be anxious about? What did she really have to fear from such a plan apart from a few hours of crushing boredom?

Selina stood up. An ingrained sense of etiquette dragged Edward to his feet likewise, and they faced each other across the expanse of table between them.

'I said I don't want to go.'

'Even if it will make our lives easier if you do?' Edward fought to keep the edge of frustration from his voice. 'Would you *really* rather half of society descends on this house to peer at you like a creature in a zoo?'

Both voices were tense. The old dog took one look at each of the set faces, tucked his tail between his legs and crept beneath the table.

'Of course I don't want that. I won't be seeing anybody, anywhere. I'm not one of your kind, Edward.' Selina shook her head, her eyes filled with that strange emotion Edward couldn't seem to place. She looked almost haunted. 'I can't—I can't walk among them and pretend I belong.'

Edward raked his hand through his hair, struggling to restrain his exasperation with his determined wife. There was high colour in her cheeks now, a dusky pink that, despite the depths of his ire, Edward couldn't help but note suited her.

The thought only fanned the flames of his irritation. 'Why are you doing this? Why must you make this simple thing so difficult?'

'You think me difficult because I won't be a good wife and do as you demand? Don't forget you were the one who never wanted a *good wife*.'

It was all he could do to bite back a growl. He was well aware of the unsentimental terms of their marriage, despite his confusing stirrings to the contrary. Surely it was Selina who needed a reminder of her part in their scheme.

'You didn't answer the question. Why are you so set on denying me this request? Is it simple spite? What?'

She was moving away from him. One part of Edward's mind reeled at her poor manners—turning one's back in the middle of a conversation?—while another merely raged at her obstinacy. She couldn't possibly have a real rationale for her actions; she simply wanted to wound him.

The realisation stung.

Selina paused in the doorway, one hand resting on the handle. She turned back to him, an expression of intense feeling written upon her face. 'Nothing I do is ever born out of spite. *I* was raised better than that.'

'Then what *is* your reason?'

Edward knew his voice was raised more loudly than a gentleman's should ever be, but the provocation was too much to bear. He flung the words at her back, but she had already thrown open the door and disappeared from his sight.

Selina's heart thudded in her ears as she swept down the cobbled path to the stable yard.

How could he?

Wasn't it enough that she'd sacrificed so much already? That she'd already swallowed her pride and tasted the bitterness of leaving her home, her family, her entire way of life to help Edward claim his precious inheritance? Certainly he had aided her in return, and for that she was grateful, but surely he was demanding more now than she could ever be expected to give.

The sound of her footsteps on damp cobbles rang out across the yard, and the two stable lads dipped their heads in respectful greeting as she strode past. Even that added fuel to the flames of her fire. All the servants were by now aware of her origins, she knew that for certain, and yet they still *'yes, ma'am-ed'* her as if she were a born lady. It was all so false. Everything of Edward's class was so insincere, so built on illusions and glamours. And now he wanted her to embrace it even more, to mingle with those but for whom she would still have a mother.

Djali flicked his ears at her as she approached, his huge grey head poking out over his stable door. Well used to his moods, Selina could tell just by looking that he was irritable at being cooped up. Roma horses were allowed much more freedom than gentry mounts, and Djali didn't seem to be taking to the upper-class way of life any better than his mistress.

Selina unbolted the door and stepped inside, closing it behind her. The horse eyed her for a moment before turning to his trough, and Selina perched on the edge of it, her arms folded across the worn fabric at the bodice of her dress.

She hadn't seen Edward close to losing his temper before, and she would confess she hadn't enjoyed the experience. Following their dance lesson, and his wholly unexpected kiss, she had noticed his behaviour towards her undergo a subtle change. Whereas previously he had been polite but distant, he now seemed more inclined to seek her out during the day for innocuous conversation—conversation that, mortifyingly, Selina found she was beginning to enjoy.

Returning to her room after the events of that morning, Selina had seated herself in front of her looking glass and gazed long and hard at her reflection. Her mirror image had stared back unflinchingly, almost challenging her to voice the confusing array of thoughts that chased each other through her mind.

She had danced with Edward. And she had liked it.

Even worse: he had *kissed* her. And she had *liked* it.

Despite herself, her better judgement and all her attempts to squash it, her worrying attraction to Edward showed no signs of diminishing. Her thoughts of him *would not* cease to plague her day and night. The memories of how good his hand had felt on her waist, how his lips had moved on hers so urgently, were burned into her mind like a brand, and nothing could free her of their grip. It was an unexpected complication to feel her weakness for him increasing rather than the reverse, and the knowledge that Edward would be horrified by her fledgling feelings for him only made her feel worse.

Hadn't he made it plain that he wanted a wife who would form no attachment to him? His kiss must have been some strange lapse of thought— a thing of no importance that she ought to try to forget.

Tears pricked at her eyes. Sitting in the calm stillness of the stable, surrounded by the heady scent of hay and horse, Selina felt a sudden wave of powerful homesickness threaten to engulf her. The smells were of her childhood, when Papa would take her with him to market to look over some new pony, and for a moment she wondered if she should just take Djali and ride back home to Zillah. Hang Edward and everything he stood for—why should he be allowed to make her feel such confusion?

A shadow sliced across the cold sunlight filtering through the stable door.

'Selina?'

Edward's voice was quiet. Glancing up, she saw him looking over the split door, an unreadable expression on his infuriatingly handsome face. She said nothing as he entered the stable and leaned against one wall; his silence matched her own.

Tiny motes of dust danced in the shaft of light that streamed through the doorway and outside Selina could hear the stable lads sweeping the cobbles, one of them humming to himself as he worked. Djali stood close by, the grinding of his teeth against oats his only contribution to breaking the strained silence that neither Edward nor Selina seemed willing or able to end.

After what felt like half a lifetime Edward spoke. He wasn't looking at her. Instead his attention was fixed on the marked flanks of the steadily chewing horse.

'I keep meaning to ask you. How did Djali get his scars?'

Selina felt herself tense. She knew he was just trying to break the tension between them, but of all the questions he could have asked he *would* have to stumble across the one she would have given anything to avoid answering. Her heart rate, already raised at his entrance to the stable, picked up speed.

'It's not a story I like telling.'

Edward scuffed the toe of one immaculate boot through the straw strewn at his feet. 'Why is that? Was it an upsetting event for you?'

'Oh, yes.' Her voice was low and bitter. 'You might certainly say that.'

How could she tell Edward the truth of it?

She risked a glance in his direction—a quick sideways cut of her downturned eyes. He seemed to be waiting for her to elaborate, and Selina turned her face away. There was no way of explaining what had happened to Djali without revealing all: how the fate of her mother was tied to it, and the role his own family had played in the whole sorry business. To confess the full story to Edward would be to reveal his uncle's wickedness—surely he would not thank her for that.

'I'm not sure you would enjoy hearing about it.'

She stared down at the floor, noticing a new

tear in the hem of her dress. *Another thing to repair.* If only her heart was as easy to mend.

The familiar dull ache she felt whenever her final day with Mama was recalled settled beneath her breastbone again, a weight in her chest she had grown used to carrying since childhood. Perhaps she *should* tell Edward exactly why the Roma hated his class, she thought, a sudden feeling of hopelessness stealing over her. It wouldn't change anything, but then he would know why she couldn't bring herself to walk among those responsible for causing so much pain to her people.

At least then he would understand—and besides, wasn't there some secret, shadowy part of her that wanted him to know she wasn't as heartless as he obviously thought her to be? She shouldn't care what he thought—she knew that—and yet that small part of her was undeniably there, and its whisper caused her to make up her mind.

'I'd like to think I could cope with whatever you have to say.'

Edward sounded far away, although he couldn't have been more than a few yards from where Selina sat stiffly, hunched slightly as though in pain. She forced herself to look up at him, watching her from across the stable floor. 'Would you truly like to know?'

'If you would be so good as to tell me.'

Selina could feel the jumping of her pulse at her throat, but her voice was calm and cold. 'Perhaps I should. I hope then you'll see why I can't bring myself to mix with the people you think of as friends. Only...' She tailed off for a moment as worry gnawed at her.

I hope he won't react too angrily. I can't imagine he'll like me calling his uncle a murderer, even if I suppose it was an accident.

'Only recall that I warned you first you wouldn't enjoy this tale.'

Edward opened his mouth to reply, a frown appearing between his brows, but Selina began to speak, forcing him into silence.

'Djali was a gift from my father to my mother. Mama broke him in herself. Papa told me it took her weeks to get a saddle on him, but she was the only one who ever could have done it. Papa bought Djali cheaply, because of his bad temper, but Mama managed to see the best in him and he loved her, too.'

She swallowed, her mouth dry as she considered how to proceed. Edward watched her closely, the frown replaced by a look of wary concern.

'A good horse is worth its weight in gold to the Romani; it makes things a little easier as life on the road is hard. There are times when there's no food, no coal for our stoves. Winters are always the worst.'

The edge of the trough was digging into her thighs. Selina stood up and moved across to the doorway, standing with her back to her waiting husband.

'The winter when I was eight years old was the coldest I can remember. Papa was out trying to find work and Grandmother was sick with a fever, so it was just me and Mama who went hawking. We thought we'd test our luck at the nearest gentry house, see if anybody would buy our wares. We tied Djali up not far from the house.'

She swallowed hard. *Just say it.* There was no going back now.

'In fact, it was this very house. Blackwell Hall.'

Edward started, straightening up immediately from his position leaning against the stable wall, but Selina allowed him no time to speak.

'It was a freezing, iron day. We were so, so cold, and so, so hungry. I knew Mama was desperate. When the front door opened I swear to you I believe she thought our luck had changed.'

'But it hadn't.' It wasn't a question. Edward's voice held a world of grim foreboding.

'No. It hadn't. At the first sight of us standing on the doorstep your uncle bellowed at his men to release the dogs.'

Her chest was rising and falling faster than she could control as she saw Edward's mouth drop open, his face rigid with naked horror.

'So we ran. We ran as fast as we could away from those hounds and we heard your uncle Charles *laughing* as we went.'

Her voice was thick with emotion. How ugly it must sound to Edward, some distant part of her thought, but she couldn't stop now—not until the whole tale was told.

'We ran back down the drive and through the gates, and we were almost back safely with Djali when Mama slipped on the frost and fell down. The dogs were still coming. I could hear them barking as they got closer and closer, and Mama was still on the ground—'

It was as though she was living it all over again. The sounds, the sight of the pack of hounds almost upon her, and the worst, the very, *very* worst of it all: Mama lying among the sharp frosted blades of grass, so terribly, unnaturally still, her lifeless black eyes gazing upwards with no earthly way of knowing what they were seeing.

'I thought the dogs were going to tear us apart. I tried to help Mama up but she didn't move. I know now that she hit her head on a rock, killing her instantly, but at the time I just couldn't understand it.'

Tears were coming thick and fast now, falling from Selina's burning eyes. She could no longer see the stable yard beyond the door, her vision blurred and her mind fixed on the horror that consumed her.

'But then Djali leapt out in front of us. I still don't know how he managed to break free from where he was hitched, but he put himself between me, my mother and the dogs and he took the savaging they would have given me onto himself. He saved my life. I remember every moment: how the dogs snarled and howled and lunged at him, over and over again, and how he fought them back, biting and kicking until they ran away— and then how he stood over Mama so quietly, touching her with his nose so gently. He must have known she was gone. From him. From me. From both of us. Forever.

'After a little while he came over to me. He was covered in blood and so many bites I don't know how he survived. I heard them tell Papa later, when they thought I was asleep, that I had followed Djali back to camp and then he had guided them to where my mother was lying. I don't have any memory of that. Only of what went before.'

The world seemed to have splintered into jagged fragments of light, shining in the flow of her tears. She leaned forward and grasped the stable door with both hands, overwhelmed by the grief and terror that threatened to fell her.

Selina felt Edward's arms come around her just as her legs gave way, all the breath escaping from her bursting lungs as he held her close to the firm column of his body. She knew she should push him away, force him to keep his distance, but the strength of his embrace was impossible to resist, and she allowed him to cradle her as sobs racked her body and grief overcame her powers of rational thought.

Don't let him, Lina! her subconscious screamed as she felt one of his hands come up to smooth the ebony silk of her hair away from her face, raising goosebumps on the sensitive skin of her neck with the power of one gentle touch.

But it just felt so good to be held. The unshakable circle of his arms held her swaying body firmly upright, and as her sobs quieted she became aware of the beating of his heart close to her ear, a steady rhythm she found unaccountably soothing.

'I am so sorry, Selina. More sorry than I can ever say.'

One of his hands stroked her back, gentling her in the same way she would calm a frightened foal, and she gave herself up to the comfort it brought. Of all people, how was it that this man should be the one whose arms felt the most secure? she marvelled, half dazed by grief and innocent wonder. Each movement of his hand down her back left sparks in its wake, drawing a tingling line of fire down the column of her spine, and she found herself speechless in the face of her uncontrollable desire to remain there, safe in the protection of his arms.

Some small part of her started at the realisation that she had never been held so close by a man before. Papa was the only male ever to have gathered her into his embrace, making her feel loved and protected from all who might wish to harm her. The sensation of utter security was the same now as it had been when Papa's strong arms had chased away all her childhood fears, so complete and unquestionable that all words were stolen from Selina's mouth.

Pressed up against the warm planes of Edward's body she could hardly move, but the horror of her last day with Diamanda felt more manageable now, the pain somehow more bearable, and the unlikely fact that it was Edward she had to thank left her stunned.

He was looking down at her with the same intent expression he had worn when they had begun to dance, his attention so completely fixed on her that she felt her cheeks begin to burn. The deep hazel of his eyes held a world of compassion, and she saw her own sorrow reflected back at her in the mirror of his face.

His lips were mere inches from hers. Selina felt something inside her will her to move, but to move towards him or away from him she couldn't quite tell.

The voice whispered louder. *You could be the one to lose control this time. Why not just try...?*

Seeing she had stopped crying, Edward gently put Selina from him. Delving into the pocket of his coat, he drew out another white handkerchief and passed it to her.

She took it with one unsteady hand. 'You won't have many of these left at this rate.'

'No. You're amassing quite a collection.'

Watching as Selina rubbed at her eyes in an unpolished movement took Edward straight back to the day she had found Ophelia. Then, standing in the gently stirring woods, he had been struck by her unrefined loveliness. His appreciation of her beauty had not diminished since. In fact, it seemed to be deepening—a fact that was becoming more and more difficult to fight.

No wonder she was reluctant to tell me her story.

Edward's head spun as he tried to make sense of Selina's words, their terrible meaning slotting into place like jigsaw pieces in his horrified mind.

The Roma woman Charles had been rumoured to have harmed was Selina's mother. It was *his* family's fault that she had been forced to grow up without her mama. It was a horrible twist of fate, almost unbelievable, and yet no part of him suspected her of telling anything but the truth. Her emotion, so real and unashamed, could never have been faked. His own feelings swelled with pity, and with a burning guilt that tasted like bile in his throat.

It had been a reflexive move to take her in his arms, driven by the sight of the tears that had torn at him in a way so unexpected it had almost caused him to gasp aloud. Selina's grief was raw and true, not constrained by any upper-class notions of respectability. She had given him a glimpse into the deepest secrets of her heart, quite unlike any true-born lady, and Edward couldn't help the way his own heart had leapt at this unfamiliar show of honesty.

He had never before felt such compulsion, or been so instinctively moved by a display of emotion. Urged into action by the depth of her distress, he had felt himself richly rewarded by Selina's surrender into his embrace.

She'd felt so small and soft in his arms, so unlike the fiery creature he had argued with earlier. Both versions of her were lovely in their own way, each so different from the other, but nothing could have prepared him for how protective he'd felt as she'd cried against the silk of his waist-coat. In truth, as much as her tears had caused him a deep and very real concern, he could not deny that the chance to take her in his arms once more had been too tempting to ignore.

'I came to tell you that I'm sorry. I shouldn't have raised my voice to you and I shouldn't have tried to force you into doing something you don't want to. I was so set on escaping my own problems that I didn't fully consider your feelings. I apologise.' He cleared his throat. 'Especially now, after what you've explained about your mother... For my uncle's part in your family's distress I have no words to express my shame and sorrow. I had no idea he was responsible for such a thing.'

Selina was still playing with the damp handkerchief and she shook her head, avoiding his gaze as she spoke. 'I should apologise, too. You only wanted me to fulfil my part of our arrangement. You couldn't have known what happened to Mama.'

Edward rubbed the back of his neck, unsure of what to say. What *could* one say to a woman who had just poured out the worst experience of her entire life to a man who had, only minutes earlier, been cursing her for her apparent pig-headedness?

A fresh current of guilt coursed through him, alongside the intense pity. No wonder she had mistrusted him, had hesitated before accepting his hand. No wonder her entire camp had looked at him as though he were a monster prowling among them, related as he was to the one who had caused them such grief.

To undergo such an appalling ordeal at all was abhorrent; to be aged eight at the time was even worse. Another wave of sympathy for the devastated woman he had cradled in his arms crashed over him. Edward thought back to his own childhood, casting through his memories for pictures of himself at a similar age. His mother hadn't left yet; that had come later. Edward had only dim memories of flavoured ices in summer and candied fruits at Christmas, interspersed by a jumble of Roma playmates and fat, placid ponies. No tragedies at all.

'Even so. I should have behaved better.'

Selina had moved to stand at Djali's head and was blindly stroking his wiry forelock. She still looked so small, so fragile, and so unlike her usual self that Edward felt a powerful burst of protectiveness roar up inside him, rising to mix with the disgust for his uncle that circled in the pit of his stomach. It was close to nausea, what he felt for the man who had caused so much harm, and he could have growled in grim satisfaction at successfully keeping the Blackwell inheritance out of Charles' hands.

He will never be welcome here again, he resolved, even as he tried to swallow down the renewed urge to take his wife in his arms and hold her close once again. The moment had passed. There could be no excuse to allow himself such dangerous weakness now. He had indulged his secret desires too far already, and it was with an unpleasant jolt he feared his touch might have been unwelcome.

How could she bear for him to be near her after what she had just revealed?

'Where does this leave us?' she asked.

Edward wrenched his attention away from his unwanted thoughts. 'Leave us?'

'Yes. You wanted me to venture out with you. Publicly.'

Was that a blush he saw cross her cheekbones? 'Do you still?'

He shook his head with all the conviction he could muster. There was no way he would pursue his previous aim—not now he knew the reason for her reluctance. The sight of her face, still tearstained and slightly ruddy with distress, increased the guilt twisting in his gut.

'I would never expect you to accompany me

to the assembly rooms now, in light of your revelation.'

'But it would make things easier for us if I did?'

Edward hesitated. There could be no pretence: Selina knew how set he had been on the idea, and he knew her well enough by now to realise she wouldn't appreciate being lied to. 'I can't deny that it would.'

'I see.' Half of Djali's forelock had been braided into a neat plait by her careful fingers. 'So it truly would be in our best interests to establish this connection in the minds of others?'

She appeared to be considering something. Edward waited.

'Perhaps I could propose a compromise.' She glanced at him—a swift, cautious look, as though taking his measure. 'In light of your apology.'

Edward's spirits rose just the tiniest fraction. A compromise? From the distinctly uncompromising Selina? 'What would you suggest?'

'I would be prepared to accompany you on a walk. I don't want to visit anybody, and I won't be displayed like a fairground attraction in any assembly rooms either.' She held up a warning hand. 'But a walk… That I will do.'

Relief mingled with puzzlement surged within him. A walk would be better than nothing; indeed, it might even turn out to be better than his own original scheme. They would see more people out walking than sitting in some stuffy room, and Selina would be far more relaxed out in the open air. It was an excellent suggestion. But why had she changed her mind?

'I would appreciate that very much indeed.' He knew the relief must have shown on his face.

Selina gave him the smallest of smiles before wiping it quickly from her lips with a touch of what struck him as confusion.

'Very good. I shall leave it up to you to decide where and when we shall have our outing.'

Edward bowed with all the courtesy he had been trained to show. The idea of half of society clustering at his home was unpleasant. Many of them were the same faces he had encountered on social calls with Letitia, and Selina's willingness to oblige him was as welcome as it was confusing.

'I didn't think you would change your mind.'

The look she gave him was strange. Not challenging, as had been her usual expression, and not anxious, either, as it had been earlier that afternoon. It was closer to thoughtful.

Edward felt the hairs on the back of his neck stir under her scrutiny, unable to read the expression in her dark Romani eyes.

'Neither did I. My only hope is that I won't live to regret it.'

Chapter Eight

Warwick was teeming with people, and Edward felt Selina's anxiety as they continued their stroll along the busy street.

He took in the sight of his wife, more demure than he had ever seen her before in the respectable navy cloak and prim bonnet rescued from Maria's expansive pile of cast-offs. Selina had raised an eyebrow when Dinah had helped her into them, but she had eventually accepted their necessity.

Gossiping servants were one thing, but Edward would not have Selina exposed to upperclass ridicule when a simple change of clothing could prevent it. Nobody glancing at her would guess she was anything other than a lady born and bred, and he felt a wry appreciation for the way the dark blue served to enhance the raven of her hair.

Of course you'd notice that. Why does that come as no surprise?

'Would you take my arm? I can see you're not enjoying this. We won't stay much longer.'

Edward caught the flash of gratitude in the glance Selina threw him, accompanied by a quick nod. Her small fingers reached up and slotted into the crook of his arm, sending a thrill of that unnamed *something* skittering beneath his skin, and he took a moment to marvel at how far their relationship had come.

On the night the Roma camp had been attacked, she had only touched him under the greatest duress; now she barely hesitated before entrusting him to guide her along the busy street. He wasn't sure whether to smile or frown that her trust in him had evidently increased so much, or that his chest swelled with something suspiciously close to pride at the thought. Ever since she had told him of her mother's fate he had tried harder still to repress his growing regard for her, more certain than ever that any hint of it would be unwelcome.

Selina was all eyes as they made their leisurely progress past shops and houses. Everywhere she looked there were new things to be seen, and her curiosity made Edward feel as though he too was surveying the scene with fresh eyes. Selina's head moved back and forth as she took in the carriages that trundled past, the enticing displays in shop windows, the costly fabrics of passing ladies' clothes—all things Edward had taken for granted for twenty-four years and rarely given a second glance.

Perhaps, although her almost childlike interest was tempered by the wariness he could feel radiating from her, he might dare to wonder if she might not be finding their outing such an unbearable ordeal after all…

'Good morning, Mr Fulbrooke!'

Edward felt Selina flinch as an older man and woman suddenly cut across them, the man's voice ringing out above the rattle of a passing barouche. He brought his hand up to cover her fingers, pressing them closer to the material of his coat, and felt them grasp tightly.

'Good morning, Mr Egerton… Mrs Egerton.'

Edward tipped his hat to the elderly couple, still feeling the vice-like grip of Selina's fingers on his arm. He saw how the woman's eyes widened in powerful curiosity, apparently absorbing every detail of Selina's face and clothes—in order to tell her friends about them later, Edward had no doubt—before they had passed by and moved out of sight.

Edward looked down at Selina, at her hand still gripping the material of his coat. 'That was Mr and Mrs Egerton. I was at school with their son Henry, the biggest blowhard you might ever have the misfortune to meet.'

He saw the corners of her lips twitch a little, the unease draining from her face, and felt relief wash over him. She had looked so startled by Mr Egerton's braying upper-class voice—not that he could blame her. The man was known in Edward's circle to be a human foghorn.

'Mrs Egerton is a determined gossip, so the news that she's seen my mysterious new wife will be all around town by nightfall.'

Selina gave a dry laugh. 'I'm glad to know it. The more people we see today, the fewer will come to call on us at Blackwell, I would hope.'

'That's certainly my desire.'

They walked on for a while in companionable silence, until Edward felt Selina give a small shiver. 'Are you cold?'

'A little.' She peeped up at him, eyes dark beneath the brim of her bonnet. 'I understand they would have seemed a little out of place, but no cloak is as warm as my own shawls.'

'I see.' Edward nodded, dismissing the smile that attempted to curve his lips upward.

He could just imagine the scandalised looks his wife would have attracted had she ventured out in her usual wardrobe, and Selina's indignant reaction was one he could all too easily picture.

'I think we should return to the carriage. You've indulged me quite enough.'

Selina's pert expression told Edward exactly what she thought of *that* notion, but she said nothing as he turned her gently and guided her back through the busy streets. She had more than upheld her end of their bargain, even going so far as to muster a passable attempt at a smile for some of the acquaintances they had passed during their walk. Edward couldn't fault her in that regard, and it was an enjoyable sensation to know that Selina had undertaken such a thing for his benefit when at one time the idea would have been unthinkable.

As they approached the place where the carriage awaited them Edward saw his coachman standing with hands on hips, looking over one of the pair of handsome black horses with a frown.

'Is something the matter?'

The coachman, a stout individual named Greene, looked round at Edward's voice and paced towards him, dipping a bow in Selina's direction. He nodded, a look of concern on his weathered face.

'Aye, sir. This one's gone lame.' He gestured at the nearest horse. 'I thought she was favouring her back right hoof on the way here, and now it's grown worse. She won't be able to pull the carriage back to the Hall in this state.' He patted the horse's flank with rough affection. 'I'm not sure what to make of it.'

Edward frowned, and was about to speak when Selina stepped up to the horse and smoothed her hand along its gleaming back.

'May I look?'

Greene's eyebrows raised in surprise. 'If you'd like to, ma'am.'

He lifted his hat and rubbed the back of his head. Edward saw how doubtfully he eyed Selina as she moved to stand behind the horse.

'Be careful, ma'am—she might kick...'

The coachman's sentence died in his mouth as Selina flung her cloak out of the way and firmly seized the horse's back leg, bringing it up to clamp it between her knees. Edward started in shock. *What kind of woman did such a thing? And in public?*

He looked about him quickly. More than one passer-by was looking askance at the otherwise respectable young woman who now bent to inspect the hoof, her practised fingers running across the shoe as she frowned in expert concentration.

'Hmm...' Oblivious to the mute disbelief of both watching men, Selina turned the hoof and pressed gently at the tender underside, searching for something. The horse gave a soft whinny, as though in pain, and Selina placed the foot back on the ground carefully. 'She's got an abscess.'

Selina straightened up, moving back to stand at the horse's head. She ran a hand down the animal's face, softly stroking the blaze of white splashed across jet-black.

'A mustard poultice will draw the heat out, and she'll be walking normally again quite soon.'

Greene blinked at her, obviously at a loss for words, and Edward felt himself scarcely less surprised than his coachman. Her complete lack of self-consciousness stirred his immense admiration—who else would throw quality propriety to the wind and, careless of anybody else's opinion, do such an unladylike thing in the middle of a heaving street?

Edward knew from the aghast faces of the well-dressed strangers walking by them that they were appalled at Selina's apparent lack of decorum, but Edward only felt an absurd glint of pride that his wife was so unbothered by their stares, intent only on helping the suffering horse.

That's the Selina I met in the woods all those years ago. Never one to ignore a poor wounded creature.

Selina brushed her hands together neatly. 'Do you know how to make up a poultice? I have a recipe, if you'd care for it?'

The coachman still stared at her with a combination of shock and no small degree of respect, and it was only when Edward audibly cleared his throat that the man seemed to find his tongue. 'My wife makes them when the children have toothache, ma'am. I'll ask her for one as soon as I return home.'

'Excellent. She'll be good as new directly.'

Edward clapped the man on the shoulder, seeing Selina's satisfied nod out of the corner of his eye. All that remained now was to work out how he and Selina would find their way back to Blackwell themselves, now the carriage was unavailable. Greene would walk the injured horse home slowly, and return with a fresh pair to retrieve the carriage in the morning, but how would they manage now?

Edward made up his mind. There was really only one option, and it was one that made his heart begin to beat quickly against his ribs. 'I think Mrs Fulbrooke and I will ride home on the other horse. Would you be so good as to see her saddled?'

'Of course, sir.'

Greene moved off in pursuit of his task, leaving Edward with the suddenly warily quiet Selina.

Selina watched with round eyes as Greene prepared the fit horse and brought her to stand at the mounting block. Edward climbed up at once, and it was all Selina could do to bite back a squeak of anxiety as she realised her first suspicion had been correct.

Heaven help me. Selina stared up at him, seated high above her with such natural elegance it was as though he'd been born into a saddle. *He wants me sit between—?*

She could hardly finish the thought, her breath catching in her throat and mortification stealing over her. He truly expected her to share his seat. It was so *intimate*, so *close*. She would be able to feel those strong legs she had admired for so long on either side of her, pinning her between them, while his arms would have to reach around her, drawing her close to that firm chest that she didn't dare allow herself to think about.

It wasn't proper to have such thoughts, but Selina couldn't help it as Edward looked down at her and raised a questioning eyebrow.

'Are you coming up or not?'

Greene was standing at her elbow. 'Allow me, ma'am.'

He extended a hand and Selina took it with a moment's hesitation. She didn't have much choice, but it was with no small amount of embarrassment that she allowed the coachman to help her up onto the waiting horse.

Selina swallowed down a rising sense of discomfort as she settled herself between the warm spread of Edward's thighs. The feel of his legs touching hers through the material of her dress made her heart skip faster, and when his arms came around her to take hold of the reins she felt a furious blush come roaring up from her neck to burn the previously cold skin of her cheeks.

'Are you quite comfortable?'

Edward's lips were close to her ear. Selina steeled herself not to shiver as the feel of his breath stirred the hairs on the nape of her neck, deliciously sensitive. She nodded mutely and took hold of the pommel to anchor herself to the saddle.

'Very good.' Edward twitched the reins and gently touched the horse with his heels, raising a hand to Greene in farewell. 'Walk on.'

Selina held herself stiffly, determined not to allow herself to sink back against Edward's broad chest as they trotted through the town, Edward nodding politely to his left and right as they passed people he knew. It seemed to Selina he had an extraordinary number of acquaintances, and she thanked her lucky stars that he didn't pull the horse up short to speak to any of them.

A mile or so into their journey Edward leaned down to speak into her ear again, sending another delightful rush of sensation tingling through her nerves.

'Why are you sitting so oddly? You can't be at ease, holding yourself so unnaturally upright like that.'

Selina gritted her teeth on her alarm. *I can't very well tell you it's because I don't dare come any closer.*

The instinctive reaction of her body to Edward's proximity was hardly subtle, she feared, and her face grew warm again at the thought that Edward might notice the effect his all too enticing masculinity had on her.

'No, no, I'm quite well. This is how I always sit when I'm riding.'

She heard Edward's snort of amusement. 'I've watched you ride on a number of occasions, and I beg your leave to disagree that this is in any way normal.'

Selina opened her mouth to reply, but instead only a gasp escaped her lips as Edward took one hand from the reins to place it on her waist and draw her backwards, pulling her closer to the solid pillar of his body as easily as if she weighed nothing at all.

Shocked, Selina said nothing as sparks erupted in her stomach at the feel of his hand on the intimate curve of her waist, overcome by scandalised delight as Edward's very male heat warmed her back. She leaned against him, apparently powerless to move away.

'That's better. We have a fairly long ride ahead of us. I don't want you spending it looking so uncomfortable.'

Unseen by the satisfied man at her back, Selina shut her eyes tight in secret disagreement. If Edward thought nestling closer against him had decreased her discomfort, he was entirely wrong. Her shameful appreciation for the strength of the thighs that rubbed against her own with every movement of the horse was enough to make her blush all the more, and the place where his hand had gripped her waist felt as though it was on fire.

She was almost dazed by the whirl of sensation such proximity created inside her, and so she said nothing as they rode onwards, each footfall only increasing the delicious friction between her back and his chest that made her every nerve stand to attention.

'I was very impressed by how well you dealt with my poor horse.'

Selina felt the words vibrate through Edward's chest as he spoke.

'I've never seen a woman with such—ah—*skills* before.'

Selina could have sworn she heard a note of surprised admiration in his tone, and it pleased her more than she knew was entirely sensible. 'Thank you. I've been working horses since I was old enough to walk. My mother had just started teaching me her remedies before she passed away—' She broke off for a moment as a sudden wave of intense sadness washed over her. 'Her knowledge was my only inheritance when she died.'

She heard the note of curiosity in Edward's voice at her back. 'The only inheritance? Did she not leave anything else to you?'

Selina swallowed down a flicker of pain and shook her head. 'No. That is not our way.'

Flames had consumed Diamanda's body and all her worldly goods along with her, as was Romani custom. Everything that had remained of the woman who had shaped Selina's young life had been reduced to a towering column of smoke. Diamanda's dresses, her jewellery, even her hair combs had been piled around her slight body and set alight, while her family and all who loved her had stood with dancing flames reflected in the tears that rolled down their faces.

'We leave nothing behind.'

Edward was silent for a moment. When he replied his voice held genuine sympathy, its warmth so sincere that Selina felt something within her rise up to respond. It was almost a physical stirring, although nothing could quite force back the tide of grief that still welled inside her.

'It must be difficult, having no keepsakes. Was there nothing you would have liked to save?'

Selina sighed, her shoulders moving in a hopeless shrug. 'It hardly matters now.'

'But there was something?' he asked softly, interested but not imposing. 'A memento you would have liked to keep?'

A small smile twisted Selina's lips—a wistful thing that would have broken her mama's heart. 'There was a brooch she used to wear. Only gilt and paste stones, but she used to let me play with it and I was always the one to pin it to her dress.'

She held her fingers a couple of inches apart, seeing as she did so the memory of the brooch fixed firmly to her mother's chest. The picture made her smile stronger.

'It was about this big, and shaped like a flower. One big central stone surrounded by smaller ones like petals, and two metal leaves underneath. I'll never forget it.' She sighed again, so quietly this time that she knew Edward couldn't have caught the tiny sound. 'Never.'

There was another silence as Selina sifted through her memories, recalling all the times when her childish fingers had toyed with the brooch she ached to see just one more time. Her father had brought it back with him from some market or other, and slipped it beneath Diamanda's pillow for her to find…

Her papa's face when he and Selina had stood watching as his beloved's pyre sent sparks tumbling through the air was one she had never been able to forget. The thought of Papa gave Selina pause, and she felt a fresh knot of unhappiness rising to sit heavy in her chest. How was he faring, away working so hard? Had he heard the news of her marriage? Was he even now breaking a sweat while the pain of his daughter's actions weighed him down from within?

She felt her lips tighten and looked down at her hands, increasing their grip on the pommel until the knuckles gleamed white.

'You don't talk about your father.'

It was as though Edward had read her mind. His voice was quiet, hardly audible above the chill wind that rushed about them as they rode. They had long since left the town behind, and now all Selina could see in all directions was the patchwork green of fields.

'It's difficult for me.' Selina flexed the fingers of one hand, relieving the stiffness her iron grip had created. 'I miss him. I miss all my people.'

Edward said nothing for a moment. Selina was just beginning to wish she hadn't opened up at all when she felt a clumsy pat on her arm, and she twisted in surprise to look up into Edward's face.

'I understand.' Edward's expression looked a little strained and he gave Selina a tight smile.

'My relationship with my own father wasn't easy, but even so...' He tailed off, looking away from her across the open fields.

Selina waited for him to finish, but he didn't seem inclined to carry on. The look in his eye was almost sad, and Selina felt sympathy rise up inside her for the man she longed to comfort. Would he allow her such liberties? she wondered as she twisted back in the saddle to look over the horse's head. He had spared no time in soothing her when she grieved for her mother, and she felt another glimmer of that inexplicable comfort Edward's arms had given her.

But perhaps he would not appreciate her drawing attention to his moment of sorrow. Grief was a deeply personal thing—she knew that from bitter experience. He might rather she didn't say a word. Still, the glimpse of pain in his look had moved her, and it was by some unthinking instinct that Selina reached out to take Edward's hand in her own and squeeze it in wordless sympathy.

She felt rather than saw Edward's jolt of surprise, covered by a quick-thinking cough. *Perhaps I shouldn't have done that.* She turned her head slightly to the side, hoping to catch another glimpse of his face, but she could see nothing but a vague blur.

They rode on in silence, covering the few

miles left to Blackwell Hall with neither one aware of the racing thoughts that swirled within the other.

Chapter Nine

Selina looked out at the frost delicately patterning the glass of the drawing room window. Winter was well and truly underway. The mornings were raw and uncompromising, and clouds moved across an iron sky. She could just make out the tiny forms of little birds huddling together for warmth in the skeletal branches of the grounds' trees.

She turned from the window and began to move in the direction of her bedchamber. Edward had expressed his intention of seeing his steward that morning, on estate business, stating that he wouldn't be returning until the evening, and he had left soon after breakfast, riding away down the long drive on his shining chestnut mare. It seemed to her the perfect time chance a visit to the Roma camp, without any accompanying questions.

She'd been relieved at his departure for other reasons, too.

There didn't seem to be much use in trying to hide from it anymore: her feelings for Edward had changed, and the knowledge chilled her to the bone.

She had always thought he was handsome. Even on the first day they had met, when he had coaxed her down from her hiding place and she had wanted to run from him, to be anywhere other than facing him across a carpet of fallen leaves, she had been struck by the knowledge that his face was the most comely she had ever seen. That initial attraction, a product of the most basic animal instinct, had been tempered by her utter contempt for his class, his way of life and everything he stood for.

His class hadn't changed, and neither had the life of privilege that was all he had ever known—but it seemed to matter less now, the gulf between them, and that was what frightened her. He'd given her glimpses of the real man behind the good manners and polite smiles, and she liked what she had seen. His grief for his father had shown her his vulnerability, and his care for her in the face of her own sorrow had left her in no doubt as to the kindness of his heart.

While she had felt nothing but mere physical

attraction to him, she had been safe. Now she wasn't sure how close to danger she was straying.

Out in the yard she saddled Djali herself, with automatic swiftness, although the stable lads hovered a short distance away. Ever since she'd refused their offer of a side-saddle some weeks previously they had watched with undisguised fascination each time she'd mounted, half aghast and half admiring of her insistence on riding astride.

Passing them now, as she rode out from the yard, she raised a hand in greeting and saw their heads bob in reply.

Once out of their hearing she leaned forward to pat the horse's grey neck. 'Isn't this better, Djali? Out in the open air, just you and me?'

The horse flicked his ears at her voice and lengthened his stride. He cantered easily down the long gravel drive, bearing Selina smoothly through the imposing wrought-iron gates and away from Blackwell Hall.

Try as she might to ignore him, Edward wouldn't leave her mind as she rode. He seemed to impose upon her more and more inescapably—both in real life and when she laid her head down on her luxurious pillow to dream—and it seemed even the freezing late-November air couldn't shock some sense into her.

I had hoped a day away from him would help me gather my wits. It seems I was wrong.

She didn't want to feel this way. No good could come of it. She was under no illusion that Edward felt anything for her other than a duty of care, and she shouldn't allow herself to think otherwise. A marriage of convenience was what he had wanted, specifically with no finer feelings involved—and that was what she must give him, despite any stupid, confusing, ridiculous thoughts to the contrary.

Her determination to disregard her feelings, however, hadn't stopped them from betraying her at every turn. Small, insignificant gestures from Edward insisted on taking on greater magnitude in her despairing mind. Each time his hand brushed hers as he helped her into the saddle her heart would skip a beat, and his smile as she played fetch with old Tips was endearing.

But he wouldn't want her affection, nor welcome it if she were foolish enough to let it show, and it was growing harder day by day to keep secret the stirrings she feared would so disturb her stoic husband.

The Roma camp looked just as it had the day she'd left it. The *vardos* still stood in a semi-circle around the cooking pits, their painted wooden sides gleaming in the wintry sunlight and their owners milling about busily, and the camp's horses still grazed in the makeshift paddock or were tethered to stakes driven into the ground.

At the sound of Djali's approaching hoofbeats one of the women—Selina's cousin Florentia—looked up sharply. Selina saw the apprehension in her kinswoman's face change to surprise as she registered who was riding into the camp, and she felt her spirits soar as surprise was in turn replaced by a wide beam of welcome.

'Cousin!' Florentia dropped the knife she had been using to peel vegetables and rushed towards her, arms outstretched.

Selina dismounted and reached out towards the other woman, who enveloped her in a tight embrace.

'Cousin. My poor cousin. You don't know how good it is to see you. We've all been so worried about you, all alone up there in that great house!'

'I am well.' Selina smiled as Florentia's daughters recognised the newcomer. They threw down their dolls at once and ran towards her as quickly as their little legs would carry them, and she bent to receive them into her arms.

'Lina! Lina!'

'Lina! Are you come back? Are you come to live with us again?'

'Not quite yet, dearest.' She hefted the youngest onto her hip and held out her hand for the other girl. 'But it won't be much longer.'

The other women had begun to crowd around her. The older ones touched the worn fabric of her dress, the wool of her shawls and even her hair in silent blessing, thankful for her return to them, while the younger rattled off questions more quickly than she could reply to them.

'I'll answer you all very soon.' Selina looked around at the rapt faces. 'First I would like to see my grandmother. Where is she?'

'The other end of the meadow. Another one of the babies has been ill, and Zillah went out to gather some herbs for medicine.'

All of the breath left Selina's body. 'Another one of the babies?'

Surely not. Their survival had been one of the most desperate reasons she had consented to become Edward's wife and thrown her entire existence into chaos. If a child had succumbed despite her actions all her struggle would have been in vain. The cruel irony was not lost on her.

'They have been unwell?'

'Yes. My son has been gravely ill, but he's a little stronger now.'

The child's mother, a young woman Selina knew had only been married a year, gave her a shy smile.

'He wouldn't have survived his fever if we'd

been on the road. I have you to thank for saving my boy.'

'I can't take the credit for that.' She smiled back at the woman, relief coursing through her. So the children were safe? That was good news indeed. 'It was my fault we would have had to move in the first place.'

'Nonsense.' Florentia's look was stern. 'Those evil men would have found the camp eventually. If you hadn't sacrificed yourself for us we would have had to run anyway—and probably even faster.'

Selina shrugged off her cousin's words. Whatever they might tell her, Selina knew in her heart that she was responsible for the calamity that had almost befallen her people. It was good to know that they didn't blame her, but she could never allow herself any reprieve from the guilt that had haunted her ever since that night.

Zillah's back was to her as she approached, bent over to inspect what to most would have looked to be a clump of weeds, and the old woman spun round in alarm at the touch of Selina's hand on her shoulder.

'Selina? Oh, my Selina!'

Zillah's arms came around Selina in a hug that might have crushed bones had the old woman been a fraction stronger. Her grandmother held her for several long moments, gently rocking back and forth, before letting go to hold her at arm's length and peer up sharply into her face.

'Why are you here, child? Is aught amiss?'

'No, Grandmother. I simply missed you, that's all.'

'But is it not dangerous for you here? What of those men?'

'Peace, Grandmother.' Selina smiled down at the lined face and the old eyes that gazed into her own. 'They know I'm under Edward's protection—he has made sure they are aware of our marriage. While I am his acknowledged wife they won't dare harm me. If you have suspicions that they've returned I will tell Edward and he will deal with them, have no doubt. But I'm confident they won't risk their jobs by hunting me until they feel safe to do so.'

Selina realised her mistake as soon as the words left her lips. Using Edward's given name, and in a tone a shade too warm, had been a fatal error. She saw a shadow of suspicion flit across the old woman's countenance and felt her heart sink.

'I see. Well… Come to the *vardo*, girl. I'm sure you've much to tell me.'

Selina followed the slight form of her grandmother back to their caravan. Mounting the steps and crossing the threshold, she was at once assailed by the bittersweet familiarity of the compact space inside the cabin. It was only the size that surprised her. Had the cabin always been so *small*?

Her time at Blackwell must have affected her more than she'd realised, she thought, and her heart gave a lurch at the notion she had become adrift from her true way of life. She frowned to herself, feeling guilt in the pit of her stomach. Of course it wasn't the cabin that was too small. It was the fine rooms of the Hall that were too large.

She sat and waited as Zillah busied herself stoking up the fire to make tea. Cups in hand, granddaughter and grandmother regarded each other across the narrow space between their bunks.

'So.' Zillah's gaze was unwavering as ever. 'You are well?'

'As well as I can be. And yourself? How have you been faring?'

'Oh, you know me. I am as I always am.'

Selina sipped her tea, aware of a growing discomfort nagging at her. Zillah's careful scrutiny was nothing new, but the wary gleam in her eye was one Selina hadn't seen before. An unsettling feeling of being measured was creeping over her—but measured for what?

'And Papa? Have you seen him?'

'No.' Zillah looked away from her, instead

watching the curling flames that flickered in the grate. 'He has had no time to visit. A few of the young men returned briefly, to see their wives, but your father has been promoted to foreman of a team and wasn't able to come with them.'

'He doesn't know—?'

'About your marriage?' Her grandmother still studied the fire. 'No. No—heaven forgive me—I couldn't bear to send word to him. I just couldn't do it.'

Selina stared down into her teacup. How was she to respond? Of course Zillah was right. Papa would be distraught at the knowledge of how his only daughter had wed. But it could only be a matter of time before he would have to be told, and the thought of his anguish made her tea turn to ashes in her mouth.

'But enough of that. I want to know everything that has befallen you since we last met. Have you been well treated?'

Zillah's voice was calm enough, but Selina knew her too well to be fooled. Worry had etched new wrinkles into the old woman's lined face since she had last set eyes on her.

'Yes, Grandmother.' Selina crossed the tiny gap between their bunks and took the frail body in her arms, feeling Zillah sag with relief at her words. 'I have been treated with nothing but respect and courtesy. You have no reason to worry.'

'That—that is good to know.'

Zillah patted her cheek with something like a smile, although Selina was sure she saw a shadow of unease still clouding her grandmother's eyes.

'I won't deny I have been concerned.'

'It's the truth.' Selina covered the bony hand with her own and squeezed gently. She wanted Zillah to think well of Edward, she realised with a rush of embarrassment. It mattered to her more now than she would have thought it could. 'Edward has been very good to me—better than I ever would have dreamed. In fact, he has been kind.'

Zillah was silent for a moment. She continued to hold her granddaughter close, but Selina could sense that the atmosphere had changed. Tension permeated the air of the cabin, replacing the tenderness of moments before.

Zillah was the first to draw away, and Selina saw immediately that she had not been wrong about the unease in her grandmother's expression.

'You speak as though you're fond of him. Of Edward.' Zillah's brow was pinched with wariness. 'Is that so?'

Selina felt her breath catch. Had she really been so transparent? She felt the slow tick of her pulse pick up speed. 'I didn't mean—' She stumbled for an answer, words evading her as she cast about for a way out of what she realised too late was a sprung trap.

'I know well enough what you mean.' Zillah passed a gnarled hand over her face, suddenly looking every one of her eighty-three years. 'It is as I feared.'

Selina's palms were damp as she clenched her hands into fists. *Keep your composure.* Her choice of words had been a mistake; she saw that now. How could she extricate herself from a situation that had already begun to spiral out of control?

'I don't know what you can be referring to. There's nothing for you to fear.'

There was another silence. Selina looked down at her balled fingers and forced them to straighten out, to relax on the worn fabric of her lap. The fire in the stove crackled quietly, casting an orange glow on the polished *vardo* floor.

Her grandmother's face was almost sad as she shook her head slowly, and in the silence her voice held a world of gruff pity. 'That's where you're wrong. I have a very real fear that you've made the same mistake as many a young girl and fallen for a man you cannot hope to have.'

Selina swallowed hard, panic rising within her. Her throat felt dry, tight, but she couldn't bring herself to take a drink from her cup. Her stomach fluttered with some unnamed emotion.

How had this situation arisen? She should have guarded her tongue more carefully. Zillah was no fool. From a few hasty words she had guessed at the depth of feeling for Edward that burned within her granddaughter's heart, at her secret joy and pain rolled into one.

Selina forced herself to speak, all the while wary of betraying herself further. 'If by *fallen for* you mean developed a kind of friendship with—then, yes, I suppose I have. But—'

'Selina.' Zillah's voice cut across hers, halting her stuttering reply. 'Let us speak plainly to one another, as we always have. I believe that you have developed more than a friendly liking for this man, and I believe that if you continue on this path it will end badly for all concerned.'

Selina stared at her, her heart beginning to jump. *Too close. Far too close to the truth.* It was so like Zillah to get right the point of an issue, to see through Selina's protestations as though they were no more substantial than autumn mist. 'I—*No*— That is to say, he— I—'

Zillah sighed, long and deep, and when she peered into Selina's face there was a complex look of pain that sent a shard of ice through to Selina's soul.

'He is *gentry*, Selina. *Gentry*. I will not try to pretend he is as abhorrent as the rest of his kind—indeed, I will admit to you that I am grateful to him for his help in our time of need. But even so… You must know that our worlds are too separate, and always will be.'

Her grandmother's words stung.

'I don't say I have a special regard for him. I only say that he has treated me well.'

Selina tried to keep her tone indifferent, but all the same she could hear something beneath the surface and felt a lump rise up in her throat. Zillah was right. They *were* from different worlds, and all the wishing in the universe couldn't undo that. But that wasn't the reason she and Edward could never find happiness together.

The short laugh Zillah huffed out was entirely humourless. 'It isn't your words that betray you, girl. I see that look on your face so many young women have worn through countless generations. But, however handsome your Edward is, however kind, he is still gentry and you are still Roma, and the two are like oil and water. You cannot have forgotten that fact?'

Wordlessly Selina shook her head. Of course she had not forgotten the differences between them. The differences she had once thought it would be impossible to overcome. Now, however, they paled into insignificance in the face of Edward's desire for a cold marriage, his desire that they should annul it as soon as it had served its purpose. It whispered to her each time Edward pulled out a chair for her at the dining table, or laughed in genuine amusement at something she had said.

Each time he behaved towards her in a way that strengthened her esteem for him she would snap back with that knowledge: their marriage was on paper only and had no more depth than that. Zillah's words, misguided as they were, only served to bring home the truth to Selina in harsh black and white: *a man you cannot hope to have.*

'I am well aware of how things stand between us. There has been no impropriety, and for my part I can promise there will be none.'

The words almost choked her. It was all she could do to speak, with lips that did not want to move and a tongue that rebelled at the thought of naming the sadness that writhed inside her. Her grandmother was right, as she so often was. How much Selina would have given for her wisdom just once to be wrong.

'I think only of your happiness.'

The gentle way Zillah spoke almost brought tears to Selina's eyes, so different was it from her usual bluntness. She would never want to hurt her granddaughter; Selina knew that, but the words were like pinpricks to her heart nonetheless.

'It is far better for you to accept now that your marriage to Edward is based on convenience and nothing more. If you say he is a kind man I am

willing to believe you—but never allow sentiment to cloud your eyes to the truth.'

For a long while neither woman spoke further.

What complex jumble of thoughts was twisting through Zillah's mind Selina didn't know.
All she could be sure of was the turmoil inside
her own. Staring down at the polished wooden
floor, all she could do was surrender to the ceaseless procession of images that cycled through her
head: Edward's intense face as he had taught her
to waltz; the compassion in his look when she
had cried for her mother; the closeness of his
face to hers, tempting her to reach up and touch
it with her lips.

Every single instance in which his goodness
had been displayed before her clamoured for attention, but she had to turn away. Because what
Zillah said was true. She was a means to an end
for Edward and nothing more, no matter how
gently her grandmother had tried to phrase it.
They had struck a bargain and he would fulfil
his obligation to her. Anything further could only
ever be a fanciful notion on her part, no matter
how much she now wished, despairingly, that
things could be different.

Edward rolled his aching shoulders as he cantered towards Blackwell. The day had been long
and the estate business laborious and dull. He

was looking forward to a good supper, a glass of port and his comfortable bed. He was just wondering if Selina would still be downstairs when he caught sight of the woman in question not far ahead of him, riding her distinctive grey horse around the side of the Hall toward the stable yard.

A smile crossed his face before he could stop it. There was a curious kind of pleasure to be found in returning home to a wife, and one he was increasingly powerless to resist. He had come to that conclusion the last time he had been away on business, and had subsequently spent the next hour studiously avoiding said wife by retreating to his library. It was getting exhausting, this persistent regard for the woman who haunted his thoughts despite his best efforts. He didn't seem able to master himself.

He hadn't been helping himself—that much he would have to own. He should not have instructed her to sit beside him at the pianoforte, for example, and attempted to teach her the notes, and he *definitely* shouldn't have felt a prickle of *something* shiver its way down his spine when he took her hand and placed each finger on the correct keys to play a simple tune.

He tapped his thigh lightly with his riding crop. It would have to stop. *He* would have to stop. He was getting carried away, and it was only a matter of time before somebody got hurt.

Edward knew it could only be himself.

Physically she stirred him in ways he fervently hoped she wasn't aware of. The image of her beautiful face and lithe figure taunted him at the most inappropriate times, but worse, much worse, was the reaction she caused in his heart and mind. There were flickerings there now—embers of feeling that her kindness and humour had crept in to ignite inside him—and it terrified him. However hard he tried to suppress them they would not be extinguished.

Her smile, so open and honest, in direct contrast to his mother's bland smirk, was becoming more and more contagious to him as the days went by. Her sweetness, hidden from him for so long, had begun to show itself—so different from Letitia's sharp cynicism. Everything about Selina was poles apart from the two quality ladies who had damaged his faith in women so completely, and it was so tempting to believe she could be trusted. But surely danger lurked behind the dark Romani eyes that watched him so closely, and the ability to wound him as he had been hurt before.

And besides, his own private thoughts were hardly relevant anyway. Selina would never reciprocate those feelings. She loathed the gentry, and with good reason. Certainly their relationship had blossomed of late, but surely on her side only into a brittle friendship, which might easily be broken by any hint of his esteem for her. She might have overcome the worst stirrings of her mistrust of him, but he wasn't naive enough to think she would ever forget his class, or forgive his kind for the loss of her mother.

It was this that would keep him safe and allow him to escape the perils of getting too close to a woman—just as he had always planned. He should be thankful to her for remaining so steadfast in sticking to their solely convenient marriage, for helping him to bolster his own defences when he felt them attempting to slip. To give in to his alarming weakness would be to invite the sting of rejection—something he never wanted to experience ever again.

She had already dismounted by the time he drew closer, and he called out to her as his mare's hooves clattered noisily across the cobbles. 'Good evening. Have you been out?'

Edward knew she must have heard him by the way her eyes flickered across to him before looking away again. Indeed, he could have sworn he saw her mouth twitch as though about to reply. Instead, however, she lowered her head and quickly left the stable yard, for all the world as though pretending she was ignorant of his presence—or that he was a stranger to whom she didn't wish to speak.

He watched her go, his face creased in surprise and more than a touch of confusion. *Have I managed to offend her somehow?* Surely there was no reason for such sudden and unexpected coldness.

Edward cast his mind back to their brief greeting that morning as he had passed her in the hall on his way out. There had been nothing out of the ordinary in their exchange and he frowned to himself as he dismounted and passed the reins to the waiting stable lad. What could have happened in the intervening few hours between then and now to make her so apparently displeased with him?

The notion of having upset Selina, even unconsciously, was uncomfortable—and the usual whisper that it was unwise to care for her good opinion had grown quieter of late. He found himself wanting to know what could have transpired that was making it necessary for him to swallow down a sharp disappointment at her newfound reserve. He would have to find out what was bothering her, and indeed where she had been.

A slow creep of suspicion began to steal over him, and it was with heavy feet Edward climbed the stone steps up to the Hall's front door— firmly closed only moments before by the wife whom he suspected had just had malice whispered into her ear by those with good reason to dislike him.

Chapter Ten

Edward ran his eye over the small white rectangle of parchment covered in elegant script. To anyone else it would have looked like an invitation—*he* knew it was more of a summons.

Sir William Beaumont.

So his annual Twelfth Night ball was almost upon them again.

Edward had hoped rather than believed his father's death would excuse him from having to attend, but now, with the invitation in his hand, he had to face facts. His own aversion for high society parties made no difference: Ambrose Fulbrooke and Sir William had been boys together, and the presence of the Fulbrookes at each of the old knight's gatherings was considered essential to the occasion's success.

The real question, he mused as he moved from the hall towards his private study, was how to proceed with regard to Selina. She would have

to accompany him—of that there was unfortunately no doubt. Word of his marriage had spread
so far and so wide that for his wife not to attend
the ball would register as a snub. It would also
be a good opportunity for more of his acquaintances to see her, to see them together, so nobody
would contest him having met the terms of his
father's will.

Despite the potential benefits of the plan, the
prospect of having to break the news to her almost made him groan out loud. She'd been acting so strangely of late, and his announcement
would only make things worse. Any warmth between them seemed to have evaporated, and it
was a source of constant frustration that she refused to tell him why.

*I wonder what the old woman said to her to
make her behave so oddly.*

Edward had reached the safety of his study
and he paced the floor with irritable strides. He
could date the change in Selina from the day she
had ventured out to visit the Romani camp, and
the only explanation could be that her grandmother had filled her head with new doubts. Now
she turned away when he greeted her with only
the barest of acknowledgements, and she had
taken to dining alone in her rooms.

Her avoidance of him stung. He knew he
should be glad that she was making things eas-

ier for him in a way—wasn't that old saying 'out of sight, out of mind'? She would never feel the flicker of longing for him, coming as he did from the class who had done her people such wrong.

Instead of managing to withdraw his affections, however, Edward found they were intensifying day by day, apparently undeterred by their object's indifference. He had cursed his feelings, and himself, roundly and repeatedly. *Why* could he not break the spell of this madness? Even when she hurried away from him Edward was struck by the captivating shape of Selina's body, by the fine darkness of her eyes as she turned them from him. Was he to torment himself forever?

Of course not. She would be leaving as soon as spring arrived; that had been their bargain. The fact that he would be sorry to see her go only made her departure all the more necessary. He feared the power she had begun to hold over him. When a man cared for a woman he handed her the ability to wound him in ways too painful to imagine—as he knew all too well. Even if the prospect of her leaving was more unpleasant than he would have imagined, knowing she would be taking with her the fresh life she had brought to the brooding Hall, he knew there could be no alternative.

She would never choose to stay with him, and

every one of the defences he had constructed around his battered heart reminded him that he should not desire it.

Selina was in her cosy drawing room when he managed to locate her, curled up in the depths of the most comfortable armchair and gazing into the fire that danced in the fireplace grate. She glanced up as he entered the room, and Edward saw her cheeks flush as she recognised her visitor.

'May I speak with you?'

'Of course.'

Selina gestured vaguely to another of the chairs that stood by the fire—the one furthest away from her, Edward noted in frustration. He settled into it, taking a moment to warm his hands before the flames as he considered how to proceed. The poker stood propped against the hearth and he seized it irritably. She was so difficult to talk to of late—how was he to know the best way to go about it?

'We've been invited to a Twelfth Night ball. My father's oldest friend has one every year, and I'm afraid my attendance is compulsory.'

Edward thrust the poker into the flames, stoking them higher. Out of the corner of his eye he could just make out Selina watching him, her face carefully expressionless beneath her raven nest of curls.

'Given your feelings on the landed gentry, I understand you might not be delighted at such a prospect. I would never try to force you into attending, but I should tell you that it would be considered an insult to the host if you didn't.'

She said nothing for a long while, instead looking down at her slender hands as they lay in her lap. The crackle of the fire and gentle ticking of an ornate clock on the mantle were the only sounds, the only movement the soft swirling of snowflakes against the windows.

Edward waited. It was her silence that bothered him the most, he'd come to realise. At least when she railed at him he knew what she was thinking. When she sat there so quietly, looking demurely down into her lap with her eyes veiled behind long lashes, he had no idea of what was happening inside her head.

How was it he found himself *wanting* to know? The ceaseless task of fighting against it was starting to wear him down, and the seductive temptation to give in to it and abandon his restraint whispered to him, its voice sweet in his ear. Edward shook his head quickly, to clear it, but an echo of that whisper still remained.

'How many people would be there? Is it a very grand occasion?'

Edward rubbed his jaw, hesitating before he answered. He couldn't lie to her, but he knew she wouldn't like his reply. 'Unfortunately, yes. Sir William extends an invitation to all the old families—there will be a good number of guests, all of them exactly the type of people you'd rather avoid.'

'I see.' The clock ticked in the quiet that settled between them for a few moments. Then, 'What would be required of me?'

'Required?' Edward had dropped his head into the cradle of his palms at her silence, but now he looked up from his hands. 'Why, nothing—aside from perhaps pretending my company isn't too distasteful to you. If such a thing can be managed.'

He realised as soon as they left his lips that his words had come out entirely wrong. He had meant for them to sound darkly comic; instead he'd heard an edge of bitterness, and he saw Selina's expression change as she too caught the dour note.

Perhaps it was too close to the truth for both of them? he wondered. He feeling slighted and she unwilling? He cursed internally at making such a mistake.

He saw her open her mouth to speak—to defend herself or upbraid him? he wondered—but she evidently thought better of it, for she closed it again and returned to staring into the flames.

He thought he saw tension in the way she held

herself stiffly upright, but when she eventually turned to him her voice was restrained.

'If you think it would be for the best, you may accept the invitation. For both of us.'

'Oh?' Edward attempted what he hoped would turn out to be a normal smile, although a warm flood of relief washed over him. Perhaps he hadn't made such a grave error after all. 'Excellent. I shall reply to Sir William at once.'

Selina nodded, although Edward saw that the line of her jaw looked a little tight and a shadow of something like unease dimmed the usual sparkle of her black eyes.

'I'll look over my best dress. It isn't quite the height of fashion, but it might do with some fresh lace and a flower or two—if you can spare some from the hothouse.'

'I can do better than that.' Edward felt his smile become less fixed as an idea crept into his mind. 'I'd appreciate it if you'd allow me to buy you a gown for the occasion. I know you don't like the idea of me spending money on you, but I would consider it a favour if you were to oblige me in this.'

Selina's brows twitched together, but Edward could have sworn he saw her hesitate before she replied. 'We've talked about this before. I don't wish for you to waste money on me.'

'It wouldn't be a waste. It would be my way

of thanking you for doing something I know you have little inclination for.'

He watched as Selina thinned her lips and fidgeted with the tasselled edge of her shawl, apparently wrestling with her thoughts. When she finally looked up her cheeks were tinged with the slightest hint of colour.

'Very well. If it means that much to you.' She toyed with the woolly trim again, her eyes hidden by the black sweep of her lashes. 'I can't pretend it wouldn't be a relief not to have to wear my shabby dress to a gentry ball. Thank you.'

In a sudden movement Selina uncurled her legs from beneath her and stood up. Spurred on by his usual good manners, Edward rose likewise, and watched as his graceful wife crossed the room, moving away from him. She was wearing the same outfit she'd worn when he had first ordered her down from that tree, he realised belatedly, and the contrast of scarlet against the black of her hair was just as striking now as it had been then.

He felt the now familiar stirrings of that *something* he still couldn't name move within him at the thought.

Selina had never seen such a stunning display in her entire life.

The inside of the dressmaker's shop was like

something out of a picture book: shining rivers of silk gleamed in the wintry sunlight that streamed through large windows, and mirrors reflected the jewel tones back to dazzle her with their lustre. Long rolls of muslin, some plain and some printed with intricate patterns, were laid out carefully according to colour, demure next to the more flamboyant gloss of satin.

The shop assistants were far more welcoming than she had expected—but how much of that was due to Edward's presence on the other side of the painted willow screen was open to interpretation. He was seated in a fine chair, calmly perusing the morning's news sheets, and she could just about make out his silhouette against the barrier the ladies had so thoughtfully erected to save her modesty.

Apparently it wasn't usually the *done thing* for a man to invade such an exclusively feminine space, but the winning combination of Edward's handsome pocket book and even more handsome face had apparently been enough to overcome that particular obstacle.

Her own feelings at Edward being in such close proximity while she wore nothing but her slip were more complicated, and the thrill that crackled down her spine at the idea didn't bear thinking about. It wasn't decent, and it certainly wasn't proper, but some secret part of Selina wondered how warm his hands would feel with only one flimsy layer of material between them and her sensitive skin.

It was enough to make her breath come a little faster and that ever-ready blush to threaten to flood her cheeks once again. He was close enough to cross the room in a handful of those slow, long-legged strides. It would take him mere moments to reach her, to pull her into another heated embrace—

'And if you'd turn just a touch to the left, please, madam...'

The dressmaker knelt at Selina's hem, a measuring tape dangling from her practised fingers. Selina jumped guiltily, flushing scarlet as she hoped her train of thought hadn't shown on her face.

'Very good...thank you...almost finished...' The woman sketched a quick note on a piece of paper with a silver pencil and got to her feet. 'Excellent. Perhaps if madam is agreeable we could now pick out what fabrics might suit?'

Edward's voice issued suddenly from behind the screen, as firm and decided as ever. 'She'd like silk, if you'd be so good as to pull out your finest. Satin, too, and also lace—and perhaps some embroidered detail in places?'

Selina bit back a retort and instead arranged her face into an expression of calm interest as the girls fussed around her, leaping to do Edward's bidding and bring swatch after swatch of rich fabric for her consideration. She just *knew* he would be smiling that confident smile at having the last word, and it was with a twinge of irritation that she could picture just how much the upward curve of his lips suited him.

He seemed almost *pleased* to be indulging her. It was as though it wasn't merely a necessary evil for him to be spending the time and the money—enough to buy several weeks' worth of food for a Romani camp, she thought regretfully—needed for her to play what she knew was only a mummer's role.

For wasn't that all her wifely position amounted to?

She had been considering that very question when he had found her in her drawing room the previous day, striding in to interrupt her solitude with his all too alluring presence. Zillah's words had echoed in her ears as he had explained his reason for disturbing her, stoking the fire as he did so with such vigour that he had caused a shower of sparks to rain down upon the hearth rug.

He'd seemed distant, ill at ease, and Selina had wondered how much of his manner was her fault.

Don't be ridiculous, Lina. Her rational mind

rejected the notion. *As if Edward cares two straws whether you've been avoiding him or not.*

But something about that immediate dismissal didn't ring true. Edward *had* sounded sour in his remark about her aversion to his company— surely she hadn't imagined it. His face had been set, too, in an expression of studied indifference—perhaps a little *too* set to be genuine. He had meant to sound comical, of that Selina had no doubt, but could it be that his real feelings on the matter had been laid bare instead?

She sighed internally. Was that why she now found herself here, pretending to have an opinion as to which of four almost identical shades of silk was the most fitting for a gown to wear to a landed gentry ball? Out of some misguided regard for Edward's feelings?

The very idea that she had agreed to his request was absurd. Sir William's ball would be everything she loathed: filled to the rafters with gentry folk, a pit of lavish excess and vain chatter that would make Selina sick to her stomach.

There were so many reasons for her to refuse to attend. But the bitterness of Edward's words had forced her to confront her own most secret thoughts, and after that how could she have resisted the powerful urge that had risen up within her, whispering in her ear that to grant him his request would please him? And—damn it all—

wasn't that what she seemed to want these days, somewhere in the darkest recesses of her heart?

'I think perhaps this one? Would this be the best choice?' Quite a pile of swatches had built up before her. Selina hesitantly patted one of the fabrics, feeling its sheen beneath her fingers.

The dressmaker clapped her hands together softly. 'Perfection. Madam has a very fashionable eye.' She waved her assistants away and stepped a little closer to Selina. 'Now, if we were to move on to cut... As it happens, madam, we have a gown at the moment that was ordered but is no longer required. Perhaps trying it would give you an idea of the style you might prefer?'

'An excellent idea. She'd be delighted.'

Edward's voice drifted across the shop once again, and once again Selina bit down on her tongue to silence her reply.

The gown was brought forward from a gilded armoire—borne towards her with such reverence it might have been made of pure gold. Selina was forced to submit to the attentions of the army of assistants as they dressed her deftly, praising the slim shape of her waist and the slender length of her neck, until she was encased in the silky garment, complete with some gilt hair accessories that nestled within the softness of her curls.

'There, madam.' The dressmaker stepped back to admire the effect, satisfaction clearly written across her face. 'It's almost as though it were made with you in mind. Would you care to take a look in the glass?' She paused for a moment. 'Or perhaps you would prefer your husband to take the first look? He has been very...*involved* in the process, so far.'

Selina forced her lips into what she hoped would pass as a sweet smile. 'He most certainly has. Indeed, why would he stop now?'

She flicked her eyes towards Edward's silhouette. He had paused in the action of smoothing the page of his newspaper. She turned her back. He would have to see her in such ridiculous rig eventually—at least if she allowed him to observe her at this point he could tell her how far short of the image of a perfect lady she fell. He would likely be far more honest than the complimentary ladies who peered at her, good-natured but disturbingly unblinking.

'I suppose it's only fitting that he sees it through to a conclusion.'

'Very good, madam.'

Behind her, she heard the dressmaker instruct an assistant to bring Edward forward. When the heavy tread of a large pair of fine leather boots grew closer Selina sighed and turned around to face him. There was no going back now, and she could do nothing but wait for his verdict as she peeped into his face.

* * *

The sight in front of him was so wholly unexpected Edward found he couldn't speak.

The woman who peered up at him, half uncertain, half challenging, was the picture of a born lady. Her raven hair sparkled with golden accessories, the empire cut of her satin gown showcased the lissom lines of her figure and the square neck allowed the most tantalising glimpse of what lay beneath.

The cream of the fabric contrasted beautifully with the deep shade of her flawless skin and lent a radiance to her complexion—the finest that Edward had ever laid eyes on. Selina's back was straight and her chin held high, and it was only because he knew her, had studied her despite his every rational or sensible thought, that he could see the discomfort with which she wore what to her must only feel like a costume.

'You look—' Edward could almost feel the watching eyes of the delighted assistants boring into him as he struggled to form a coherent sentence. Even Selina's eyes were uncomfortably intent on his own, although for a very different reason. He roused himself with a small bow. 'You look wonderful.'

'Do I?' Selina's tone was doubtful, her insecurity plain. 'I feel…somewhat strange.'

'You don't look it. Here, see for yourself.'

Edward stepped to one side, revealing an elaborate mirror standing against a wall behind him. He watched as Selina approached it slowly, cautiously—and then couldn't hide his smile as her mouth dropped open in naked shock.

'That cannot be me!' She gaped at her reflection, standing stock-still in front of the glass. 'That doesn't look anything like me!' She stared, a combination of wonder and horror mingling in a vivid expression that lit up her face as though the sun shone behind it.

'Don't you like it?'

'I—I'm not sure.' Selina turned slowly, tracking her movement in the mirror. 'It's just so strange!'

She had never looked more beautiful. That was the only thought that rang through Edward's mind as he watched her turn this way and that, surrounded by a ring of entranced dressmaker's assistants. The loveliness of her face and the exquisite shape of her in the luminous cream gown eclipsed them all.

He could scarcely speak, and he certainly couldn't look away. Something in the back of his mind nagged at him, muttering some kind of warning—but against what? Falling for the charms of this Roma girl who had, quite accidentally, charmed him already? He was powerless to resist, and now he was powerless to deny it.

It happened before he could stop himself. One moment he was merely standing in front of Selina, having stepped forward to help her with the fastening of a gilt bracelet around one wrist, the next her hand had found its way into his own and he had lifted it to his lips. And then he had pressed a kiss to the smooth skin of her knuckles and she hadn't pulled away.

The rest of the room seemed to fall back as they gazed at each other. Selina's lips were parted on a tiny gasp that sang in Edward's ears and her eyes were round, the shock in them reflecting Edward's own. For a moment there was no other reaction, and then her cheeks were suffused with a rosy blush that crept up her neck and spread across her skin, stealing over her as he stared down into her face.

Get a hold of yourself, man!

That nagging warning growled again. His heart had begun to thump a rapid tattoo against his ribs and the warmth of her slender fingers beneath his own was scalding. He was on a dangerous path, and every second that he touched her was a second closer to the weakness he had always feared.

He released her hand. She drew it back to the safety of her body, holding it against herself with the other. But it hadn't been the lightning-fast movement of rejection, as it had been when he'd proposed and she had ripped her hand from his as though his touch were made of flame, and the horror of that night was missing from the complex expression he now saw dancing in her eyes.

There was no disgust there, he realised with a start; only the kind of half shy, half daring look any young woman might turn upon the face of her favourite, he having acted so boldly, and Edward felt his own eyes widen in surprise.

She was not displeased by his rash action?

Even as Selina was hustled away by the ring of delighted women Edward's mind raced with questions. He should not have kissed her, but never in his wildest dreams would it have occurred to him she would *like* it. The look on her face had imprinted itself into his mind, and the silks and satins of the dressmaker's shop dissolved into nothingness as he stood, dazed, with only the vision of Selina's open-mouthed expression in front of his eyes.

Why had she not flinched away from him? Wasn't his touch repulsive to her now, thanks to the intervention of her grandmother? There was no sense to be made of it, of her dizzying contrariness, and Edward cursed inwardly at his own lack of self-control. Had he not just made an already confusing situation a hundred times more unclear?

It was bad enough that he had lost his head

and kissed her once before, in the quiet grandeur of Blackwell's ballroom. He'd reprimanded himself repeatedly since then, and used it as a lesson to guard himself against venturing any further. But now he had once again been foolish, and this time it was worse. His need for Selina to feel the same rush of desire for him as he felt for her had increased tenfold, and his confusion at the intensity of that need was almost breathtaking.

The rise and fall of too many excited voices grated on his ear, adding to the cacophony of thoughts that spun through his mind, and Edward felt a sudden need to escape into silence. He wanted to think, to process what in blazes had just passed between himself and his wife, and he could no more do that surrounded by bird-like chatter than he could join in with it himself.

A handful of blind strides took him to the door, and his last glimpse of Selina as he stepped through to take a deep lungful of crisp winter air was of her blank face, still mute with the shock of his thoughtless action.

Chapter Eleven

Sweeping boughs of winter greenery were spread across every available surface in Blackwell's entrance hall, and as Selina descended the curving staircase she saw balls of ivy hung in each of the doorways that led from it. A closer look at the little white berries that studded each one showed them to be mistletoe, and Selina felt the colour rise in her cheeks at the implication of what *that* implied.

Not that Edward needed one of these Christmas kissing balls to make his mark on her; that much she'd learnt already and it had been a damnably confusing lesson.

She allowed the thought to rise up in her mind for a moment as she reached the bottom of the stairs, before pushing it aside and moving through the huge front door into the snow-covered wonderland beyond. She and Edward had agreed she would spend part of the day with her people, before returning to Blackwell to take Christmas dinner with him and Ophelia, and Selina felt a curious sense of anticipation at the thought.

The weight of the small box in the pocket of her cloak acted as a constant reminder of its giver, gently knocking against her thigh as she rode in the direction of the Roma camp. With every movement her desire to know what lay within grew stronger, but she urged Djali on, watching the horse's breath blowing out in clouds that matched the white-covered ground.

Christmas Day had dawned bright and chill, the pale sunlight powerless to thaw the icy tendrils that had hung from Selina's window ledge as she'd looked out at the bleached beyond.

Edward had caught her just as she'd been leaving her rooms. She had clutched her gift for him under cover of her cloak and felt her palms prickle at the prospect of presenting it to him. Nerves coiling in her stomach, she avoided his gaze as they swapped parcels, hers looking so clumsily wrapped next to the neat blue box he'd deposited carefully in her hand. She had heard the note of surprise in his voice as he'd thanked her, and she had muttered a swift pleasantry of her own before escaping, feeling his eyes on her back all the way down the long corridor to the stairs.

She had decided to keep Edward's gift unopened until after her visit to the camp. That way she would be spared from being caught in an uncomfortable lie should Zillah ask—as she would, Selina knew—if Edward had presented her with anything for Christmas. She would be able to answer no with an almost clear conscience, for until one actually *opened* the box how could one say one had truly received a gift?

But he has already given you the gift you truly want, hasn't he, Lina? Another kiss. Only you would have preferred it to have been on your lips, rather than your hand...

The voice in her ear made her grimace, and she gripped Djali's reins a little tighter. It was a low, mean thought, and she wouldn't entertain it. And yet...

Even now, with the cold December air stinging the tips of them, she could feel the warmth that had blossomed in her fingers at the first touch of Edward's lips, gently brushing them in a sensation so sweet it had taken her breath away. Selina could still see his head bent over her hand, low enough that she could have stroked the golden thatch of his hair, and feel the flames that had licked up her spine burst into a conflagration upon reaching her chest.

It had been as though somebody had dropped a lighted match into the bonfire of her heart.

Cantering through fields and past quaint workers' cottages, Selina felt it again, jumping against her breastbone as though trying to break free from the cage of her ribs, the memory of Edward's mouth against her skin the cause.

Edward's expression had reflected what she imagined her own had shown as she'd stood, speechless, staring up into his face. He had seemed entirely taken aback by his own actions, and Selina had been able to do nothing but watch as he released her hand quickly, as though suddenly coming to his senses, and shot her a hurried, uncertain smile before retreating outside, away from her and the cluster of captivated women who surrounded her.

Had her breathless wonder shown on her face? The very idea made her burn hot with mortification. Had Edward seen the effect his kiss had had on her? Perhaps heard the gasp he had dragged from her lips or felt her sway at the sensation of his mouth on her?

He couldn't know—he *mustn't*. It was one thing to confess the truth to herself…quite another for him to be party to the maelstrom of emotion he roused in her with his touch.

But why did he behave so? the voice whispered to her again.

Selina shook her head to dispel it. There was nothing to be gained in asking why. For all that Edward's gesture had shocked her, delighted her, robbed her of all rational thought, there could be no deeper meaning. It could not have signified so much to him as it had to her, and Selina knew it. It had surely been a spur-of-the-moment act, kindly meant, no doubt, to reassure her in what he must have known she found an uncomfortable situation.

If only she could persuade herself to listen to reason and cease replaying the moment in her mind time and time again. The pointless exercise made her chest ache with the knowledge that his kiss had meant so little to him, at the same time as it had meant so much to herself. It was a senseless torture, and one she knew she should not endure.

The line of trees that camouflaged the Roma camp hove into view and Selina took a deep breath in. She was almost there. Zillah would be waiting for her—although perhaps 'lying in wait' was a better phrase to describe the old woman's watchful welcome.

The air was so cold it burned her lungs as she inhaled, long and hard, but she held it there as she approached, narrowing the distance between herself and what had once been all she'd ever known.

* * *

Edward twitched a blanket across to cover Ophelia's sleeping form. She mumbled something he couldn't quite catch, her arm tightening its grip on her new woollen bear, but she slept on without interruption and he smiled to himself as he moved away from the sofa in front of the drawing room fire.

In truth, he'd been waiting for this moment ever since Selina had placed the parcel in his hands early that morning, with something like shyness in her eye as she had avoided his gaze. She'd left immediately afterwards, and the whirlwind that was his sister on Christmas Day had taken all his attention since.

Now she had finally collapsed into an overexcited stupor he could retrieve the intriguing bundle from his desk drawer and take a peep beneath the inelegantly wrapped paper.

He withdrew the parcel from the desk, wondering at the soft weight of it. Whatever was contained within seemed fluid, pliable, and he half frowned in puzzlement. *I didn't think she would give me a Christmas gift. How could she afford such a thing?* As far as he knew she hadn't come into any new riches—so what had she handed to him so uncertainly?

One of his many letter openers lay on the desk top, and he slit the twine that bound the paper with its sharp edge. The printed wrapping fell open and Edward stared down at the objects in his hand with brows raised in surprise.

Four crisp white handkerchiefs nestled among the paper folds. Each was edged with intricate embroidery of a kind he had never seen before, curling into a decoration of vines and leaves, and the sides were hemmed with a slim border of fine lace. Picking one up to hold it up to the light, Edward saw as it unfolded that his initials had been carefully worked in one corner, the letters picked out in scarlet thread to gleam against snowy fabric.

The embroidered leaves glinted in the light of the fire as Edward stared at this most unexpected Christmas gift. When had Selina crafted these for him—and why?

Across the room Ophelia murmured in her sleep. Edward glanced at her, but she didn't wake, and he propped his elbows onto the leather top of the desk. A picture of Selina sitting in her little drawing room, her face pinched in concentration as she bent over her task, rose up in Edward's mind.

Had she worked by candlelight? he wondered. Or had she sat at the window, placing each stitch as snow had fallen the other side of the glass, her work serving to keep her slender fingers warm? Had she taken a secret pleasure in knowing she would take him by surprise with her gift? And was she even now smiling as she rode back to Blackwell in time to take Christmas dinner with him and Ophelia as they had agreed?

Edward passed a hand across his face. *I thought all the progress we'd made had been ruined. Perhaps I was wrong.*

He stared down at his initials, worked red on white, and traced the neat stitches with his fingers. A small bubble of hope, fragile but tentatively holding its own against the doubts that attempted to crowd it out, rose within him.

This would have taken her hours. Surely if she disliked me she wouldn't have taken the trouble?

A sudden desire to see her washed over him and he rose quickly to his feet. She would be back soon, fresh-faced and windswept from her cold ride down to the Roma camp, and his mind buzzed with the questions he wanted her to answer.

What does this mean, Selina? Has your opinion of me changed?

Of his own feelings he was now sure. His reluctant wife had somehow, despite all the obstacles he had placed in her way, worked herself deep into the fortresses of his heart and mind, breaking down the walls he had constructed as though they were no more substantial than paper.

Her face had been the head of the arrow that had first pierced his defences, but her wit, defiance and kindness had forced it through, and now he found himself vulnerable, unprotected by the armour of indifference he had cultivated for so long.

Another thought struck him and he sank back into his chair. *You know you can't really ask her any of those things.* The glimmer of hope within him dimmed a little, some of its sparkle fading to grey. *Even if this means she likes you a little more than before, that is still a far cry from the kind of feelings you would be a fool to believe she could ever have for you.*

Edward closed his eyes briefly. The little voice inside him could be right. Even if Selina *did* have some small regard for him, how could it ever match the depth of feeling he would only now truly accept burned within him?

It was a painful prospect, and one that made him grit his teeth—but it was true, nonetheless.

How long he sat, his head cradled in his hand and staring blindly down at Selina's gift, Edward couldn't tell. All he knew was that for a long while the only sounds were the crackling of the flames in the grate and Ophelia's gentle breathing, occasionally punctuated by the rustle of her new dress as she fidgeted in her sleep. His only company was his own confusing thoughts.

* * *

The little blue box had felt as though it was burning into Selina's skin like a brand the entire time she had spent with Zillah and the other Romani, and she could hardly bear it a second longer as she rode back up the sweeping drive to Blackwell Hall.

She'd been right not to open it before. Even as the rest of the Romani had surrounded Selina, blessing her safe return and exchanging the season's greetings, Zillah had hung back slightly, watching with all the keenness of a knowing old cat.

She had asked the question, exactly as Selina had known she would, and had looked thoughtful at the reply. Edward had not been mentioned again, although the atmosphere between the two generations of Agres women had been tense throughout their modest Christmas feast. Even now, as she cantered into the stable yard and dismounted from Djali's wide back with the ease of many years' practice, Selina was aware of the uncomfortable mixture of defiance and guilt that circled in the pit of her stomach at her deliberate deception.

She found Edward in his cosy drawing room, with Ophelia tucked up beneath a blanket in front of the hearth, still clutching the crimson bear Selina had knitted for her with wool unravelled from one of her own shawls. Diamanda had made Selina a similar creature when she was young, and it was a bittersweet memory that echoed now as Edward looked up from his desk at her entrance to the room.

'Ah, Selina. How was your visit?' He rose to greet her almost hurriedly, holding something in one large hand. 'I hope your grandmother is well and your people are enjoying the festivities?'

Selina was about to answer when she realised what it was that Edward held so carefully: one of her handkerchiefs, its lace edge peeping from between his fingers.

She felt a slow blush begin to climb up her neck. *He has opened my gift already, then.* Her heart quickened a fraction. *I wonder if he liked them?*

Seeing the direction of her gaze, Edward gave a small smile and opened his hand, spreading the little white square on his palm.

'I want to thank you for such a thoughtful gift.' He ran a finger over the red shapes of his initials. 'I've never known such craftsmanship—the lace alone is some of the finest I've ever seen.'

Selina glanced up at him. His face was sincere; he looked genuinely pleased. She couldn't help the glow that blossomed in her chest as a result. *That answers my question, I suppose.* He seemed truly to appreciate the lengths she had gone to in making his gift, and a tingle of satisfaction warmed her insides.

'I'm so glad you like them. Lacemaking has been passed down through my family for generations.'

Edward nodded, again running a fingertip across the delicate material. He seemed absorbed by the tiny details, his face intent, and Selina could have sighed aloud at the way the seriousness of his look enhanced the chiselled lines of his handsome features. They were more than handsome to her now. In all honesty beloved would have been closer to the truth, and the thought made Selina's throat contract in an involuntary swallow.

'I'm very grateful you took the time to make such things for me. Thank you.' He smiled down at her, with the barest suggestion of warmth in the rich hazel of his eyes.

'It was my pleasure. Besides, it was my fault you barely had a handkerchief left in the first place.'

Edward laughed—a short, low thing that seemed to take him a little by surprise. 'I can't argue with you there. I had no idea taking you on as my wife would cost me so dearly.'

Ophelia mumbled something. She was still fast asleep before the fire, but all the same it saved Selina from having to reply. This was the most friendly conversation they had enjoyed since her unhappy visit to Zillah, when her dreams had been destroyed by the old woman's reminder of the truth—although not the way she had intended. To laugh with Edward was a wonderful thing, and she wished they could stay in this moment forever, with him smiling down at her and she feeling a glimmer of happiness that she would have given almost anything to be able to keep for the rest of her life.

'And have you opened my gift to you? I wasn't sure—I hope you like it?' Edward looked away from her, suddenly quiet in his uncertainty, his hands moving to clasp behind his back. 'You are a difficult woman to buy for.'

The little blue box that has caused me to be so secretive.

She'd momentarily forgotten it in the haze of delight created by Edward's praise of her skills, but now she blinked and patted at herself, feeling for the pocket in which she'd felt it necessary to hide her prize from Zillah's close scrutiny.

'I haven't yet had a chance. I'll open it now, of course.'

She drew the box from her cloak, glad to have an excuse to look somewhere other than up into Edward's face, so watchful and intent was his expression. A tiny gold clasp held it closed, and with her heart beating in her ears Selina flipped it up and lifted the lid.

For a moment her mind couldn't process what her eyes were seeing. Lying before her, cushioned within a bed of white tissue, was the brooch she had last seen pinned to the bosom of the dress her mother had worn on her funeral pyre.

Selina's hand shook as she lifted the brooch from its wrapping. She saw, once her brain had caught up with the rest of her senses, that of course it was not the same piece that had accompanied her mother on her final journey. This brooch was new—the gilt setting of the original was replaced with real gold, and what had been paste stones glittered in the firelight as only diamonds could—but the design was identical to the one she had touched countless times as a child. How had Edward—?

She gaped up at him, no words at all coming from her open mouth. *How? How has he done this?*

His eyes searched her face, his expression almost wary. 'Is it not to your liking?'

Dumbly she shook her head, still unable to find her tongue as realisation suddenly swept over her, mingled with doubt. Could it truly be that he had *remembered*?

She turned the brooch over, feeling with nerveless fingers the achingly familiar contours of metal and stone. Mama's brooch had featured a simple design of small oval paste crystals arranged around one central gem, fashioned to look like a flower with gilt leaves beneath. The sparkling copy Selina now held in her hand managed to replicate it exactly, and for some time her mind was silent in simple wonder at how Edward had managed such a feat.

He remembered every word I said.

The voice in her ear was filled with quiet amazement, and the same feeling ran over her like a shower of cool water, a complex tumult of emotion that would have taken any words from her mouth had she even been able to form them. She couldn't remember ever having felt so touched by a gesture in her entire life, and the overwhelming intensity of her wonder almost moved her to tears.

He had listened, and then he had used her words to commission a gift for her that tied Selina to the memories she had of Diamanda: a gift beyond price. The fact that Edward had gone to such lengths for her took her breath away. Why had he given her such a gift?

Some corner of her consciousness ventured an answer, and she swallowed hard at the notion. Could it be, against all her rational beliefs to the contrary, that he had developed some measure of fondness for her despite his initial intentions?

Selina didn't dare look at the idea directly. Worried that doing such a thing might cause it to flee, she instead considered it from a distance, watching it out of the corner of her eye.

He had given her such a thoughtful gift, one an indifferent man would never have dreamed of, and as for his behaviour towards her... Selina recalled how his first kiss had seemed so instinctive, so surprising to him even as he'd held her body close to his own, and how his arms had come around her so protectively when she'd cried.

A dozen tiny moments, each meaning nothing on its own, built up into a perfect montage of something deeper—something Selina could scarcely comprehend or dare to believe could be true.

'This is the most wonderful gift I've ever been given. I don't know how to thank you.'

Edward smiled, a shadow of something like relief passing over his face. 'I'm so glad you like it. I remembered how you described the piece belonging to your mother and thought a replica might please you.'

Selina nodded, her fingers still stroking the polished metal. The urge to rise onto her tiptoes and kiss Edward full on his upward-curving lips was almost overwhelming. There were no words strong enough to express her thoughts—only the touch of her mouth on his could hope to explain the depth of her appreciation.

Blinking back the tears that sparkled in the light of the fire, she instead settled for a light brush of her lips on the warm plane of his cheek, and watched as a look of surprise—but not displeasure—flooded Edward's face. Selina felt her pulse skip at her own daring, but the precious gift she held in her hand was worth any small embarrassment.

'I'll treasure it always. Thank you, Edward. Thank you a hundred times over.'

His eyes were warm with some unspoken thought as he smiled down into hers, black and hazel meeting in the orange light for one long, meaningful moment that stretched out between them, neither voicing what secret desires might be hidden within.

'You are most welcome. Merry Christmas... wife.'

Chapter Twelve

Edward felt the tremor in Selina's fingers beneath his own as he handed her down from the carriage. In any other woman he might have suspected a chill, but Selina's rigid face throughout the duration of their journey to Sir William's estate had been an indication of determinedly suppressed anxiety, and he knew her hand's unsteadiness was not a result of the freezing January evening.

Candles blazed in every window of their host's grand house, bathing the guests who mounted the stone steps up to the front door in a soft orange light. The sound of musicians playing a lively tune floated through the night air towards them, carrying with it the buzz of a hundred conversations and the faint thud of footfalls as the guests within the manor moved in time with the music.

All around carriages rolled to a halt and

streams of people stepped out into the cold, the men standing tall in their best knee breeches and stockings and the ladies glittering in the candle-light like birds of paradise, their gowns shining in jewel colours and feathers swaying in their headdresses.

No small number of them greeted Edward as they passed, some looking with barely disguised curiosity at the woman who stood next to him, silently gazing up at the Beaumont ancestral home with an unreadable expression in her dark eyes.

Edward looked down at her and marvelled yet again at the miraculous powers of an expensive wardrobe to entirely transform the wearer.

It wasn't that she hadn't been beautiful before—far from it. It was more that now, swathed in the rose silk that ghosted the lush shape of her figure, falling in an empire cut from below her bosom in such a way as to emphasise the captivating curves pressed at the square neckline above, Selina radiated an almost ethereal femininity that had been previously hidden beneath layers of woollen shawls.

The soft colour that peeped out from beneath her cloak was the perfect complement to the tawny cast of her skin, and the ebony of her hair—braided and twisted into the most elaborate style Dinah had ever had free rein to create—was offset by ribbons intertwined with gilt flowers that gleamed in the light spilling forth from the house.

Her only other ornamentation was the brooch pinned to the centre of her chest, at which Edward glanced in secret satisfaction. She hadn't been lying, then, when she had said it was the most wonderful gift she had ever received. In turn he had carried one of Selina's handkerchiefs with him ever since that day—partly out of necessity, but largely for the feeling of confused delight he felt each time he looked down at the gifts she had given him.

He still didn't know what she had meant by it and had yet to muster up the courage to ask. There was still the possibility that he wouldn't like the answer.

She was silent as he guided her up the steps and allowed a servant to relieve her of her cloak, busy taking in her surroundings with eyes round with wonder.

'Are you well?' Edward murmured into Selina's ear, close enough to brush the delicate shell with his lips. The idea was tempting, and he swallowed hard.

What she needs tonight is a friend. Not you trying to find excuses to kiss her.

'Yes.' Selina's smile was small but determined. 'This is the grandest house I've ever set foot in. I don't think I could feel more out of place if I had arrived in my usual clothes.'

'You needn't worry about blending in.' Edward bowed to a passing acquaintance, noting how the man's eyes slid from him to Selina's face. 'You look quite the high-born lady.'

Stepping within the ballroom, Edward looked about him. People he had known his entire life were scattered in all directions—some seated at small tables dotted around the walls, some dancing, and still others standing in clusters, talking and watching the dancers with critical interest. Chatter and laughter rang throughout the room and the musicians' airs vibrated in his ears, their instruments clearly audible above the hum of conversation. Despite the wintry chill outside, the ballroom was extremely warm, and more than one lady was fanning herself with a little more enthusiasm than elegance.

'It's rather close in here. Would you like a glass of punch?'

Selina nodded, still looking this way and that in a combination of curiosity and distaste, and Edward moved away from her towards a table on which stood a bowl and several fine crystal glasses. On his return he saw a small group of ladies standing a short distance away, casting furtive glances at Selina's luxurious gown. Obviously they were wondering who such a fashionable stranger could be, and they dissolved into rapid whispers when Edward appeared and handed her the drink, their eyes shining with curiosity.

One of them, a young woman he vaguely recognised as a former friend of Letitia's, looked at him with particular interest, her gaze straying across him with a little more appreciation than was strictly polite. He was just about to turn away when he felt a jolt of surprised delight crackle through him at the sensation of Selina's fingers settling lightly on his forearm. It was a subtle movement, accompanied by a pleasant smile on her full lips, but there could be no mistaking it.

Selina's expression was serene, but Edward saw the determined angle of her chin, raised in the faintest suggestion of challenge, and his heart sang. She had staked her claim on him—out of injured pride, perhaps, but the notion was still absurdly pleasing. He had to fight back the urge to preen as the other woman's face fell and she pointedly turned her back on him and his quietly elegant wife.

There was a brief lull while the orchestra arranged their next piece, and when the music began again Edward leaned down to speak into Selina's ear.

'Is that the opening for a waltz I hear?'

'I believe it is. I sincerely hope I can remember the steps—I'm a little afraid for your toes.'

Edward took Selina's hand and steered her firmly in the direction of the dancers. Their progress was slowed by Edward's having to greet various acquaintances, bowing and smiling and introducing Selina to so many people he was sure he could see her anxiety increase. It was a relief to finally reach the dance floor and be able to hold her close to him once again.

She felt almost weightless in his arms, slight and instinctively graceful as she stepped to the music as though having had a hundred lessons, and Edward was powerless to resist as the memory of the first time he had held her so closely sent a flash of heat through his every nerve. She had been so stiff then, so patently uncomfortable with their proximity, but now, as they moved across the floor, it was as though they had been designed to be partners. Her small hand fitted perfectly into his grasp and her ear was close to his rapidly beating heart. Her awkwardness with him had entirely dissipated, Edward realised as she peeped up at him, a smile of genuine appreciation only enhancing the beauty of the face he now knew he held most dear.

'Thank you for rescuing me. I don't think I could have survived yet another introduction.'

* * *

Edward's laugh rumbled through his chest and Selina felt its vibrations against her cheek as she drew nearer still to the silk of his waistcoat. Perhaps it wasn't entirely proper to be *so* close to the broad chest that haunted her dreams, but the press of bodies around her and the braying of upper-class voices made her nervous, and nowhere felt so safe as being close to Edward.

Held in the unshakeable strength of his arms, Selina felt the knowledge that there was nowhere else she would rather be rise up in her again, and she made only the most half-hearted attempt to dispel it.

'No? But there's still—oh, I don't know—another two, maybe three hundred of my closest friends for you to meet.'

Selina shot him a narrow look that was entirely ruined by the wayward curve of her lips. 'I most certainly hope not. I couldn't stand the scrutiny.'

They danced a few steps closer to another couple, the male half of whom fixed Selina with an unnervingly bold stare.

She twitched her brows together and drew a little further into Edward's hold, murmuring up into his ear. 'Why do they stare so? Ever since we arrived I've felt too many eyes upon me. Is something about my appearance really so troubling?'

Edward glanced across at the other man, who dropped his gaze at once. 'They've been staring because you are, without doubt, the most beautiful woman in the room.' He turned her deftly, calmly continuing their dance as they began to sail back in the direction from which they had just come.

Any activity in Selina's mind stuttered and died and her eyes flickered up to meet Edward's before she could stop them.

He looked down at her with the most serious expression in his hazel eyes she had ever seen. There was no laughter now—no twinkle of humour in the greenish gaze that had settled on her more and more frequently over the past weeks and months, in a scrutiny she had tried in vain not to enjoy. Instead he was solemn, earnest, as though he had meant every one of the unspeakably delicious words he had just murmured in her ear, and Selina felt her breathing become ragged as she stared up into his face, robbed of the ability to recall any language in order to respond.

A slow creep of pleasure began to steal over her as she turned his words over inside her mind. He had called her beautiful, and now, with his hands holding her close to him, a thrill of something dangerous crackled beneath her heated skin. His touch was like a flame and her nerves the touchpaper, and the combination of the two called to the secret longing Selina had tried so hard to conceal.

She couldn't drag her eyes away from his. They were mere inches apart. If she were just to reach up onto her tiptoes she could rise high enough to claim him with her lips, and a powerful yearning to do just that swept over her as unrelentingly as a tidal wave.

Edward seemed to be bending down. His face was growing closer, the look in his eyes sharpening into an intensity that would have made it impossible for Selina to move away from him even if she hadn't been a willing captive in his arms. She could do nothing but wait breathlessly, dazedly, as his arm tightened on her waist and brought her closer still to the firm column of his body, for his mouth to meet her own. For surely that was his intention?

Their faces were almost touching as they danced, oblivious to any other people in the room. The vague notion that it might not be socially acceptable to explore Edward's mouth with her tongue crossed Selina's hazy mind, but there was nothing she could do to quell the burning she felt beneath her skin, or the desire for the man who held her so closely against him that blazed in her every sinew.

Etiquette be damned, Selina's subconscious whispered as she felt her eyes drift closed and

Edward's lips finally meet her own, the heart-stopping culmination of all the hours she had spent dreaming of this very moment, hoping and yet fearing it would soon come to pass.

If their first kiss had been heated, this one was an inferno. Selina felt herself set ablaze with the burning desire to hold Edward against her, to feel the touch of his hands on her skin as his lips moved over hers and she opened her mouth to receive him.

His grip on her waist tightened further, forcing her as close to the heat of his body as it was possible to be, and his other hand moved to cradle the back of her head—which was just as well, for Selina's bones seemed to have turned to water, and but for Edward's unshakable arms she might have collapsed entirely.

Her own hands twined into the fabric of his coat, trying to pull him closer still, and the whole world seemed to dissolve in the riot of sensation Edward's lips on hers were lighting up in every nerve in her trembling body.

Edward's breathing was coming hard and fast as his hand snaked down from her waist to splay over the small of her back, pinning her to the front of his towering frame. He deepened the kiss. Selina heard herself gasp as his tongue danced with her own in a movement so unspeakably sensual she could almost have stopped breathing had she any thought to spare for such a trivial thing as *that*. Her arms tightened around him, locked in an embrace that sent sparks of pure desire to writhe within her stomach—

'I say...is this really the place?'

Selina started violently at the sudden voice, too close to her for comfort. Eyes flying open, she saw an older gentleman looking at them with barely suppressed amusement, and stumbled backwards out of Edward's hold. All the breath had left her body and she felt winded by the blistering fire that seemed to have replaced it in her lungs.

She blinked rapidly, trying to bully her brain back into action. 'Oh, I—I—I'm most terribly sorry.' Selina heard how breathlessly the words escaped her but had no power to make them sound stronger. 'I don't know—'

'Sir William.' Edward extended his hand and the other man shook it, a gleam of humour still clearly visible on his lined face.

If Selina hadn't known better, she might have suspected Edward felt as stunned by the unexpected turn of events as she. His own breath seemed to be coming fast, reminding her of Djali's after a long ride, and his cheeks were flushed with colour.

'So good of you to invite us. May I introduce my wife, Mrs Selina Fulbrooke?'

'Aha...' Sir William looked at her closely, dawning understanding filtering into his expression. 'Enchanted, I'm sure. A rare treat to meet such a beautiful lady. Madam...' He bowed over her hand, lightly holding her fingertips in a cool grasp.

Selina nodded mutely and attempted a smile, although her heart still pounded from Edward's touch and no words would come into her racing mind. Whatever must their host think of her, putting on such a shocking display? Edward was just as much to blame as herself, of course, but it was on her that every scandalised eye seemed to be fixed, and Selina's blush deepened as she heard loud whispers about their brazen behaviour from more than one direction.

'I'm so glad you and your lovely new bride could attend tonight. This is the first gathering I have had since your poor dear father left us, you know, and he is very sadly missed.' Sir William didn't seem to hear the muttering surrounding them as he sighed and patted Edward on the shoulder. 'He would be pleased, I think, that you came to honour us with your company. And I hope you won't think me too forward when I say you have grown into a fine young man, most worthy of your new position as Squire.'

'Thank you, sir.' There was a touch of something like emotion in Edward's voice, and Selina had to restrain herself from reaching out to touch him.

Sir William glanced about him and lowered his voice conspiratorially. 'You know, I never agreed with that condition old Ambrose included in his will, and I told him so. You're a grown man with a sensible head on your shoulders; you can be trusted to make your own way.' He nodded reassuringly. 'I'll be willing to say the same to your uncle when he arrives here, too, should that be necessary.'

A shard of ice shattered the warmth that mere moments before had burned in Selina's chest, slicing through to chill her to the bone.

What does he mean—when he arrives here?

Her eyes flew to Edward's face, and she saw his brows drawn tightly together in confusion.

'My uncle, sir?'

'Your Uncle Charles—has he not written to you of his forthcoming visit?' The older man was at once unsure, hesitant. 'I received a letter just last week, stating his intention to return to Blackwell and help you run the estate. Perhaps I was not to mention it...?'

'Indeed, I have received no such letter.' Edward's voice was quiet suddenly, seeming to come from far away. 'Did my uncle mention when he is intending to visit?'

Selina barely heard him speak, lost in the cold

grip of dread that had begun to squeeze her in its fist.

'Within the month, as I understand it.'

Within the month. That could be any day...
with no warning.

Selina backed away a little, narrowly avoiding a collision with another pair of dancers. Her head swam with sudden nausea and her hands felt clammy with horror, fear choking the air from her lungs.

Charles Fulbrooke, Mama's killer, is coming back to Blackwell.

It was every one of her worst nightmares come true, and panic rose up within her like an unstoppable flood. The room seemed as though it was spinning, and suddenly she could no longer breathe.

'I feel a little warm. Please excuse me while I go to take some air.' She managed to force out the words, only dimly aware of how raspy they sounded issuing from her dry mouth.

She felt Edward's eyes on her as she retreated through the crowd, but she knew better than to look back over her shoulder. He would see the blank terror on her pallid face.

Selina quickened her step on unsteady feet as she left the ballroom and tottered out into the hall. The light of the candles was suddenly too bright, throwing her into blind confusion as she fought her way towards the front door, dumb and unresponsive with images of unspeakable horror tumbling through her mind. The music that issued from the ballroom was suddenly too loud, and the press of bodies claustrophobic. And had it always been so *hot*?

A woman nearby laughed—a shrill, whinnying sound that made Selina shudder—and a gentleman's speculative look at her as he passed by made her skin crawl. She had to get out. *She had to get out.*

It was as though a dam had given way inside her—one that had been shielding her from the worst of her recollections. All the fear and disgust she had been struggling to quell since hearing Charles's name now threatened to pour forth, and image after image of the reason for her revulsion flickered through her mind in unstoppable cruelty. The man responsible for her pain would soon be closer to her than he had been in twelve years, and the memories spun faster.

She was surrounded. Gentry stood close on every side, and suddenly she couldn't *bear* it.

Selina knew she would have to fight to push her way through the crowds that thronged Sir William's Great Hall, but even the idea of touching them made her stomach turn. Perhaps she ought to go back to Edward, she thought as she felt her throat begin to close with anxiety and a fresh wave of nausea wash over her. He would surely escort her outside, help to guide her past the people who now sickened her with every glance.

But then Zillah's words echoed through her mind, mingling with the fear that squeezed her in its iron grip. *A marriage of convenience and nothing more.*

Selina's mind stubbornly replayed the image of his face, growing closer to her own as they danced, the look in his eye, determined yet tender, as he closed the distance between them and his lips sought her own. Edward was better than that, and her faith in him would not be so easily shaken.

And yet... Selina's shoulders slumped as the cold sting of reality turned her blood to ice. Charles was Edward's kin—almost the only relative left to him. Hadn't she seen the glint of sadness in his eye when he'd talked about his father and sensed that, despite all their differences, Edward regretted the late Squire's early passing?

Charles was Ambrose's brother, despite his cruel acts, and tied to Edward by blood. Surely he would rather his uncle returned than hear Selina's tale of woe yet again. The tale of a wife he had taken only for their mutual advantage. After the death of his father Edward must want to draw nearer to the family he had left. Of course he regretted his uncle's behaviour, but wasn't blood thicker than water? Especially if that water had only been married out of cold necessity?

Shame, fear and regret washed over her, tumbling her in the maelstrom they created within her. She was tossed by the waves of her unhappiness, and supremely conscious of it being all her own doing.

A man you cannot hope to have.

Those had been Zillah's words—and they had been entirely right. Edward would never return her feelings now, despite the precious gift he had given her and the breathtaking passion of his kiss—not now Charles was returning to Blackwell, to undermine her at every turn.

What poison he would whisper in Edward's ear she didn't yet know, but there could be no chance of the happy future she had so foolishly hoped for, despite her better judgement.

'Ma'am? Ma'am, are you quite well?'

An elderly gentleman stood close to her, watching her breathless confusion with genuine alarm. His concern for her might have struck her as kind, once upon a time, but now all Selina desired was to be as far away as possible. With her heart hammering, and tears gathering at the corners of her eyes, she did the only thing she could think of to do.

Selina turned and ran.

Chapter Thirteen

～～～～

'Any sign of her?'

'Not yet, sir.'

Edward cursed aloud as he scanned the frozen wasteland of the Beaumont estate that surrounded him and his coachman on all sides. Deep snowdrifts covered the ground in every direction as far as the eye could see, and Edward pulled his coat closer about his body, gritting his teeth as another blast of freezing air tried to wend its way beneath his clothes.

'Mrs Fulbrooke is out here somewhere, without a cloak in this bitter cold. We must keep looking.'

'Aye, sir.'

Edward lowered his head against the biting wind and ploughed onwards, sinking almost knee-deep into the snow. His breeches were soaked and he could feel the chill beginning to reach his bones. Each step was getting more and more difficult as the cold seeped into him and squeezed his chest in its icy grip.

Where the hell are you, Selina?

He brought a hand up to shield his eyes from the moonlit glare of snow all around him as he peered across the great expanse of white, searching for any clue as to the direction in which she must have travelled.

An elderly gentleman in Sir William's hall had said he'd seen a woman matching Selina's description bolt past him and out into the freezing night, without even so much as a cloak to warm her. Her flimsy ball gown would give her no protection at all against the unrelenting cold. If he didn't find her soon, he shuddered to think what might become of her.

Edward tried to tamp down his rising panic. He thought back to her face, how it had looked when poor, well-meaning Sir William had given her the worst news she ever could have heard, and the picture made him grimace.

She looked like a hunted animal. I don't know when I've ever seen a person look more afraid.

Of course she feared Uncle Charles returning to the estate. The death of her mama might have been a tragic accident, but Selina would always hold him responsible for what had happened, and Edward didn't blame her. Charles Fulbrooke would stir memories within Selina she doubtless would have given anything to forget forever, and her horror at the news that she might risk seeing him again would have been too much to bear.

No wonder she had been spooked at the notion and had run into the night like a fox from a pack of hounds.

'Sir! Over here!'

The coachman's voice carried to Edward on the chill wind. Turning at once, he saw Greene crouching by a snow-laden hedge at the border of the field and stumbled towards him, his heart beating so fast it was almost painful. Whatever Greene was looking at was lying on the ground, and Edward felt a sharp twist of fear that they might be too late.

I'll never forgive myself if—if—

He couldn't bring himself to finish the thought as he reached a small shape stretched out in the snow, half covered by a soft sprinkle of white.

Selina's face was pale in the moonlight, and frost sparkled on the tips of her long eyelashes. Her hair had come undone from its elaborate style and fanned out around her, a dark splash on the pristine white of the snow, and as Edward swiftly wrapped her in his own coat he felt her skin was as cold as death.

Her chest still rose and fell with quiet breaths, but they were slow and shallow, and as Edward gathered her into his arms and lifted her from the ground she made no sound, her eyes still closed as though in the deepest sleep.

Edward carried her towards his carriage in pained silence. She weighed little more than a child, and under any other circumstances he knew he would feel a thrill at holding her so closely against him. Instead, however, he felt only dread as he reached the carriage and climbed inside, still bearing her as if she was made of glass. He sank down onto the richly upholstered seat and gathered her into his lap, feeling the jolt as Greene geed up the horses and turned their heads for home.

My stubborn, headstrong Selina.

He looked down at her silent face, her lips blue and cheeks paler than he had ever seen them before.

Couldn't she have waited? I would have taken her home myself. If she never wakes—

He swallowed—a painful convulsion of his burning throat. A complex mixture of despair and frustration churned inside him as he chafed at her hands, seeing how her fingers were blue at the tips.

Running off into the snow. Who would go running off into the snow without so much as a cloak—apart from Selina?

It was just his luck to have lost his heart to such a wild creature, he thought with grim acceptance. An upper-class woman would never have acted with such instinctive rashness. But it was her difference from those of his own class that had made him, despite his best efforts, her most devoted servant, and it was with worried eyes that he watched her unconscious face as the carriage swept him and his wife through the night, back to where Edward felt sure they both belonged.

He would have strong words with her when she awoke—*if* she awoke. The prospect of her never again opening her dark eyes was enough to twist his insides so hard he could have cried out in pain. She *had* to wake up: the alternative was simply unthinkable.

The pillow beneath her head was soft, and Selina enjoyed the delicious sensation of waking slowly from a deep sleep for several long minutes before attempting to open her eyes. She had been having the most wonderful dreams, and was in no hurry for them to end, but she surfaced gradually, feeling their sweetness linger until her eyelids flickered open and a grim face swam into focus before her.

'Edward?'

He was seated in a chair drawn up to the bedside, so close that the red coverlet she lay beneath touched his knees. But her own bed was always swathed in powder-blue, and Selina's brow furrowed as she took in the decor of a room she had never seen before. A swift glance down showed she was wearing her nightgown, and a furious blush roared hotly up from her neck at the question of who had dressed her in it.

'Where am I? What happened?'

There was no preamble to his anger.

'Selina. What in seven hells were you about, running off by yourself into the snow without even a cloak to warm you?'

Selina attempted to sit upright in the bed, but Edward checked her with one strong hand.

'Don't try to get up. The doctor said that when you awoke you would need to rest.'

'The doctor? Why has he been here? I am quite well.'

'*Quite well!* Are you indeed, madam?' Edward's eyebrows were raised so high they were almost lost in the flax of his hair. 'You must forgive me if the evidence to the contrary was quite compelling!'

Flames danced in the grate of a grand fireplace not far from where she lay, their light hurting Selina's eyes. A slight ache was beginning to niggle at the back of her head, and she sighed at Edward's angry words. What she wouldn't give to be allowed to drift back into the dreamland she had so recently visited, where she and Edward had existed in perfect harmony without his furious voice ringing in her ears.

She remembered now, as she took in the set of his expression, why she had been trudging through the snow. A sudden weight settled beneath her ribs and she attempted once again to sit up. Once again, however, she was stopped by a large hand.

She pressed her own hand to her chest, feeling the place where that knot now lay heavy over her heart. 'I'm sorry, Edward. I just—I had to get out. If I gave you cause to be worried—'

'Worried?' Edward stood up from the bed and paced the floor in front of the fire, the flames casting shadows on his hair as he moved. 'Do you have *any* idea what passed through my mind when I found you lying on the ground, covered in frost and with your lips completely blue? You didn't move for the entire journey home. I didn't know if each breath would be your last!'

Selina winced at his tone. It was unsettlingly similar to Zillah's when she delivered a scolding. The comparison only served to remind her of the words that had haunted her just before she had sunk down into the snow.

A man you cannot hope to have.

'I'm sorry. It was never my intention to get into such trouble when I left Sir William's house.' Edward glanced at her but didn't cease his fretful pacing to and fro. 'I just couldn't stay there a moment longer. I suppose I should have told you, but I didn't think you would mind my leaving.'

Zillah's words echoed louder in Selina's mind as she looked across at her tight-faced husband, and fresh sorrow began to ache in her chest. The dark shadows beneath his eyes touched her heart and made her want to reach out and pull him to her, to allow him to chase away the final vestiges of the winter's chill with his masculine warmth.

Zillah's words echoed louder still—*convenience and nothing more...a man you cannot hope to have*—and she forced the urge back. She could never now tell him how she longed for his touch, or how living without him would be daily torture. He had never sought her love, and with his uncle's return Selina's feelings could only grow more and more irrelevant.

It was time for her to voice the decision she had come to moments before the cold had overcome her and she had sunk into a heap on the ground, so icy and so still that Edward had mistaken her for dead. Selina knew there would never be a better moment, and yet the words fled from her as she struggled to speak.

'I had not the smallest idea of you being so moved.' She spoke quietly, her eyes fixed upwards on the red embroidered canopy of the unfamiliar bed in which she lay. 'I have no wish to be a further burden on you, and therefore I shall be leaving Blackwell as soon as I am able.'

Edward had moved to stand close to the fire, one arm leaning on the mantel as he waited for her to answer, and the expression Selina saw flit across his face as he turned sharply towards her was unreadable.

'You mean in the springtime, as we agreed?'

'No. I mean now—as soon as I'm able to leave this bed.'

Staring upwards, Selina missed the shadow that clouded Edward's features.

'That was not our agreement,' he said.

'I'm aware of that. Given the circumstances, however—you must understand why I can't stay?'

'If it is only on account of my uncle's return, I—'

She cut him off with a shake of her aching head. Intense unhappiness welled up inside her and she bit the inside of her cheek to prevent her mouth from trembling. 'It isn't *only* that.'

The terrible truth returned to pinch at her again and she was powerless to push it aside. The return of Charles Fulbrooke was indeed a horrible prospect, but so was the notion of how close she had come to allowing herself to believe her deepest, most secret wish could ever come true.

There was no room for both her *and* Charles

at Blackwell Hall, and she was under no illusion that Edward would choose her—a necessary evil—over his own flesh and blood. She and Edward would never be together in any real way, and the knowledge made her want to weep. The fact that she couldn't tell him the real reason for her suffering only made it more painful. He must never know how truly she had fallen for him, and there was only one lie she could think of that would explain her sudden decision she knew he would believe.

Her eyes burning with supressed emotion, Selina forced herself to speak. 'I—I have realised the truth of my presence here.' That much was true at least, but the rest of her falsehood tasted bitter on her tongue. 'I have seen the reality of my situation and now I know I cannot stay.'

Edward's blood ran cold in his veins as his mind struggled to process Selina's words.

It was as though he had been suddenly doused in a bath of icy water, and his thoughts spun uncontrollably, unable to comprehend the dizzying turn of events that now unfolded before him.

She intended to leave him.

The image of Selina's rapt face staring up into his own as he bent towards her lips burst upon him, and he involuntarily tightened his grip on the mantel.

I pushed her too far. I frightened her, and now she wants to run from me as well as my uncle.

She was silent as she lay, unmoving, in the splendour of the carved oak bed—the bed in which Edward had spent so many sleepless nights thinking of her, wondering if there was a way to break down the walls Selina seemed so determined to build between them.

His first thought upon seeing her raven hair fanned out across his own pillows had been how badly he wished he could see the same sight every night, and the realisation that such a thing could never come to pass sat in his stomach like a stone.

'What do you mean, the reality of your situation?' Edward crossed the room towards her and dropped unceremoniously into the chair at her side. The urge to seize one of her little hands, now tracing the embroidery at the edges of the blankets with tense fingers, almost took his breath away.

'I have been pretending to be something I'm not.'

Selina's fingers paused in their activity. Edward gripped his own in his lap to prevent himself from reaching out.

'I wore those clothes, and smiled, and danced— all the while denying who I truly am.'

Edward saw her throat move as she swallowed, his eyes tracking the movement of her slender neck even as he fought the desire to touch it. He passed a hand across his face, hiding the emotion he feared he could not contain.

'You have denied nothing. All your people know you married me only as part of a bargain to save them—surely anything else you have done has been in the same vein.'

When Selina raised her eyes to his Edward was surprised to find them dimmed, dulled by a look of hopelessness he couldn't understand.

'Yes. That was why we wed, was it not? There was no feeling there. If I recall, you thought our mutual indifference could work to our advantage.'

She smiled at him, a sad, thin thing that somehow managed to make her look much older than her years.

'That was the only reason you could possibly have welcomed me into your home.'

Edward frowned, his brows drawn tightly together as he forced himself to stem the automatic contradiction that rose to his lips. The urge to deny her words was strong.

How could she still think she mattered so little to him, even after all this time? After they had shared such a heated embrace and he had comforted her as she cried? After he had lifted her from what he had feared was her icy grave and laid her down in his own bedchamber, knowing it was the warmest in the house, and taken up a bedside vigil that had lasted long into the night? Did that strike her as meaning nothing? Despite these actions, she still attributed to him so little feeling... Perhaps to her he was still, deep down, the same as all the other faceless gentry she feared.

Her face was lovely in the firelight, despite the strange sadness that sought to undermine the beauty of her eyes. Edward looked away when she avoided his gaze, staring instead at his hands as they lay in the broad spread of his lap.

'I wish you would reconsider.'

Even as he spoke the words he feared they were worthless. The heaviness in his gut increased with every second that passed, and he cursed his inability to tell her honestly that he would be lost if she left him, his existence without her like a living death. But the fear of rejection roared up within him again, the mocking faces of his mother and Letitia sneering at his pain, and he lapsed into silence.

'I cannot. I realised this evening I have no place here, living among my betters.'

'Your *betters*?' Edward stared at her, incredulity creeping into his voice. What new nonsense was this? 'This cannot be. When have I ever treated you as anything other than my equal? Or

given you the impression I think you are somehow beneath me?'

Selina still refused to meet his eye. Vexation
beginning to pump through his veins, Edward
abandoned his restraint and reached for her, circling one fragile wrist with the fingers of his
right hand. He felt the rapid tick of her pulse beneath the thin skin, and marvelled at how warmth
had returned to what had before been so cold—
before she pulled away from him.

'Never in word, but I am not a fool. I see now
how truly wide the chasm is between us. I am not
and never will be a real lady, no matter how expensive a gown I am hidden beneath. Our worlds
are poles apart and can never fit together. I do
not belong here.'

Edward sat back in his chair. They had finally reached the crux of the matter, he thought
in fierce frustration, and it was in no way flattering. The injustice of her words hit him with
cruel severity, and he felt what tenuous control
he held over his temper begin to slip.

So that was her opinion of him: that he was
every bit as bad as the shallow society he took
such pains to avoid, and that the only woman
who could ever satisfy him was a vapid, fashionable, upper-class lady.

The spectres of his mother and Letitia rose up
before him again, even as Edward stared at his

stone-faced wife. The contrast between the three women had never been more stark than at that moment. How could Selina possibly imagine *she* was the one lacking? Her warmth and instinctive kindness might be a different kind of fortune, but Edward had never been so certain that such riches were the only ones truly worth having.

But what was the point in such idle thoughts? The treasure of Selina's goodness would never be his. That much was now painfully plain, Edward lamented as the shadows from his past loomed ever more largely. Letitia's presence in his mind disgusted him, and yet there was nothing he could do to banish her from stalking through his head, unlocking memories he had kept hidden for so long.

He balled his hands into fists, clenching them tightly as though faced with some physical assailant. 'Damn it all, Selina. Is this how you think of me? That I judge your value on how high you were born or how well you look in a silk gown?' Edward's voice was low as he struggled to maintain his composure. 'I value a good soul above all else, madam, which is one of the reasons I hold you in higher esteem than any woman I have ever met.'

Selina's eyes flew to his face and he saw the glimmer of uncertainty that flickered within them.

'You know you don't mean that. We both know a Romani has no place in your home—'

'Will you stop telling me the contents of my own mind?' The final thread by which Edward's temper hung snapped, and he turned to Selina in real anger. 'I and I alone am party to what I do and do not know, and I tell you this: I would rather a Romani in my home than any number of young ladies of my own class. Do you truly think it's the ability to tell one spoon from another or speak flawless French that impresses me? I once knew two women with those accomplishments and more—the epitome of perfect gentlewomen—and their conduct scarred me for life.'

He swallowed. Selina's gaze never left his own.

'I am in no rush to repeat the experience.'

A silence stretched out between them, filled only with the crackle of flames as they writhed in the grate. Edward flexed his fingers, uncurling them from the angry fists they had made, and out of the corner of his eye he saw his wife watching in wordless contemplation.

She would ask questions now—of course she would. Any woman would be curious, but Edward knew Selina well enough to understand the depths her curiosity could run to. His mind began to work, running over possible falsehoods and diversions from the truth. How could he ever find words to explain how between them his mother and Letitia had left him unable to love? To the one woman on earth he now felt he would love for the rest of his life?

'Who were they, Edward?'

Selina's voice broke the silence, quiet against the stirring of the fire. Edward glanced at her, and all thoughts of deception melted away at the genuine concern in her eyes.

He felt her gaze on him, warm as he shook his head. *You don't have to answer. She doesn't have to know.* But the look in her eye was so gentle, so sweetly concerned, that the dam within him broke and he muttered the words he had thought never to share with anyone.

He sighed. 'My mother and my former fiancée.'

The concern in her face softened further into an expression of such deep compassion Edward felt his breath catch in his throat.

'And what was it they did to scar you so terribly?'

Edward leaned his head back onto the top of his chair, staring up at the ceiling as he marshalled his thoughts.

Two paths lay ahead of him. The first one—to minimise the damage Mother and Letitia had wreaked upon his ability to trust in the constancy of women—was tempting. He could keep his demons hidden from Selina and offer her some fake tale. The other path was that of complete honesty. It would be to trust Selina with the knowledge of the pain he had kept buried deep down within himself for almost his entire life, to lay bare to her the inner workings of his heart and mind.

Could he take that step? Certainly she had shown him time and again that she possessed great empathy with the troubles of others—her devotion to her people was evidence enough of that—but could it be that her sympathy would extend to him, a member of the class that had done her such a terrible, life-shattering wrong?

A sudden burst of fire erupted in the fingers of his left hand. Edward started, looking down quickly for the cause, only to see Selina's fingers entwined with his own and her dark eyes watching him with silent understanding.

Sparks exploded in the pit of his stomach as he watched her small hand gently fold over his, and he released one ragged breath. How was it that she managed to unman him so? Even after the long months of their marriage his reaction to her still took him by surprise.

Edward began to speak, wondering even as the words passed his lips by what witchcraft Selina dragged them from him.

'I was twelve years old when my mother left my father for another man—only a week or so before I met you for the first time in the Black-well woods. She was never the most attentive parent, but I loved her as fiercely as any boy loves his mother, and thought she felt the same.'

He frowned, a crease appearing between his fair brows. He should stop talking, he knew, but Selina's soundless encouragement gave him reason to continue.

'I realise now, of course, that I never mattered to her very much. She was proud of me as an extension of herself, and for what I would become: a rich country squire with a huge estate, once I inherited.'

Edward paused, looking down at Selina's hand held tightly in his own.

'I know now that it was her arrogance that prompted any affection she had for me, and it ceased as soon as she found another, more valuable prize. The man she left us for was a foreign nobleman, with a fortune ten times the size of my father's.'

Edward heard Selina's soft intake of breath and allowed a grim smile entirely devoid of humour to twist his lips.

'She left without even saying goodbye and I have never heard from her since.'

Selina's eyes were filled with wonder as she shook her head slowly, compassion radiating from her so strongly it was almost palpable. 'I am so, so sorry, Edward.' He saw her throat move as she swallowed, evidently at a loss for words. 'I had no idea. I assumed your mother must have died—I never dreamed...'

'No. You could never imagine such an unnatural mother when your own loved you so fiercely.' The light from the fire stung his eyes and he rubbed them roughly.

'And your fiancée? Did she—?'

'Leave for another man? Just as my mother left my father?' Edward's laugh was short and bitter. 'Your instinct is uncanny.'

Selina said nothing, apparently waiting for Edward to continue.

I might as well tell her everything. She already knew half of his shame—why not finish the sorry tale of why his heart had been so cold?

Edward gazed deeply into the fire, ignoring the burning in his eyes. 'Letitia was everything a man in my position could have wished for: beautiful and accomplished. When she set out to catch me I found her captivating, despite myself, and it wasn't long before I believed myself sincerely in love.'

He glanced towards Selina's intently listening face.

'I was lonely, I suppose. I was living in London to escape the daily wars with my father, and for a while Letitia seemed like the answer to my empty life. We were quickly engaged and my father was thrilled—until three days before the wedding, when I received word she had eloped with another man of our acquaintance and was lost to me forever, taking my faith in gentry women with her. You asked me once why I did not choose to marry a woman I could love. The truth is I feared it. Certainly love for a woman in any way reminiscent of my mother or Letitia.'

He traced his fingers down the back of Selina's hand, noting the contrast between the tone of his skin and hers.

'Do you see it now? I *value* your difference from the people with whom I was raised. Your kindness, your honesty and complete lack of guile... If you are unlike a gentry woman it is only to your credit. It's because of who you are that I—that I—'

That I love you, he concluded silently, knowing without question that he could no more voice his thoughts aloud than he could grow wings and fly.

She might be feeling some modicum of sympathy for him in that moment, but the knowledge that Selina's opinion of him had previously sunk so low stung. The fact that she had wanted to leave him could only be taken as proof that her feelings did not match his own.

Selina's brow furrowed slightly, but she did

not pull her hand away as his fingers lightly sketched the network of veins at her wrist.

'Where are they now?' she asked.

'Both out of the country.' Edward shrugged. 'Mother moved abroad with her noble lover, although where I do not know. After their divorce Father banned any mention of her—even her name. All her portraits were removed, and now it's as though she was never here at all. As for Letitia—her new husband owned a fine chateau in France, and they settled there after their elopement.'

There was a short pause, during which Edward silently admired the slender shape of each of Selina's tanned fingers. She appeared to be thinking, but it was only when she began to speak that Edward realised the direction of her thoughts.

'We both mourn for our mothers, in a way…'

Selina's voice was soft, almost shy. Edward inclined his head slightly to look into her averted face and wondered at the rosy blush he saw spread across the smoothness of her cheeks. His heart rate picked up, beating quickly inside the prison of his ribs.

'I would never presume to put the manner of my mother's absence in the same category as yours,' he said.

'Even so.' Selina turned back to him and Edward saw new emotion dawning in her eyes. 'You know how it is to feel that pain.'

'I do. I felt it keenly.' He tried to smile, but his heart was hammering so fast it hurt him to breathe. 'In truth, I feel it even to this day.'

It happened too quickly for him to see—or perhaps it was more that it happened so gradually he didn't notice. All Edward knew was that Selina reached for him, and this time when their lips met there was nobody there to interrupt.

Chapter Fourteen

It was as though Edward's hands were made of flame as he touched Selina's skin, leaving behind trails of fire as they traced the slender length of her neck. A strangled cry was dragged from her lips as his fingers continued their steady progress downward, and Edward smiled unseen against the warmth of Selina's throat.

Her nightgown lay in a heap on the floor, entangled with the shirt she had helped remove from Edward's chest with fingers that trembled with desire. She gritted her teeth on a whimper, unable to stop the telltale roll of her hips at the sweet sensations that coursed through her.

'Edward…'

His name escaped her lips like a plea, although what she was pleading for Selina hardly knew. She had no awareness of anything other than the desperate need within herself that only *he* could satisfy: her husband—the aggravating, confusing, beautiful man who smiled at her whispering of his name and bent his head to kiss the shivering peak he had awakened, drawing from her another breathy sigh.

She reached for him with hands made clumsy by want and pulled his face towards her own, her heart pounding in her ears as he captured her lips once more.

A nagging voice in the back of her mind needled her, whispering for restraint, but Selina could no longer understand the need for her to do anything other than slide her tongue past Edward's own and feel a rush of heady satisfaction as this time it was his turn to groan, to show her more clearly than words ever could how much his desire for her had grown. His arms wrapped tightly around her, melding her slight frame against the power of his own, and Selina held him to her and felt the muscles in his back shiver beneath her touch.

His physique was just as impressive as she had dared imagine, although the hair that roughened the broad expanse of his chest had taken her by surprise. It was so much darker than the flaxen thatch on his head, and she had wondered at it momentarily, as she'd pulled Edward's shirt from his body, leaving only his breeches intact. But then he had taken hold of the hem of her nightgown and begun to inch it higher, sliding his hands against her skin as he followed its progress upwards, and all sensible thought had been chased from her mind by animalistic craving.

She clung to him, feeling the final dregs of self-control leave her. *You shouldn't be doing this*, some distant corner of her mind insisted, its panicked voice sounding far-off and foggy. *What would Zillah think? Or Mama? How will you explain yourself?*

The questions were fair ones, Selina conceded with her last ounce of rationality as Edward's tongue found her ear and traced the lobe, creating splinters of want that lanced through her and turned her limbs to water; but she could no longer fight a losing battle. Her desire for Edward's touch was too strong, and her newly discovered connection to him as a fellow hurt and frightened child too profound. They had at last found some common ground on which something might be built—something *real*.

Selina had found herself reaching for Edward before she even knew what she was doing, spurred on by the powerful sorrow in his face that she knew she so often wore on her own.

Edward drew back a little, his eyes never leaving the soft landscape of her curves, and ran one strong hand down the length of Selina's leg. She bucked immediately, her fingers clutching at the sheets that lay tangled beneath her, and when she gazed up at Edward his eyes were burning.

'Have you ever—?'

Selina stared at him, her chest heaving. Sweat had begun to gather on her skin, its sheen gleaming dimly in the firelight, and she could have sworn she felt the temperature of the room rise at his question. She shook her head, and almost gasped at the intensity of Edward's answering look.

'No. In my culture, too, that honour is reserved for a woman's husband.'

'I see.'

Edward's voice was low with want; Selina felt herself stir in reply.

'In that case I shall endeavour to make it worth the wait.'

His eyes devoured her as she lay before him, tawny skin and raven hair laid bare to his hungry gaze. Selina wondered if she ought to feel some sense of shame in being so exposed, in allowing Edward's eyes and hands free rein to wander where they pleased, but the notion died at the reverence with which he watched her rapt face and she gave herself up to the pleasure that glittered within her body, sparkling through her blood and turning her to pure gold.

His hands were skilled, urgent and yet gentle, and when they strayed to the secret part of her that nobody else had ever known she shuddered and gasped, her back arching against the pillows where Edward had lain sleepless for so many nights, his mind full of the woman who now writhed in his bed.

Selina's brows drew together in an expression of pained ecstasy as Edward's fingers moved against her sensitive flesh, her breath escaping in a staccato rhythm that matched the frenzied beating of her heart. Her eyes drifted closed and she felt rather than saw Edward lean down to scatter melting kisses across the cage of her ribs, working up from her navel until he reached her fragile collarbone.

She tried to lift her arms to pull him closer but found all strength had left her. She was rendered immobile by the heat of Edward's caress. A tiny thread of sound, somewhere between a moan and a sigh, fell from her lips as Edward delved a little deeper, pulling her further and further out to drift in the sea of sensation that he created within her.

Dimly, as though in a dream, she thought she heard him groan in reply, and she made another attempt to reach for him. This time her hands connected with the firm breadth of his chest, and her eyes opened to see him watching her with undisguised hunger written across his handsome features. The same glint of sweat that ghosted over Selina's skin seemed to gleam on Edward's, serving to highlight the contours of his defined muscles despite the snowflakes that swirled against the windows of the chamber and the wind they could hear whistling through the trees outside.

Splaying her trembling hands against the heated sheets beneath her, Selina pushed herself up, rising unsteadily to her knees. Edward's gaze never faltered from her face. 'I think you're being a little unfair,' she said.

'Unfair?' Edward's voice hitched, his breathing uneven as Selina's fingers moved to trace patterns across the smooth linen of his breeches.

There was so much to explore, so much to see, she thought as she stretched up to cover his willing mouth with her own. She didn't want to waste another moment.

'You seem to be wearing far more clothes than I am. Doesn't that strike you as a little unjust?'

She felt him smile against her lips. The deep ache he had awakened within her intensified as he rose from the bed and stood before her, hesitating for the briefest of moments before loosening the fastening at his waist and allowing Selina to see, for the first time other than in her most fevered dreams, the full marvel of his masculine form.

Some last remnant of propriety caused Selina's cheeks to burn with fierce heat, adding to the conflagration Edward had inspired inside her, and for several seconds she found herself speechless, unable to conjure up a single word with which to break the taut silence that stretched out between them. He gazed down at her from his great height, eyes molten with need, and Selina could do nothing but drink him in as he stood, tall and proud, with the proof of his desire for her evident for all to see.

He dropped down to kneel in front of her on the red coverlet he had so carelessly torn from her, grasping her hips to hold her firmly to the hard planes of his body as once again he explored the cavern of her mouth with his clever tongue.

Selina was aware of the evidence of his longing pressing against her, and she felt the blush climb up from her neck again to suffuse the burning skin of her cheeks, even as she sifted her fingers through Edward's hair and clung to him, deepening the kiss and exulting to hear his growl of guttural delight.

Hands still firmly locked around Selina's waist, Edward gently tipped her backwards, following her as she fell and bracing himself above her on his forearms. The hardness of his belly against the soft skin of her own sent a thrill running through the entirety of Selina's being, and

she swallowed hard at the overwhelming feelings
that coursed unchecked within her.

'May I?'

Edward's words were quiet in her ear, but Selina heard the hoarse undertone of want and it
made her shiver. She looked up into the face of
the man above her, barely illuminated by the embers of the fire dying slowly in the grate. His
gaze was locked on hers, hazel on black, and
even in the depths of his intense need Selina saw
how he waited for her signal.

Her heart was beating so hard and so fast it
was almost painful, but she smiled, a slow upward curve of her voluptuous mouth that Edward's lips soon copied.

'Yes, husband. You may.'

Edward still slept.

One of his arms was beneath his head and the
other rested across Selina's waist in a gesture so
protective she felt a wave of pure contentment
steal over her. She lay quietly, unmoving, and
drank in the new knowledge of how he looked
when those hazel eyes were closed in sleep and
the muscles of his face had relaxed completely,
with no trace of his usual carefully cultivated
smile.

This was Edward as he truly was, Selina
thought wonderingly. Only when he was sleep-

ing could his guard be down entirely. His face was turned slightly away from her, giving her an uninterrupted view of his sharp profile and the scar that gleamed white on his cheek, and Selina had to lock her fingers together on the flat plane of her ribs to stop herself from reaching out to trace it softly, from reading the lines of his face with her hands.

He shifted slightly, still immersed in whatever dream was currently running through his subconscious, rolling from his side to rest on his back. The movement shifted the sheet he lay beneath, dragging its scanty cover downwards, making it close to being no cover at all, and Selina felt her eyes drift to follow it.

Whoever could have guessed that a pampered gentleman would have such an impressive physique? she contemplated as she surveyed the peaks and valleys of Edward's musculature, taut and toned beneath fair skin. His chest resembled that of a hard-working man's, and his biceps were almost as defined as those that belonged to Roma men with a lifetime of graft under their belts.

She laced her fingers together again, still fighting the urge to touch. The euphoria of the night still sang in her veins, and she was aware of a growing ache in the muscles of her limbs. It was a sweet ache, similar to the ache she felt the day after a long session breaking in a new horse:

painful, but accompanied by such a sense of satisfaction that it made the discomfort bearable.

She stretched, feeling the tension in her arms as a vivid flashback of what had caused it burst upon her. *I wish he'd wake.* A thrilling mix of anticipation and anxiety pooled in her stomach. What would his reaction be, waking to find his wife lying beside him in the great red and white expanse of his bed? Pleased, she would hope.

The reverence with which Edward had touched her burning skin could not be faked, she thought as she drummed a rhythm on her ribs with impatient fingers. They had seemed to join together not just physically but emotionally, connecting in a way she could never have dreamed of. Even sleeping next to him felt natural.

Selina felt her faith in Edward surge upwards as she waited, nerves fizzing with delicious nervousness, for him to wake. Casting her eye yet again over the sleeping face so close to her own, she tried to pinpoint the moment she had fallen so completely and utterly under his spell. Had it been the first moment she saw him? Or perhaps later, upon finding there was more to him than a handsome face and an even more handsome inheritance?

Whenever the moment had been, Selina thanked her lucky stars for it—for without the realisation that Edward was everything she had been missing from her life, even without knowing it, she would have continued on as she always had, carrying the unhappy weight of her mother's death with her for the rest of her days with no one to help her bear it.

The thought of Diamanda wiped the smile abruptly from Selina's lips. The memory of Sir William's ball crashed through her rosy daydreams: Charles Fulbrooke was returning to Blackwell Hall, and if she stayed she would have to see him.

Selina felt her chest tighten with panic once again as the spectre of the person she least wanted to meet in all the world rose up before her. To set eyes on Charles would be unthinkable, unbearable. Would she faint if he stood in front of her? Or would she simply run wild with fear?

Edward would never allow any physical harm to come to her, she tried to remind herself as her thoughts began to spiral downwards and her breath became short, but even his protective arms wouldn't be able shield her from the hatred with which Charles would look at her, and the heart-stopping terror she knew would drive her half-mad at the sight of him. Seeing her mother's killer would be more than she could bear— an all too real reminder of the nightmare he had forced her to live.

But what alternative was there? He was Edward's blood—the only kin he had aside from Ophelia. She couldn't ask him to refuse the uncle who had been a part of his life for far longer than she had herself. Even if their night together had somehow overcome Edward's reluctance to care for her, as she hoped so fervently it had, she still couldn't ask him to choose between his desires and his duty to his family.

Almost as though his mind had sensed the frenzied activity of her own, Edward's eyelashes flickered, and Selina watched as his eyes opened slowly, adjusting to the grey light that crept between hastily drawn curtains. Still lying on his back, Edward seemed to study the red canopy above his head for some moments, before rolling over onto his side and fixing Selina with the hazel gaze she had come to adore more than any other.

There was a genuine smile playing about his lips—an upward curve that made her heart swell painfully with love—but it slid abruptly from his face as he took in the anguished expression on her own.

Edward saw Selina's distress and wondered, as a tight fist of dismay squeezed the air from his lungs, what could have happened to cause it.

He had woken slowly, his mind still sluggish as he surfaced from the deepest sleep he had enjoyed in months. The feeble light of a new day assailed his still closed eyelids, and the only sound had been the gentle breathing of *someone* lying close to him on the rumpled sheets of his formerly lonely bed.

The breaths had been quiet and even—quite unlike the fevered panting of the night before—and Edward felt himself stir in response even as his brain shuffled his thoughts into some semblance of order. The uncomfortable feeling of wrinkled blankets under his back served as a reminder of how they had got into such a state, and Edward had felt the stirring grow a little more intense.

We spent the night together and she's still in my bed.

The realisation broke over Edward in a wave of amazed elation as his eyelids had finally struggled open and he'd taken in the red canopy above his head. *Whoever said miracles don't happen?*

Selina's cheeks were flushed with warmth, rosy against the untidy ebony tresses of hair that tumbled around her unhappy face. One tawny shoulder peeped out from beneath the sheet that shielded her from his gaze, smooth and perfect, and the urge to lean across to kiss it almost took Edward's breath away. *She is utterly beautiful*, he thought as his eyes roamed her face, and for the first time felt the true fathomless depth of his adoration for her mingle with his growing concern.

A powerful sense of vulnerability swept over him now as they stared at each other, neither uttering a word to break the silence. She had completely destroyed all his defences, forcing her way into the heart he had never intended to share with anyone. She had worked herself so irrevocably into his mind and soul that Edward would have nowhere to run if she were to leave him—nowhere to hide from the feelings he had declared to her so unmistakably.

If she carried on with her plan to leave with her people his heart would be ripped from his chest, but surely she would not abandon him now. They had shared the most profound experience a man and a woman could share, Edward thought dazedly, memorising the pattern of freckles across Selina's nose as he watched her lovely face intently. There was no way she would return to the Roma—not now she had confirmed, in action rather than words, how her fledgling regard for him had grown into something so precious.

I need to find out what's worrying her—I can never let her run from me again.

'Good morning, Selina. Are you well?'

Edward pushed himself up to lean back against the pillows, allowing himself a better view of her face. 'You look…troubled.' Apprehension crept into his voice and he watched her closely, as though searching for clues, some snippet of an idea as to why she looked almost on the brink of tears. Her apparent distress tore at him, his feelings still raw after their unexpected airing the night before. The urge to gather her into his arms was strong, but the unhappy set of her jaw gave him pause.

He saw her throat move as she swallowed, her slender neck seeming to cry out for him to kiss it as he had mere hours previously. Instead he tore his eyes away and waited for her to speak.

'I have been thinking about your uncle's return.' She spoke quietly, her gaze fixed on her fingers as she worried at a lock of her midnight hair. 'He could arrive any day and I— Forgive me.' She broke off for a moment, her emotion obvious. 'I do not have the strength to see him.'

Edward felt a sharp pang of relief burst in his chest and his spirits soared upwards once again. *Is that all that troubles her? Uncles Charles's return?*

It was almost an anti-climax after his dizzying despair that the cause of her haunted look could be so easily solved. It wasn't that she regretted their night together—it was something else entirely. He could have laughed aloud as the weight fell from his shoulders.

He turned to Selina, reaching out to take her

small hand in his much larger grasp. He saw her almost flinch at his touch and knew the same crackle of sensation he felt flared within her too. His body reacted at the sight, but he forced himself to set the ungentlemanly train of thought to one side in favour of reassuring his unhappy-looking wife.

'Selina. Let me make you a promise: you will never have to set eyes on my uncle ever again.'

He traced his thumb over the ridges of her knuckles and felt her hand tremble at the feel of his skin on hers. He wanted to kiss her tawny skin, to give in to the hunger for her that was beginning to stir within him once again, and the dawning hope he saw in Selina's eyes only made his appetite grow.

'I will write to Charles this very morning and tell him not to leave the Continent. Would that set your mind at ease?'

He brought her hand up to his mouth, his gaze still locked on hers. He heard her tiny sigh at the touch of his lips and smiled down at her as her frame visibly relaxed, only moments before having been held so tightly he had wondered if it hurt.

'You would do that?'

Selina's voice held a world of amazement and her face was a picture of wonder, although Edward almost narrowed his eyes at the hint of disbelief.

'I—I would not want to be the cause of you missing the chance to see your family.'

There was more than a shadow of irritation in Edward's voice when he answered—though it was not directed at the woman in his bed. 'There is no reason I can think of for his return other than an attempt to impose upon the running of my estate. My father and I fought often as a result of his controlling nature. My uncle is cut from the same cloth.'

He looked down at Selina's fingers, so small inside his palm, and marvelled with a fresh burst of dazed wonder at this second chance of happiness he had been given.

'As the Squire of Blackwell I am more than capable of governing my own estate. I have no need of anybody to hold my hand as though I were a child.' He paused for a moment before a small smile curved his lips. *You romantic fool.* 'The only person whose hand I ever wish to hold is—'

'Sir? Sir, are you awake? Apologies, but I'm afraid I need to speak with you.'

Evans's discreet knock at the door made Edward curse softly and wrench his eyes from Selina's wide-eyed face. He snatched up his shirt from the tangle of clothes and linen on the floor next to the bed and pulled it over his head, at the same time swinging his legs over the side in search of his breeches.

'You might want to pull the curtains.'

He heard Selina's giggle as she shuffled forward to draw the rich hangings of the four-poster bed into place, shielding her from Edward's glowing gaze. He was just wondering if it would be terribly rude simply to ignore the servant at the door and rejoin his wife beneath the covers when the knock came again, this time a little more firmly, and so it was with his breeches held up by one hand and his shirt untucked that Edward finally opened the door.

'Good morning, Evans.'

'Good morning, sir. I'm very sorry to wake you.'

Edward bit down on a smile. He could hardly have looked less like a man who had been innocently sleeping. Trust the old butler to attempt to maintain his master's dignity.

'Think nothing of it. Is there something you need to speak to me about?'

'Yes, sir.' Evans nodded, his expression slightly disapproving. 'You have an unexpected visitor. We found him very early this morning, attempting to gain entry to the Hall.'

The butler cleared his throat and Edward felt a sudden creep of dread at the unhappiness on the older man's face.

'We have put Mr Charles in the West Wing guest suite, where—I *am* sorry, sir—he insists he would like to speak with you at your earliest convenience.'

Chapter Fifteen

Edward quickly stepped through the door and pulled it closed behind him. 'My uncle? He is here? In this house?'

The butler nodded apologetically and Edward drew in a harsh breath.

'*Damn.*'

He brought a hand up across his eyes. Charles must have left to return to Blackwell almost as soon as he had written of his intentions to Sir William, no doubt hoping to catch his nephew off-guard.

Edward felt a hot pulse of anger at Charles's presumption in arriving unannounced and lowered his voice to mutter in Evans's ear. 'I shall see to this at once. Don't mention his presence to Mrs Fulbrooke.' Edward looked the other man intently in the eye. 'Do you understand me? Mrs Fulbrooke is *not* to be told.'

'Yes, sir. I understand.'

It was evident by his face that the butler didn't *truly* understand, but he would do as Edward ordered despite his own politely concealed confusion, and Edward clapped him on the shoulder.

'You did right to tell me. I shall go to dress at once. Please send Wellburn…' Edward hesitated, struck by the sudden thought that he couldn't dress in his bedchamber as usual.

The presence of Selina in his bed made his lips want to curve into a disbelieving smile, but he forced himself to return to the matter at hand. *There will be plenty of time to spend with Selina later—once you've dealt with Uncle Charles.*

Edward set his face grimly. It was essential that Selina didn't catch wind of Charles's arrival at the Hall. To say she would be distressed was something of an understatement, and he could hardly bear the thought of her in such pain.

'Please tell Wellburn I shall dress in my drawing room today. I will wait for him there.'

'Very good, sir.'

Evans moved off with his silent step and Edward ducked back into the bedchamber. The curtains were still drawn around the bed and, twitching them aside, he saw Selina's eyes were closed and that her chest rose and fell with gentle breaths. He watched her for a moment, wondering yet again at the dizzying turn of events that had brought them together so inseparably, and felt the same grin he had fought back earlier tug at him again.

I'll speak with Charles and then come to wake her. I think the time may have come for me to tell her...

He allowed the train of thought to tail off as a cold veil of doubt clouded his mind. To tell Selina of his true feelings for her would be to admit them out loud—something he had never even done alone in his rooms. There would be no turning back, no more hiding behind the walls he had built around his heart for so long, and the thought of laying himself bare chilled him to the bone.

She might still reject him—might take his love and thrust it aside as had happened to him twice before. Her rejection would be kind, Edward didn't doubt that, but all the same it would wound him in a way with which his previous suffering would not compare.

He turned away, smoothing the curtains back into place and allowing Selina to sleep on, her raven hair fanned out across his pillows. An uncomfortable combination of apprehension over Selina's reaction and anger at his uncle's intrusion settled heavy in his stomach, and Edward drew his brows together in a frown as he left the bedchamber and made for his drawing room.

An audience with Charles was the last thing he wanted to deal with on this surprising morning, but it would at least postpone the hour when he had to look Selina square in the eye and tell her that, despite his fears, he couldn't live without her—and then hear her reply, either making his dreams come true or crushing them beneath her heel.

The snow lay in deep drifts as Selina wandered slowly down one of the recently cleared paths that meandered through Blackwell's gardens, but even the chill couldn't dampen the warmth she felt lighting up her insides. She pulled her shawls closer about her body and breathed in deeply, savouring the crisp air as she allowed a smile of perfect happiness to spread across her face.

The image of her husband as he had looked that morning, his hair rumpled from sleep and his eyes regaining their twinkle as he woke slowly, caused her heart to turn over in her chest. The memory of the heat of his body and the achingly masculine scent of his skin made her close her eyes briefly, recalling every detail of their unbelievable experience together.

It hadn't been a dream. She truly had spent the night with Edward, and the delicious feel of his lips on her knuckles as he had assured her that she needn't fear his uncle's return still tingled on her skin.

He'd had to postpone their taking breakfast together while he dealt with some urgent business. Evans had murmured as much to her apologetically when she had emerged from Edward's chamber, respectable once again in a gown hurriedly brought in by a blushing Dinah, with her Christmas brooch pinned to it, and she had thought that while she waited for him to reappear a walk in the gardens might help to clear her head. It still ached a little from her snowy adventure, although the pleasure that sang in the rest of her nerves helped to soothe the slight niggle of pain.

Nothing could completely drown out the anxious fluttering in her stomach, however, at the thought of what she would have to tell Edward on his return.

Selina ran a hand across the frosted leaves of one immaculately kept hedge as she walked, feeling the chill beneath her fingertips. Her breath hung in the air in little clouds—a visible reminder of how her nerves had quickened it.

Surely you can be honest now? He must have guessed the truth of it.

If Edward was in any doubt as to her feelings for him now she could only shake her head in wonder at the blindness of men to female emotions. He *must* be aware of how her love for him had grown. Every touch of his hand, every kind word, every thoughtful gesture had increased her fondness for him until it had erupted into something far more powerful than the instinctive attraction any woman might feel for such an undeniably handsome man. It was deeper than that.

Selina swallowed as the sudden desire to see Edward seized her in its grip. She had to tell him—she couldn't bear the tension anymore. Even if he didn't feel the same way she had to stay true to her own heart—even if that meant risking the agony of rejection. He might have entered their marriage with the intention of mere convenience, but there was surely no way that could be his feeling now.

The sound of footsteps crunching through snow made her turn. 'Edward?'

They were definitely a man's steps: long strides made by large leather boots, unless she was very much mistaken, and they were coming from the other side of the hedge that bordered the path she had been following through the gardens.

'Edward? Is that you?'

A sudden vivid thrill of delicious anxiety flooded her and her heart began to pound. This could be the moment she had waited for, agonised over. The moment when she would finally know the answer to the question she had whispered in her sleep for months.

The footsteps grew louder, and Selina felt her

mouth shape into an instinctive smile as a figure rounded the corner before her.

The smile dropped from her lips as a blindingly painful bolt of sheer horror punched through her chest, snatching the air from her lungs and winding her as though she had fallen from a great height. She could only stare with eyes huge and glassy with terror as Charles Fulbrooke came towards her, her every nightmare made flesh, and she was fixed to the spot by legs that suddenly felt as though they were made of water.

It was in mute, heart-stopping fear that she saw Charles's brow crease into a frown, before clearing to be replaced by a look of pure, arrogant contempt. His mouth twisted in a sneer, and the bow he swept Selina was so low it was clear even to her frozen mind that it was intended to mock her.

'Well, well... The new lady of Blackwell Hall, I assume?' He raised an eyebrow, elegantly amused. 'I've been so looking forward to meeting you. I am Edward's Uncle Charles—brother to his late father.'

Charles's eyes roamed across her and Selina felt herself shudder, her skin clammy with a sudden heat that made her palms prickle with sweat. He appraised her as though she was an animal at market, blatantly lingering over the shape of her figure in a way no gentleman would ever look at a respectable lady, and Selina almost gasped at the intense wave of nausea that swept through her.

He looked just as she remembered, his face imprinted onto her brain forever, and the memories he unleashed flashed before Selina's wide eyes, their unspeakable horror filling her with a dread she had hoped never to feel ever again.

She had no words with which to reply. Instead she felt the air choked from her burning throat and fire scalding hot within the prison of her ribs. A voice inside her screamed at her to *run*, in any direction as long as it was far and it was fast, but her legs wouldn't obey her churning mind and still she stood, staring at the man responsible for the death of her mother and for a lifetime of nightmares, with no way of escaping his cruel smile.

'I've yet to see my nephew. I had intended to wait for him in my rooms, but he was taking such a long time to come to me I thought I'd look over the grounds while he roused himself. It's been so long since I was last here.'

Charles spoke idly, self-assured in the face of Selina's obvious panic. She swallowed painfully, bile acrid on her tongue.

He stepped closer to her—close enough for

Selina to smell the tobacco on his breath and the expensive pomade on his hair.

'I heard some whispers about you. Rumours, stories…that sort of thing.'

Selina closed her eyes, attempting to blot out the face that had haunted her dreams. Perhaps she was asleep? Perhaps at any moment she would wake up, find herself back in the warmth of Edward's bed with his face smiling down at her?

'I heard that my foolish young nephew had taken a wife far below his station, but I hadn't imagined he had sunk *quite* so low in his search for a bride. I returned at once, to make sure he saw reason, but now, having met you here so fortuitously, perhaps I needn't speak with him at all.'

Selina's eyes flew open. Charles's chestnut hair and ruddy complexion were entirely unlike Edward's fair colouring, but the hazel eyes were similar enough to make her heart skip a painful beat. How one set of eyes could radiate such kindness while another the same shade could be so cold was a mystery, but Selina had no time to dwell on the question as Charles continued.

'No doubt my nephew has been good to you, but your time here has come to an end. He has always had the most peculiar regard for your kind—one his father and myself did *not* encourage.'

He paused to flick a scathing glance across

her, and Selina flinched as though he had touched her skin.

'I see no reason to involve him further. He has already shown how badly he is in need of my guidance and my instruction on how to conduct himself. If you had any decency...' He trailed off, once again eyeing her from head to toe with unconcealed contempt. 'Well... The less said about that the better. Still, even one such as *you* can surely see there is no place for you here?'

Selina backed away from him, never taking her eyes from his hateful face. There was such venom in his voice it made her want to shrink into the hedge at her back, but some tiny part of her spirit, small but stubborn, crept from behind her blind terror and defiantly raised its head.

They were no louder than a whisper, but Selina somehow managed to force words from her bloodless lips. 'Edward wants me here.' She almost choked on the sounds. 'He was going to write to tell you not to come.'

Cold anger flooded Charles's face and he took a step towards her, closing the gap between them. Selina pressed herself against the frosted leaves behind her and felt an icy shard of fear pierce her like a knife to her chest.

Where is Edward?

She didn't dare look away from the furious man in front of her and cast a desperate glance back in the direction of the Hall. All she could do was offer up a silent prayer that he would somehow sense her distress and appear to rescue her, as he had all those months before.

'Audacious lies!'

Charles's nose was mere inches from Selina's own and she shrank a fraction further.

'You wish to drive me off, do you? To isolate the boy from his family so you can have him and his fortune all to yourself? You think to ruin his life with your selfishness!'

Selina's heart leapt within her as though it was trying to escape her chest. Acute fear and nausea had robbed her of her senses, leaving her deaf and blind to everything other than this dangerous man who looked as though he might try to grab her at any moment, crowding into her space and making every muscle in her body stiffen in terror.

She swallowed down another hot pulse of panic, balling her hands into fists that were damp with sweat. She *wasn't* selfish. Edward had said himself that he hadn't wished for his uncle's return, and had implied he had chosen her happiness instead.

Some trace of her thoughts must have shown on her face, as with a sudden whip-like flick of his hand Charles seized Selina's wrist and dragged her towards him, his face twisted into a sneer. Selina felt her eyes grow huge with word-less panic and her breath shortened into shallow pants, as if all the air was being expelled from her lungs in tiny painful bursts as her heart hammered harder than she had ever known it to do before.

'Listen to me.' Charles tightened his grip on her arm, fingers biting into the skin. 'My nephew has no father and his own mother abandoned him. His own *mother*! I am almost the only family he has left. Now, thanks to you, people are whispering about him, shunning him. He will find himself friendless and alone, and it will all be *your* fault. If you cared about him at all you would leave and return to where you belong. You have no place here—ruining my nephew's reputation and that of this great house.'

Selina wrenched her wrist from his hand, cradling it against her chest. The skin was red and sore, but it was the pain in her chest that made searing tears rise up behind her horrified eyes.

Edward's face as it had looked the night before, when he was telling her his most secret sorrows in a voice so low and pained it had hurt her to hear it, flashed through her mind. He had felt the agony of rejection twice already and it had made him turn away from the world, even to go so far as to choose a wife he had hoped would never love him. The idea of being the cause for him to be cut off again from those he might care about was like a fist in her gut, and Selina felt herself wince as a shard of burning realisation cut through her.

'Surely you can see the truth of your situation? Edward only married you to secure his inheritance—an unfortunate circumstance forced on him by his father. Do you truly wish for him to pay so dearly for something he couldn't avoid? To see him humiliated and alone because of your selfishness? Besides…' He tossed the words at her with casual malice. 'There has only ever been one woman for whom Edward cared—a beautiful, accomplished, high-born woman—and she betrayed him with another. What makes you think he would risk his heart again for a low creature like you?'

It was the confirmation of all her previous doubts and insecurities, laid out before her in brutal clarity. Edward might have some measure of fondness for her, but would that survive if she was the reason for his downfall and disgrace in the eyes of his people? All her plans for their future lay in ruins at her feet, and as she looked up into Charles's face through the starburst of her tears Selina thought her heart might break in two.

There was a glimmer of triumph in Charles's smirk as he sighed and shook his head. 'Poor, silly creature. Save yourself the grief. Go now—

you needn't see my nephew. He might try to persuade you to stay out of some misguided attempt at gallantry, and it would be pointless to delay the inevitable.'

He reached out a hand and a powerful wave of intense loathing broke over Selina's trembling body as he placed a finger beneath her chin and jerked her head upwards to meet his cold gaze.

'Let there be no misunderstanding. Whatever pretty words he may have spoken to you, and whatever hopes you may have had, I have returned to guide Edward in a position that should by all rights be mine, and I have no wish to set eyes on a Roma peasant girl in *my* home ever again.'

Selina pushed his hand away from her, terror and revulsion clouding the ebony of her eyes. Her legs felt weak with distress and she longed to sink to the ground, but the fear of being unable to get to her feet again held her upright, although she swayed slightly beneath the weight of her horror. Bile rose up in her throat again and she forced it down, the taste burning her tongue.

A person could live without a fortune and be happy—the Romani were proof enough of that. It was the lack of *people* that led to real misery, and Selina almost flinched at the thought of Edward alone, without anybody to surround him. Would society's disgust at his actions extend to little Ophelia? Would she be tainted by association and grow to resent her brother for his choice?

The notion of Edward being deprived of the only warmth in his life pained her more than she had ever thought possible, and she knew in that moment what she must do.

To turn her back on the man she mistrusted more than anybody else in the entire world took all of Selina's willpower, but on unsteady legs she forced herself to push up from the hedge against which she leaned and to stumble away, her feet slipping over the wet gravel with each wavering step. She was sure she heard a satisfied grunt from behind her but didn't turn to look, instead focusing all her energy on reaching the garden border and the stable yard beyond.

Each one of Charles's cruel words rang in her ears—spoken proof of her every insecurity and secret fear. He had dragged her lingering doubts from the darkest recesses of her mind and flung them into the light, naming them out loud with harsh triumph. With every word he had shattered the foolish dreams she had clung to, confronting her with the truth.

Ever since she had learned about his mother's abandonment Selina had not been able to wipe from her mind the image of the young Edward, sitting alone, wondering when his beloved mama would return. It was enough to make her heart ache with sorrow and a lump rise in her throat. He had already suffered abandonment twice at the hands of those supposed to love him. Selina would not allow herself to be the cause of history repeating itself and inflict such suffering on the man she loved: in leaving she would save Edward from himself and his misplaced regard for her.

That was the most she could hope for, and she clung to the thought like a lifeline.

To leave Blackwell never to return, never to see Edward again, was more than Selina thought she could bear. Her chest felt as though it would burst with the ocean of grief she felt welling up within her as she lost her footing and almost fell, but she forced herself onward, down another path and towards the stable gate.

She was only dimly thankful that nobody lingered to witness the anguish she knew must be present on her face, to see her lips twisting in distress with every agonised step she took towards a future she no longer wanted.

Chapter Sixteen

'Edward, my boy!'

Charles opened the door to the guest suite with a confidence Edward could only wonder at. How was it possible for him to arrive at another man's home without so much as an invitation and walk around it as though he owned the place?

Edward felt his lips set in a grim line, but he rose from the armchair in which he had waited with growing annoyance for a full hour and extended his hand to his uncle out of ingrained politeness. 'I was wondering where you had gone, sir. I understood you were waiting for me here, but I found the rooms empty.'

'Aha.' Charles moved towards the crystal decanter of port standing on a nearby table and poured himself a generous measure. The fact that the sun was barely up was apparently unimportant, as he drank it down with relish and flashed Edward an expansive smile. 'You kept me waiting too long. I thought I'd entertain myself with a jaunt about the grounds.'

Edward nodded shortly, knowing his face was rigid with dislike but unable to unlock the tension of his jaw. Seeing his uncle strolling about as though he was a welcome visitor now that Edward knew the consequences of his despicable actions made his pulse skip a little faster, and his disgust and irritation with his unwanted guest were plain to see. Edward could even feel a slight tic in the tight muscle of his jaw—an outward sign of the rising temper he sought to quell beneath icy good manners.

'An unexpected pleasure, Uncle. How long had you intended to stay?'

Edward's voice was as polite as ever, but his mind was full of Selina as he waited for his uncle's reply. He would have to get rid of him quickly; Selina must never be allowed to feel the overwhelming horror that would surely consume her should she stumble across their unfortunate visitor.

I will not risk her running again. After how far they had come together, and how close they now were to the potential of finding real happiness, Edward felt a sharp dart of anxiety at the notion that anything should threaten their future. It hung in the balance, by the finest of threads—and Charles *would not* be allowed to ruin this chance of a real future for both him and his wholly opposite wife, to spoil the connection they had forged between them despite all the odds.

'How long?' Charles poured himself another drink, a frown of good-humoured confusion on his ruddy face. 'My dear boy, I'm not here for a short stay. I'm here permanently, of course.' He tossed back the port, missing the tightening of Edward's face.

'I'm afraid that won't be possible.' Edward heard the note of barely concealed dislike in his voice but was powerless to restrain it.

I think not, Uncle. This is not your home. There was no chance in hell that he was allowing Charles to stay indefinitely, and even his uncle seemed to realise his nephew's feelings as he turned to him with a challenging scowl.

'Come now. Don't be absurd. I have every right to be here. Why, if you hadn't so rashly taken a wife the estate would have fallen to me anyway—and quite rightfully so.'

The mention of Selina made the hairs on the back of Edward's neck stand up like the hackles on an angry cat. The memory of what Charles had done to her and her mother rose up before him, and he shook his head with cold firmness.

'No, Uncle. You do *not* have the right. As you said yourself, I have taken a wife—she and I will live here together with no interference from anybody else.'

He saw his uncle's face flush with temper, his good humour of minutes before evaporating in his indignation.

'Oh, your *wife*. I had the pleasure of meeting her only an hour ago in the gardens, while I was waiting for you to finish dressing and attend me.'

His look was scathing, but Edward hardly noticed as the sensation of his heart dropping into his boots hit him hard.

Selina has seen Charles?

It was enough to make his mouth open in horror, but his uncle ploughed on, regardless of his nephew's blank dismay.

'That was a shocking and disappointing lapse in judgement on your part, which it fell to *me* to rectify, and it only serves to prove to me that I am right in returning to guide your hand in the estate. Evidently you cannot be trusted to behave properly.'

Edward's eyes narrowed in cold suspicion. His pulse had begun to jump in apprehension, and worry loomed ever larger in his mind. 'What do you mean by *rectify*?'

The words were almost a growl, quiet with menace. A dawning sense of dread crept over him; he knew instinctively what answer he was about to receive, at the same time hoping—without hope—that he might be wrong.

'Well, I told her the truth, of course.'

Charles picked at a cuticle, affecting idle unconcern, but Edward caught the flash of hesitation that flickered over the older man's face.

'I reminded her that she had no place here and insisted that she leave at once. I'm pleased to say she listened to reason—at least one of you has.'

Edward felt his face freeze into an expression of pure horror. His worst nightmare—the one he had dreaded, that had robbed him of sleep and surely some part of his sanity—had come true. Selina had gone.

The blood in Edward's veins turned to ice. His uncle's harsh words had surely obliterated any understanding he and Selina might have reached, and she had run from him just as she had tried to flee on the first day they had met, when he had watched her ride like the wind in front of him and felt admiration for her skill grow with each beat of her horse's hooves.

That admiration had blossomed into so much more during the strange months of their marriage, and the idea of anyone seeking to destroy it made Edward's hands ball into fists. That his uncle had been successful in driving Selina away before Edward had been able to speak to her of his true feelings was more than he could stand.

He heard his knuckles crack from the pressure of being so tightly clenched, and when he raised his eyes to meet Charles's he knew they must be burning.

'She has *left*?' Edward lurched towards him, feeling the rage that throbbed inside him begin to beat like a drum. 'You have driven my wife from her rightful home?'

His uncle's cheeks flushed puce and he took a small step backwards. '*Rightful home?* If she has left then she has behaved as she ought—eventually. She knows she is not wanted here and has acted accordingly.'

Edward felt his face twist into a grimace of anger, and his voice, when he managed to find a reply, was a low rumble of barely controlled fury. 'Who do you think you are to decide whether she is wanted?'

A shadow of something dark and wild was growing steadily in Edward's chest, gripping him with rising rage.

'Who are you to arrive in *our* home—hers and mine—and make her feel as though *she* is the one who is unwelcome?'

It was his father all over again. Charles was trying to assert his control over not only Edward's estate but also his heart. How *dare* he try to destroy the tender shoots of Edward's blossoming happiness? The very idea of it made Edward want to roar.

Instead, he fixed his uncle with an eye so devoid of warmth he could have sworn he saw the other man shudder. 'You will excuse me, sir. I must beg you to postpone the rest of this discussion until after my return.'

Edward turned away, his mind already swirling with activity. There was nowhere else she would have gone other than back to the Roma camp. If they were going to move on he would have to leave quickly... Talking with his uncle had taken up too much of his time already, and the idea of wasting a single moment more on this man who disgusted him so deeply was enough to make him sick to his stomach.

'Your return? Where can you mean to go?' Charles seized his arm, clinging to him like a bad-tempered child. 'I *know* you cannot mean to chase after that gypsy woman!'

Edward wrenched himself free and bit down on a snarl. 'That *gypsy woman* is my wife. Of course I will go to look for her.' He gazed down at his uncle, into the hazel eyes that matched his own, and felt the final pieces of his life fall into place like those in a jigsaw puzzle.

He had never sought to love Selina. That had grown inside him slowly, day after day, putting down roots in his heart until it had bloomed in all its beautiful colours, chasing away the sadness he had carried within him since he was a child. Nobody would stand in his way now—he would make sure of it.

'I expect you to be gone by the time I return. You are not welcome in my home and I never wish to see or hear from you again. You have no place here. Leave.'

Edward's heart thumped within the cage of his ribs, and his face when he turned towards the door was set. Without another word to his uncle, who watched him with his mouth slack with disbelief, Edward left the suite and marched with long strides from the top of the house to the bottom, into the entrance hall and out through the front doors.

The stable lads scrambled to ready his chestnut mare as Edward stood in the yard, bareheaded and clear-eyed, and inhaled great lungsful of the damp Blackwell air. The scent of snow and wet soil assailed his senses and he almost smiled in bittersweet determination. If there was still a chance for him to win Selina he would take it with both hands. His mind felt clear, like a lake of crystal water. All doubt was washed away, leaving only the true path he knew he must now take.

It would be hard for him to leave the safety of the fortress he had built around himself for all these years—desperately hard, and nothing would ever be the same again. But against all his efforts this Roma woman had forced him to examine the true wishes of his heart, and there could only be but one way ahead.

Selina heard the buzz of conversation beyond the shuttered doors of her *vardo*, but she lay still in the nest of her bunk and continued to gaze up at the curved ceiling. The chatter was occasionally punctuated by the sharp staccato of Zillah's voice as she warned away those who strayed too close to the porch on which she sat guard. She had taken one look at her granddaughter upon her unexpected arrival and waved her into the caravan without a word, the agony of Selina's expression telling her all she needed to know.

At any other time Selina would have been grateful to the old woman for protecting her from the Roma's endless questions, but now her mind was blank with grief and her head empty of anything other than the image of Edward's face.

I will never see him again.

The same six words echoed in her ears as she lay immobile, the only movement her fingers blindly stroking the brooch pinned to her chest. She touched the metal and stone as though it were a talisman, the last thread connecting her to Edward, and felt the slow thud of her heart beneath it.

Had the death of her mother not so cruelly taught her otherwise, Selina might have wondered if it were possible to die from the pain that gripped her chest, squeezing the life out of her with every wretched breath. A broken heart couldn't kill a person—Diamanda's passing had shown her that—but its agony made her wish it could.

Her eyes were dry now—no tears left to fall. They had coursed down her face in an unrelenting stream to patter onto Djali's neck as she had ridden from Blackwell to the camp, the ache in her core deepening with each of the horse's long strides. But sorrow still welled violently within her, and only the undeniable fact that she had helped Edward secure his inheritance, and that by leaving she would spare him future pain, kept her from galloping back in the direction from which she had come.

Her life would never be the same again, she acknowledged dully as her fingers traced the brooch's golden setting. She would have to continue on, knowing that the man she loved could never be hers, his name the only part of him hers to keep.

The hum of voices from outside suddenly halted abruptly, but Selina heard it cease with blank indifference. Her world had shrunk to fit within the four walls of her *vardo*, closed in on itself in a mixture of hopelessness and pain, and she felt as if nothing beyond would ever move her again. She couldn't stay shuttered away forever, of course—but for this one day at least she would hide and give herself up to the anguish of having found love only to allow it to wither and die.

Zillah's voice sliced through the silence, her words muffled by the crochet blankets Selina lay burrowed beneath. Whatever words her grandmother had spoken were answered by a deeper tone—one that vibrated through the wooden walls of the *vardo*—and with only a half-second of disbelief it sent Selina flying from her bunk to tear open the caravan's door.

A very tall man stood a few yards from the *vardo*'s steps, surrounded by a ring of stunned Roma and looking warily at Zillah. Hearing the door open behind her she turned to address her granddaughter, but Selina was deaf and blind to anything other than the sound of Edward's sigh of relief and the sight of his achingly handsome, painfully familiar face.

His eyes found hers and it was as though the sun had come out from behind the clouds to shine through Edward's face from within. His smile reached all the way up to illuminate the hazel of his gaze, and Selina felt the breath leave her body as she was pinned to the spot by the upward curve of his mouth.

'Edward…?'

His name dropped from her lips as though murmured in a dream. She could hardly believe he stood before her, brightening the dull winter day by the power of his smile. Even a few of the Roma women looked a little dazed by his good looks, although from the way Edward's eyes never left Selina's face it was clear that to him there were no other women in the world.

'Selina. I'm so glad you're still here.' He gestured at the camp around them—a small, somewhat uncertain movement.

Selina gazed at him in mute wonder, the frenzied jumping of her heart robbing her of speech. Why had he come? There could be no reason for him to seek her. The combination of confusion and overwhelming pleasure at the sight of his face rendered her speechless.

When she did not reply, Edward cleared his throat. 'I know that I have no right to ask anything of you, but please—let me speak just once.' His voice was a fraction less steady than before. 'Then, if you wish it, I will leave and you need never see me again.'

Selina hesitated, overcome with bewilderment, all too aware of the small figure of Zillah at her elbow. Her grandmother was studying her face as intently as a scholar with a new book, scouring her features from top to bottom as though searching for some hidden clue. Selina saw how the old eyes narrowed, just for a moment, and then she caught the minute shake of her head in wordless resignation.

'Speak, boy.' Zillah tossed the words at Edward, her eyes never leaving her granddaughter's face. 'My Lina might be lost for words, but I know what is in her heart and what I suspect lives in yours. Speak, I say.'

Selina saw the surprise in Edward's expression, but he offered the old woman a courteous bow. Selina's brows rose almost into her hair when she saw it returned with a short nod from Zillah that was almost bordering on civil.

The crowd of silently watching Roma moved a half-pace closer as Edward laced together his fingers and looked down at his palms, apparently arranging his thoughts. Selina felt a lump rise up in her throat at the sight of him so quiet, so unsure, and every one of her sinews burned to slip down the steps and run into his arms. But then he started to speak, and with only the rush of blood in her ears accompanying his words Selina gripped the *vardo*'s door to anchor her where she stood.

'I have spent so many years caring for scarcely anyone but myself. Ever since my mother and Letitia left my heart had been closed, so determined was I never to let myself be broken again.

I had thought I would never love, would never allow myself to feel the things other people felt, leaving themselves vulnerable—and then out of nowhere you came into my life.'

The words tumbled from Edward's dry lips and hung in the frozen air between him and Selina, who watched in silence, the rapid flicker of a pulse at her throat the only sign she was not carved from stone. Her face gave nothing away, but her black eyes, fixed on him so unblinkingly, seemingly gave Edward the courage to continue.

'I remember as though it were yesterday. You stood in front of me that day with mud on your face and your hair so wild, and I remember thinking you were the most beautiful thing I'd ever seen. It frightened me to discover I could think such thoughts, and when you disappeared through the trees I was determined to put you from my mind.'

Selina felt her breath come more quickly, escaping her in a shallow rhythm she couldn't control. A curious warmth began to unfurl in her stomach, reaching up with golden fingers in the direction of her chest, and she almost gasped at the sensation. The warmth seemed to curl around her heart, and suddenly she felt as though she was aflame with a fierce hope she didn't dare express.

The feeling lingered there, hot against the cage

of her ribs, inviting her to accept the truth: Edward had sought her out, and he had told her she was beautiful, and still he stood in front of her with apparently more to say. She tightened her grip on the *vardo* door as her head swam with the assault on her senses, almost robbing her of the ability to stand.

'I tried to deny what I felt for you. I tried to convince myself that when you returned to ask me for help I behaved towards you the way I would have behaved to anyone in need. Later, I tried to convince myself that our marriage meant nothing to me, and that it was no more than a convenient arrangement. I failed both times.'

He took a step towards the caravan, mere paces from the wooden steps on which Selina stood. She was just out of his reach.

'It was never just that. In fact, it was precisely the opposite: it was very *in*convenient when I finally allowed myself to admit my feelings for you, knowing you would never return them.'

He must have seen how Selina's taut frame had flinched a little as she started, she thought. Her nerves were responding to him of their own accord, and now her lips had parted as though she wished to speak. She could force no words to emerge, however, and she merely tightened her fingers on the shawls she clutched to her chest.

With another step forward he spoke to her

again. 'I do not come to you as gentry. I come as a simple man who has lost his heart to you and who has to tell you how he feels—how he *truly* feels.'

The ground beneath his feet was cold and wet, but Edward paid it no mind as he dropped to his knees in front of Selina's disbelieving gaze. All around her she heard the Romani women break out into low whispers of shock, looking from Edward, kneeling in the mud, to Selina, who stood on the back porch of her caravan with her eyes as round as saucers at his sudden move.

The damp and chill must have seized him immediately, but Edward ignored the unpleasant sensation as he smiled up at the woman he adored. 'Whatever my uncle said to make you run was a lie. He will never speak for me, or know the first thing about my feelings. I swear to you, if you consent to take me as your true husband I will spend the rest of my life trying to win your heart. I can't—'

He ran a hand through the thatch of his hair and gave a short, resigned laugh.

'The simple truth is I cannot live without you. Whatever the circumstances, whatever cruel falsehoods you have been told, you are all that I want and all I will *ever* want.' Edward shrugged, the final vestiges of the weight he had borne for so long falling from his shoulders as he laid his soul bare. 'I love you.'

The entire camp was silent. Every eye swivelled to fix on Selina, who stood like a statue and then felt her limbs turn to water as the full weight of Edward's words hit her like a lightning bolt.

Edward stayed likewise as still as a rock, looking up at her from the mire in which he knelt, with mud spattering breeches that had cost almost as much as a horse and caring not one single iota that they were ruined beyond saving.

The cold winter breeze stirred Selina's raven curls, moving past her to drag the skeletal branches of trees against the dour sky. The smell of snow still hung in the air, and the chill of the evening had begun to wend its way beneath the wool of Selina's shawls. In the silence of the Romani camp she took in the scene before her, her racing mind slowing and slowing until finally, *finally*, it ceased its swirling and allowed her to act as her heart longed for her to.

There was no sound but that of her own footsteps as Selina stepped down from the caravan, crossed the barren stretch of ground between them, and flung herself into Edward's waiting arms. Every last trace of fear and uncertainty fell away as she reached down to draw his face up to her own, leaving the raw truth exposed as his mouth met hers and she felt him smile against her trembling lips.

Rising up, his arms closed around her in an embrace so tight it almost took her breath away, and then Selina felt her feet leave the ground as he lifted her as gently and as easily as he would a child and held her against the warm column of his body, one hand supporting her weight while the other blindly stroked her hair back from her face.

Edward covered her skin with breathless kisses time and time again—her closed eyelids, her cheek, even the end of her freckled nose. Each kiss set her nerves alight and culminated in him capturing her lips once more in a kiss so powerful Selina felt herself swoon, sagging in Edward's arms as she allowed feelings too wonderful to name to course through her body and set her ablaze.

The Romani's ragged cheers echoed around them, and Selina broke the kiss to look up into Edward's face and feel the delicious sensation of his tender expression warming her to her very toes. He gazed down at her, his eyes filled with the vibrant life she had once feared she might never see again, and she buried her face in the silk of his waistcoat.

It was all too much, suddenly, and the knowledge that her suffering was over was almost overwhelming. Edward was all she wanted, would ever want, and now, as he held her in his arms, it was as though every secret wish she had ever made, every whispered prayer she had uttered in the darkness of her lonely bedchamber, had come true. He loved her—truly loved her—and Selina knew her breathless happiness to be complete.

He lowered her, still holding her firmly against him as her feet hit the ground. She staggered a little and Edward's grip tightened immediately to steady her, gathering her to him more closely than ever before.

'May I take that as a yes to my request?' The smile lines at the corners of his eyes stretched as his lips curved upwards.

Selina felt her own lips twitch in reply. 'I suppose I shall allow it.'

Edward's laugh rang in Selina's ears as her friends and family closed in on them, too many hands to count reaching out to touch her, to touch Edward. Selina saw their joy for her, saw it even in the ancient lines of Zillah's face, and she felt her heart swell with pride at the warmth of her people. They welcomed Edward now as though he were one of their own. His love for her had shattered the barriers between his world and hers, and now they abandoned their pride to pat his back and pinch his cheeks and blush in scandalised delight as he bowed to the women as low as if they were the highest-born ladies.

Selina reached up onto her tiptoes to murmur into Edward's ear. 'What about your uncle?'

The prospect of meeting Charles again was enough to dim the perfect happiness that glowed within her, casting a cold shadow over the warmth of her joy. Edward would always be there to shield her, she knew, but the notion of encountering his uncle made her heart check.

Edward's expression was bordering on triumphant as he pulled her close again. His hand caressed the small of Selina's back, the movement making her toes curl in catlike pleasure despite her sudden worry. She saw the sly amusement in his face, and glanced up at him suspiciously.

'He is no longer welcome in our home. *You* are the mistress of Blackwell Hall, and my beloved wife—and nobody will ever make you doubt that ever again.'

He smiled at her rosy blush, and that slow upward curve of his lips Selina now knew so well enhanced the handsome lines of his face.

'And, with that in mind, I would like to extend my affection to the rest of your people and invite them to stay on our estate for as long as they wish. Forever, if they choose.'

Selina gasped, hardly able to take in his words

as a bubble of intense relief mingled with gratitude rose up inside her. Edward had neatly taken care of the only obstacle that could have got in the way of their happiness: now her people would have a safe haven for the rest of their days.

No Roma baby would ever gasp its last breath on a pitted and frosty road; no mother would have to choose between food or coal. Zillah could grow frail without the worry of where their next camp would be, and without the constant fear of persecution that had followed her like a shadow her entire life.

The pain of her mother's passing would never truly heal, Selina knew, and she felt the smallest pang of sorrow tinge her joy as she felt Edward take her hand in his far larger palm and squeeze tightly. But she knew, too, that Diamanda would be proud of the sacrifices her daughter had made, and glad that they had, against all the odds, led her to find real happiness. There would always be a gap in Selina's life that only her mother could fill, but with Edward by her side Selina felt a hope rise within her for the first time, and knew that he could help her feel almost whole again.

He was looking down at her and, as black eyes gazed up into hazel, Selina could have sworn she felt the love radiating from him.

'May I take you home now, wife?'

Selina swept into a deep curtsey any gentry lady would have been proud of and came up smiling. 'Yes, husband. You may.'

* * * * *

MILLS & BOON

Coming next month

THE BROODING DUKE OF DANFORTH
Christine Merrill

'You spent more time talking to my father than you ever did to me. The day of the wedding arrived and I realised that I had not seen you since the day you made the offer. But my father had spoken to you at least a dozen times.'

'We share a club,' Benedict said absently.

'And we were to share a bed,' she snapped.

For the first time since Abigail had met him, the façade of perpetual ennui disappeared and she saw real emotion on his face. His eyes darkened to the deep green of the sea in a storm and his lips parted in a smile that had nothing to do with mirth. Then, he moved closer until she could feel the heat of his body through the air between them. 'Yes, Miss Prescott, after our wedding, I would have taken you to my bed. But a meeting of bodies is one thing and a meeting of minds is quite another. I had hoped that, after some time together, the latter would develop from the former.'

'And I hoped quite the opposite,' she said, surprised. 'It cannot be possible to enjoy the marital act with a complete stranger.'

In response, he laughed. And something deep inside her trembled in answer to the sound. 'Would you care to wager on the fact?'

'It is likely different for men,' she added, taking a

steadying breath to counter the odd sensations that the question evoked.

'In a way, perhaps.' He placed a hand on the wall beside her head and leaned even closer, until she felt his breath at each word. 'In my experience, it matters little whether the woman is a friend or a stranger. But for a woman?'

His voice grew soft until it was barely more than a whisper. And against all modesty, she leaned closer to him, so she would not miss a word.

'The pleasure of the act has much to do with the skill of the partner. I can assure you, Miss Prescott, you would have had nothing to worry about.'

Then he reached for her. And without another thought she closed her eyes and waited for his kiss.

Continue reading
THE BROODING DUKE OF DANFORTH
Christine Merrill

Available next month
www.millsandboon.co.uk

COMING SOON!

We really hope you enjoyed reading this book. If you're looking for more romance, be sure to head to the shops when new books are available on

Thursday 30th May

To see which titles are coming soon, please visit

millsandboon.co.uk/nextmonth

LET'S TALK
Romance

For exclusive extracts, competitions
and special offers, find us online:

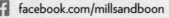